THE
LOST PIECE

A novel by
David Imrie

This international first edition published by
Divers Novels in 2024.
www.diversnovels.com

1

ISNI   0000 0005 1434 2076

ISBN   978-84-09-57992-1

<u>AI transparency</u>
This book is 100% human-written and human-edited.
Artwork for the cover and interior uses human-edited
AI-generated images (Adobe Firefly).

Typeset in Baskerville 11pt.

Cover by studioannadahlberg.com

Prologue.

Petrograd (St. Petersburg), October 1917.

The thoughts were seductive: "Who will know? Do you not wish to behold it? What harm could possibly come from assembling a jigsaw puzzle?"

Anger simmered; by what right did his patron forbid Pavel from joining together that which he had made? Forty-nine perfectly-interlocking pieces in finest pockholz hardwood, their sinuous patterns leading inwards to the two rubies.

He held the bejewelled centrepiece above the one remaining space, then let it fall. Instantly the red stones lit with fire and a yawning tunnel ruptured the surrounding world. It belched air colder than any Siberian winter, upon it the stench of burning, yet far worse was the shadow approaching through that hideous rent. It had neither face nor form, only potent malevolence. Pavel gibbered, certain he would be slain.

But something seemed to trap it. Even as he cowered, the craftsman's eye spotted the slight misalignment of that final square. Scrabbling for his tongs, he manged to grip its raised edge and pull it clear. As he did the whole maelstrom vanished.

Slowly the room and life's small background sounds returned. Had it all been hallucination? Just the effects of too long bent over the magnifier? Needing to understand, he reached out tentatively to where he'd seen the air sundered, only to cry out as an agonising stab seared down his arm and across his torso.

After long minutes, the worst of the pain had passed and Pavel sought comfort in the mechanical familiarity of his work. He cautiously retrieved the piece that had stuck. Fingers tracing the grain's curve, he sanded the offending corner. Aware his sweat could swell the wood, he brushed the dust clear before applying a sealing layer of lacquer.

The baron's commission was finished.

But should it ever be made whole again?

He sat and considered this, eventually weeping, for destroying the puzzle would ruin both his own livelihood and that of his apprentice.

"No. My hands shall not birth such evil into this Earth," he growled at last. He jerked to his feet and reached for his hammer. Then the pain in his chest hit again. This time it was a tear through the cloth of life, his sight dissolving into stars. He managed to catch hold of the workbench, but his legs beneath him had lost all strength. Thump, thump, thump went his heart, and stopped.

He lunged weakly for the only thing within his grasp. Feeling the wet lacquer stick to his palm, he enclosed the centrepiece in his fist. As he fell to the floor, his dying prayer was to let this be enough.

It was still dark when Aleksandr arrived at his master's. Collection of the baron's jigsaw puzzle was due at dawn, but not a ruble had been handed over by the nobleman. Aleksandr smelt a rat, and he wanted to be there to ensure the gentle craftsman he served got paid.

As he reached the door a dull boom came from the city to the north where the Bolsheviks were besieging the Winter Palace. Word was the order of the Tsars would fall today. That was enticing, but also a worry when the making of objets d'art for the bourgeoisie put bread on your table.

Pushing open the door, all such concerns fled when he saw the crumpled body. He rushed over, but it was already cold to the touch.

For a long while he sat on the floor next to the old man, grey sorrow flooding him. Aleksandr was an apprentice with no master now. No trade. Lots of family, but none he could fall back on. Few prospects. No money with which to buy any.

Finally he was roused by a growing noise outside: the distant clack of hooves and rumble of wheels. Swearing, he rose and ran to close the door. It must be the baron's man. Aleksandr needed that money. No-one could know that Pavel lay dead.

Muttering apologies, he pulled out the dust sheet and lifted the corpse onto it. It was already stiff and the clenched fists made wrapping it a macabre task. Aleksandr carried the body out to the sliver of land behind the house and just made it back as knocking rattled the door. He took a deep breath, went over and opened it. Waiting outside was Ivan, a grizzled veteran from his own neighbourhood.

"Where's Pavel, boy?"

"He's...er, upstairs. Fast asleep. I think he worked most of the night on a piece."

Each looked expectantly at the other. "So come on then, hand it over," Ivan snarled.

"The baron's commission?"

"Yes the baron's commission. Why else would I be down this arse-end-of-a-goat road?"

"It's ready," Aleksandr bluffed, "but the master told me to be sure to collect payment."

Ivan reached inside his coat and tossed a cloth purse to the apprentice. Aleksandr opened it and counted the notes inside, his gut turning as he did. "There's only five thousand rubles here! The commission was for eight thousand."

"Read do you?"

"But...some, yes."

"Here then." Ivan delved into another pocket and handed over a folded note.

I believe that the current political situation merits renegotiation of contracts, and with what is here I have in fact been generous to a fault. I advise you to spend rubles quickly.

There was no signature, but there didn't need to be because no-one would suspect Ivan of having written.

"Happy now?"

"No! The materials alone cost more than what's here. This is robbery!"

Ivan explored a nostril with his little finger, paused to examine his find. "Lot of it about. Did you hear they just took the palace? Makes you think, don't it. Now hurry up."

Pulsing with impotent fury, Aleksandr stalked across the shop to where Master Pavel had apparently put together the damned puzzle. Even looking at the image it formed sent a shiver down the apprentice's spine; somehow you couldn't focus on it but you felt it was focused on you. He was glad the centre with its two red eyes wasn't in place. It was a relief to take the thing apart and pack the pieces into their case.

Now he just needed that middle square his master had been working on yesterday evening. He scoured the entire bench but it was nowhere to be seen. The floor perhaps? Trying to be discreet about it he bent down and searched where the body had lain. Nothing. Panic was rising in him; five thousand was still a huge amount of money, and Ivan would have instructions to verify what was handed over.

It seemed hopeless, until the apprentice remembered witnessing Ivan's struggles at the market. The old soldier was fine for checking something if it was very big and far away. Up close, as in within two or three arm lengths, apparently not so good. Which made it possible he wouldn't notice the substitution of the test piece.

Aleksandr searched in the miscellaneous bits drawer, and there it was! Made of oak but painted to mimic pockholz, it had been a placeholder for matching the grain surrounding the centre. Master Pavel, thorough as ever, had even set two tiny spheres of cut glass into it. They were worth no more than ten kopeks apiece but still sparkled red. It was a match, if only a rough one. Too rough to pass Ivan's long-sighted inspection? Aleksandr had to take that chance.

Fixing a scowl on his face he returned to the door. "Here. And tell your master we'll accept no more commissions from him."

"You should be so lucky! Open it then."

Aleksandr undid the two clasps and thrust the box towards the big man's face. Ivan grabbed it from him and held it further away. His squinting seemed to last forever, but finally he gave a curt nod, snapped the lid shut, turned, and stumped off to his carriage.

It took all Aleksandr had to muzzle his jubilation long enough to close and lock the door. Then he glanced towards the back garden and grew sombre again.

Five thousand rubles.

According to the credit notes some three thousand was owed to local suppliers for the fine woods and jewels. Aleksandr would pay those because Master Pavel would have wanted that.

But then what? The remaining money could either be used for a funeral or for Aleksandr's start in the world.

For death or for life.

"I think you would understand Master."

The body, wrapped in its sheet and lying in the brown grass, said nothing.

"You never liked the church. Not the rituals nor the arrogant priests. And even if I spent all of the two thousand the coffin would be clumsy compared to the things you made."

Only silence.

"But this young oak here... You always liked this oak. Nature does things with wood that even your hands couldn't match, you said. I think if your bones could become part of those roots you would rest happy."

There was only so long anyone could spend trying to wheedle a blessing from a corpse, and Aleksandr knew time would be his enemy when the baron received the incomplete puzzle. He found the shovel and for the next half hour the apprentice hacked grimly at the near-frozen soil. When the hole was deep enough he laid the body inside, the tree serving for a headstone.

At least this patch of ground wouldn't cheat Master Pavel. It wouldn't abuse his kindness nor go back on its word nor use its riches as the ruling class did to steal endlessly from the poor. Instead the oak tree would make simple use of the mortal remains that were all the old man had left to give.

That felt right.

And as for Aleksandr, he would not linger in the city always looking over his shoulder for the baron's men. He would enlist. Go and make a man of himself in the great European war. Then, when it all ended, he would settle somewhere new. Find a wife. Maybe buy some tools and set up his own little workshop. Everything was being destroyed these days, but there would come a time when people built and cherished and looked forward again, wouldn't there?

He finished filling the craftsman's grave, and hid the disturbed soil with a covering of fallen leaves. "Rest in peace, dear Master Pavel," he intoned in his unstable fifteen-year-old voice. Wiping away sudden tears, he took out his pocket knife and scored a small cross into the tree's bark.

Within it he carved three initials: P.V.L.

The life just ended would have at least this one, small mark to be remembered by.

1.

London, July 2015.

Aged twenty-two, part way to being well-qualified, and widely assured he was clever and handsome, Joel Elliott knew how the world worked and what it took to get ahead. He rejected spirituality as illusion spoon-fed to the powerless, wanting better than that in life. Yet if your family lacked contacts and currency - as his did - there were no handouts, and trusting to luck was merely a tempting folly for those already losing. So you set a clear goal, you worked hard and if needs be ruthlessly towards it, and step by step you went out and you made yourself. All of which was why, sitting at this week's hot desk in Stern Johns Rubikov, International Architects, his desperate hope was that a senior associate or better might ask him to fetch coffee.

"Joel?" The voice from behind him was urbane, assured and a welcome answer to his silent plea, for he was feeling the pressure of falling behind the curve.

"Hi. Yes, that's me."

"Stephen Latham. Junior partner here. Wondered if you might be able to help me out with something?"

Perhaps twenty years older than Joel, beautifully-tailored suit and an air of being at ease with taste, money and influence. Stephen very much personified Joel's ambitions in life.

"Sure! Is it a Starbucks run?"

Stephen flashed a grin. "Not quite. Come." He beckoned Joel to follow and led him to an empty meeting room nearby.

Pulse going somewhat faster than usual, the younger architect waited as the older shut the door.

"So Joel, on your CV you've put that you speak Russian. Being blunt, is that genuine? And to what sort of level?"

"It's true, really. I have an A-star at A-level plus a lot of conversation practice with a...well, a family friend. I'm fluent." Russian came with painful memories for Joel, but it had been a free exam pass so he'd kept it up.

"Perfect. And you did your architecture BA in Manchester?"

"Yes. I'm still waiting on my degree grade but I'm predicted for a first or upper second."

"Wonderful." It was galling to see how little importance Stephen attached to the result of three very expensive and hard-working years of Joel's life. "'Fraid I don't have details about your specific course projects and suchlike, but what's your understanding of tall building pilings and foundations like?"

"Well, I mean I have a theoretical knowledge. I can read details off a plan, but..."

"That's fine. And surveying? More or less know the principles?"

"Yes. We did some site practice and I've used the tools and software."

Stephen tapped his chin thoughtfully. "Okay. Think this will work. Suppose you haven't got your passport with you today?"

Joel was annoyed to realise his mouth had fallen open. "I'm afraid I don't. I had no idea I might need it."

"Reasonable enough." Stephen laughed and reached forward to clap Joel on the shoulder. "Know I'm hitting you with this out the blue. You live in Bromley, right? Here's the plan: we'll meet downstairs in five minutes and the car will take us past your house on the way to Heathrow. Can you pack for two nights away in quarter of an hour?"

"Definitely!" Joel could scarcely believe that whatever this was was happening.

"Super. I'll ride out to the airport with you and give you the lowdown. Then before you go airside Helen from HR will bring you a laptop with all the plans and specs on and your travel visa. And some new business cards; don't for God's sake let anyone know you're an intern!"

"Okay, sure," managed Joel.

Stephen chuckled. "We are what our façade presents us to be Joel. Consider that a valuable first lesson in commercial architecture. More seriously, for the purposes of this trip you're a fully-qualified junior associate working with me on this project who we've sent out as you're a Russian speaker. Is that a problem?"

"No. I mean if you're alright with it then so I am."

"Excellent. And on the delicate subject of window dressing, what sort of suitcase do you own? What make?"

"There might be one in the attic somewhere, but otherwise I've only got an old rucksack." Joel felt himself reddening as Stephen appraised him. "It's just what with university fees and so on..."

"Please Joel, no need to be apologetic. Truth be told I admire that you've made it here without financial help and against the demographic odds." Stephen's mouth bunched at the corner, perhaps worried about straying where HR guidelines might apply. "Your generation's being royally stiffed from every direction you know," he added in a conspiratorial tone.

That was certainly a sentiment Joel could agree with.

"Now, clothes. Is what you're wearing the best you have? In fact don't answer that. Get clear of Bromley fast and you'll have time after security at Heathrow. Shopping there's surprisingly decent. Let's see, two hundred for a case, same again for a couple of shirts and a tie. Four hundred for a suit, fifty for a belt, and of course shoes. Never forget good shoes Joel."

Stephen forestalled Joel's helpless shrug with a calming gesture. "Helen will bring you out a company credit card and I want you to charge minimum twelve hundred to it before you board your plane. You'll also need it to invite people for drinks and food. Do anything you can to get them talking out there."

For some years Joel had known who, what and where he wanted to be. The problem was the gap between that and who, what and where he was often appeared insurmountable. Suddenly these two images were coalescing and it was all he could do to keep a lid on his exultation.

"Mr. Latham..."

"Call me Stephen."

"Thanks. Can I ask where 'out there' is?"

Stephen slapped a hand to his forehead. "Of course! You'll be on the afternoon flight to St. Petersburg, Joel."

The traffic through the Blackwall Tunnel, down the A2 and past Eltham was light and they made good time to the Elliott family home. Joel bounded out of the car. Even though this was a decent street for the area, he heard Stephen lock the doors behind him.

It was only as he rooted in the family's documents drawer that the possibility his passport might be out of date occurred to him. Was it five years or ten they were valid for? Hands shaking as he located it, he thumbed to the details page and was relieved to see it was ten after all and he had ages left.

But the picture! It must have been from just after he turned sixteen. He hoped Stephen needn't see it. His hair had been allowed to do its natural half-Afro thing and he'd been at the darkest end of his seasonal café-au-lait to milk chocolate colour cycle. Add that to the idiocy of wearing a hoodie for an ID photo that would endure for a decade and...well, he knew much better now. In fact he barely recognised the kid staring back at him, unsmiling as per passport photo rules.

Upstairs in the bedroom he shared with his brother, he grabbed underwear, pyjamas and T-shirts and stuffed them into a kit bag he could re-use for dirty laundry. Imagine a new suitcase! New clothes! Good clothes! He wondered if he'd get to keep everything? Surely he would, but twelve hundred pounds just for 'window dressing' for a single trip?! It reinforced how very, very much he wanted the life in which this was par for the course.

"All okay Joel?" Stephen asked as he got back into the car.

"Yep. Good to go."

"Excellent." Stephen knocked on the glass and the driver set off. "Let's get started with some background. In a nutshell the project's an international-focused five-star hotel by Pulkovo airport and they want it to be 'statement'. Things work differently in Russia and there's - how best to put it? - much less oversight. One of the investors was uneasy with things they were hearing and approached us for a discreet appraisal of the plans. Prudent decision, because there are a number of curved main load-bearing elements in the design and our view was that the calculations for these were off. We communicated this, said investor went back and kicked up a fuss, and six weeks ago Stern Johns Rubikov took over the project." Stephen paused to study a passing billboard advertising women's underwear.

"All this is by the by," he resumed. "We reworked the design to give it our own signature and beefed up the spec for the suspect bits of structure. No issues with any of that. Then the week before last we got site photos through. We can't be sure because the images are poor quality, but the foundations going in look very similar to the previous design instead of what we've calculated is necessary. We pressed the local project management subcontractor for details, but the responses seemed evasive. Are you getting the picture here?"

Joel nodded, wondering how they could seriously expect an

intern to fix any of this?

"They've dug holes and are forming steel reinforcement at the moment. Plan is to pour concrete for pilings and foundations in the next week. Once that sets, if what's there isn't right the only way we're going to find out is by waiting a year or two to see if the building cracks. Obviously I don't want that. We also took a big excess on the liability insurance to keep costs down and make this a pipeline to future projects with the same investors."

Joel was now feeling a little queasy. "Mr. Latham...Stephen. I understand the concerns, but would it not make better sense to send out an experienced ground works engineer?"

"It would, and we did exactly that last week. Do you know Kayleigh? Complete confidence in her for the technical side, but it seems she let herself be marginalised and lied to. They showed her technical details for the rebar specs and concrete mixes and so on, but nothing was in English. She also thought they were making up and co-ordinating their story as they went along. Hence I need a Russian speaker. As well as being the only one in the firm, I'm hoping you also have a keen eye to cast about the site for what might be important extra details." Stephen's architect gaze was fixed on him, scrutinising his structural qualities. "But Joel, if you're not up to this now's the time to say so."

One month previously Stern Johns Rubikov had accepted three BA graduates into their internship program. As well as being highly sought after for the Royal Institute of British Architects' one year fieldwork criterion, the role actually paid a salary of five hundred pounds per month.

Two places lasted only for the summer and would end with the hard-to-shift whiff of second-best. The third would extend for a full twelve months, setting the fortunate recipient up with their RIBA experience and possibly even a job offer after the Master's degree component concluded the six-year trek to full qualification.

The first of Joel's two competitors, Olly, had fallen into 'CAD monkeying', the computer modelling of endless tiny details that most architects detested. He showed none of the elan the profession required and so offered little cause for concern.

The second, Gemma, was the big worry. She was one of those beautiful, high-contrast white girls with chestnut hair and blue eyes offset by creamy skin. She also knew her stuff and was set to be awarded a first by Cambridge. Worst of all she'd paired her eye-catchingly long, slender legs with daringly short skirts, so of course she'd been drafted straight into one of the senior partners' teams. Joel couldn't hold that against them, because he fancied her like crazy and in their position he'd have done the same thing, but it meant that whilst he and Gemma were doing similar odds-and-sods of donkey work and fetching drinks, she was doing it for far more influential people within the company. The galling truth was that on every intern measure she outscored him.

Every measure, that is, except this unexpected Russian one.

"Stephen." Joel returned the gaze without flinching. "I'm up to this."

He simply had to be.

2.

St. Petersburg.

Fresh from the four-star room's shower - as perfectly long as he liked without brothers and sister hammering at the door or the hot water running out - and new clothes hung carefully in the wardrobe, Joel set the laptop on the desk and opened the project files folder to do some studying.

He wasn't able to settle to it quite yet though. Instead he

stood and gazed out the window. Despite the late hour there was still plenty of northern summer light to see by. It was flat here to all horizons. The thin trees were of a paler green than in England, and the distant sea was a grey-blue smear. Defining the landscape nearby and north to the city were mushrooming clusters of brutal, concrete tower blocks joined by cracked motorways. It was alien. It was exciting. And he was right here in it, masquerading as a qualified commercial architect.

Equal measure elated and scared stiff by his task, he spread his arms as if bestowing a blessing, released a strangled laugh out loud, and toppled backwards onto the massive bed.

It wasn't yet five by his body's London clock when Joel finished breakfast and went to the lobby to meet his car. The décor was all chrome and mirrored gold, and as he entered the space it took him a second before he recognised his own reflection.

How right Stephen had been about the importance of facade. Stern Johns Rubikov's twelve hundred pounds really had transformed an intern into an associate, a boy into a man. Joel worked out and had reasonable muscular definition if you looked closely, but in his regular clothes he was still afflicted by the skinny lightness of youth. Now he looked lean and athletic instead, svelte. It was the colour combinations: charcoal grey, cream and hazelnut. It was the textures: just the right amounts of rough and smooth. It was the co-ordination. The quality. It was lines that redrew nature better. It was the power of architecture and design. And that world could be his if he could just find a way to succeed today.

Each time the main door revolved the incoming air brought

a scent of petroleum by-product from the street. When it got to half an hour after the car was due, Joel thought back to Kayleigh's failure to do the necessary here. He brought up maps on his phone. The site was less than two kilometres away from the hotel. He could walk.

At pedestrian pace the surrounding area was quite an eye-opener. Although there were a number of modern buildings such as his hotel they were like flowers growing out of a manure heap. Within a few hundred metres the internationalised zone around the airport gave way to low block-built units huddled together beneath corrugated roofs. Smoking men in ensembles of tracksuit lurked around them, glancing in his direction too often for comfort. This district was an ongoing collision between two worlds, in at least one of which Joel was very unwelcome.

When he made it to the site he wasn't sure it was one. Where there would have been a full-frontal assault of health and safety notices in the UK, here there was a rusty chain. Behind it was a shabby portacabin, and only much further in were there several diggers, men standing around them nursing yet more cigarettes.

"Hey you. No entry. Don't you see the chain?"

Joel took a deep breath. "Good morning. I'm from Stem Johns Rubikov, the architect. Why didn't my car arrive at the hotel?" The Slavic syllables were rusty on his tongue.

The man's aggression became unsure. "Wait here," he instructed. He pulled out a walkie talkie and spoke into it, something too fast and thick-accented for Joel to make out.

Joel examined his fingernails casually. He felt a lot less calm inside and wished there were something shiny in which he could be reassured by his new reflection again.

After several minutes a white pickup truck crawled its way through the mud from the other side of the site and a fat man with a greying walrus moustache got out. His eyes roved over

Joel, clearly not impressed by what they saw. "I Dimitri, site manager. Only them say end yesterday person come, but still you want car, uh?"

"I'm Joel Elliott, pleasure to meet you," Joel replied in Russian. He didn't hold out a hand, fearing it would go untaken.

Dimitri gave a dromedary snort. "So last week London sends a Barbie doll to tell Russians they can't do maths, and now we have an immigrant kid fresh out of school who somehow speaks the local language. What is your hope here, Mr. Joel?"

This was the question that Joel had spent much of the night pondering. He spread his hands in a placatory gesture. "All we want is to put up a good building. We got site photos of foundations that don't seem to match the new design, so we just want to be sure there's been no miscommunication before you pour the concrete."

"You think we can't read blueprints?"

"That's not what I think. As I said, I just want to check nothing's been lost in translation. If the pilings are as specified then London wasted some of my time and their money, and everyone's happy. But if there is a difference with the plans it needs to be resolved before the works proceed. Is that reasonable?"

Dimitri's face didn't change beyond the continuance of some slow mastication, but Joel's gambit seemed to work. "Fine. Look at what you want."

"And the men will answer my questions?"

"Why wouldn't they?"

"Okay. Thanks Dimitri." Joel scanned the five acres of churned mud and gaping holes that made up the site. He gestured to the portacabin. "Do you have work boots and overalls I can use?"

Dimitri's gaze moved downwards to contemplate Joel's

brand new, two-hundred-and-fifteen-pounds suede brogues. "Regretfully all boots are already in use. Also overalls."

Even asking the question had made him look naïve. Setting his jaw, Joel tramped forward into the sucking ground.

After a half-hour walk around, Joel's first question was the obvious one: "Why is there still a tree here?"

Dimitri paused, midway into his truck. "Specialist job, a big oak like that. It was booked for ten weeks ago but the cutter got sick. They're finally coming today and as soon as it's gone we dig the roots out. Happy?"

Not the best planning, but a genuine-sounding response, thought Joel as Dimitri drove off. He turned his attention back to the tree, and it was then that he noticed the oddest thing: the entire site was a carpet of boot-prints and tyre tracks, but all of them seemed to avoid one particular spot about twenty metres from the oak. He saw traces of brick and timber around it, indicating a building had stood there once. Intrigued, he slithered his way over, and confirmed there was indeed an anomalous, untouched island in the mud.

As he contemplated it tendrils of primeval fear wormed their way into his mind. It was irrational, which made Joel annoyed with himself. Ignoring the warnings, he thrust out his hand, exploring the air above the island. Nothing. Of course. He moved his hand up. Still nothing, except a sterile wash of intellectual satisfaction. Finally down, just for completeness. That was when, at about a metre high, he felt a sharp stab that made him recoil in shock. It had been actual physical hurt, but also deeper. The aftertaste was malevolence.

"Get a grip!" he snapped out loud and angrily. What he'd felt must have been just a delusion, suggested by the footprints and exacerbated by the unfamiliar setting and the stress of his mission here. He had a job to concentrate on. "So get on with it Joel," he admonished himself harshly.

Even so, not for anything would he have reached out to that place in the air again. As the tree stood in the opposite direction, he moved towards it instead.

It had that beauty unique to a mature oak in clear pasture, but the little island of sun-dappled green beneath its spreading limbs was under dire assault from the construction work and would not hold much longer. Still discomfited by that bizarre pain, Joel patted the trunk. "Sorry. In England there would have been a preservation order on you, but I guess not in this part of the world."

Running his hand down the bark, Joel spotted a strange scar and bent to look, tracing the lines with his finger. They formed the Cyrillic characters P.V.L. with a box...no, with a cross etched around them. Someone had cut this, but a long time ago. Trees truly were the silent sentinels of centuries, and Joel felt another pang of guilt that this beautiful, historic life was seeing its last day.

What he was here to do could admit no such sentiments, though. He forced his attention away from the oak and onto the nearby pilings drill that was tearing deep holes to fill with steel and concrete. Sliding his ruined shoes back into the mud, he went to check if his suspicion about the sizes was correct.

Russian construction workers apparently didn't stop for lunch, but Joel was feeling the inadequacy of his continental breakfast when a grey sedan pulled up at the site entrance. A thin, balding man got out and jogged over to the portacabin. A little while later he emerged with the first man Joel had spoken to, who pointed in Joel's direction, and the newcomer started picking his way towards him.

"Mr. Elliott?"

"Yes, that's me."

"Thank God! I'm Anatoly Markov, the project manager. I got held up by a family emergency earlier, then you were gone from the hotel, no-one had your mobile number, and so I've been searching for you for the last hour. Please don't tell me you walked here?!"

"It was a nice morning for it."

Whistling out a breath as though Joel was lucky to be alive, the man thrust out a hand.

Joel shook it. "Please call me Joel. And don't worry, it's given me a chance to look around."

Anatoly grimaced. "I know how it must appear, but we're pretty much on schedule...heavens, did they not give you some site boots?!"

"I didn't think to ask. Stupid of me."

Anatoly eyed him. "Dimitri told you he had none to spare, I assume?" He spread his hands in something between anger and apology. "Please don't think all Russians are prejudiced like that. He didn't say anything offensive did he?"

"Nothing out of the ordinary. Look Anatoly, it's just a pair of shoes and I prefer not to cause friction. In fact what I'd love is hot food. I have a company credit card itching to be used, but I've no idea of what or where to eat round here. Can I invite you to lunch?"

Anatoly's worry transformed into a warm smile. "I'd be delighted. Thank you Joel."

By unspoken agreement the conversation was kept general and genial over the excellent food. Joel found himself taking to this quiet, considerate colleague, but when the plates were cleared it was time to get down to brass tacks.

"So Anatoly, obviously there's the tree."

Anatoly winced, and asked a passing waiter for two vodkas.

"They have the good quality stuff here and beyond a nice glow you won't know you've had it," he said in response to Joel's raised eyebrows. "Anyway, yes, the tree. As a centennial oak it should have been declared when construction was first proposed on the site, but that was...overlooked. Before it could be cut down some busybody reported it, which meant a bureaucratic mess to resolve, but we got there eventually. Then it should have been removed back in May but the specialist got injured. They're due today so hopefully the damned thing's going even as we speak."

"Right. But my concern is you can't leave any roots or the soil will compact as they rot. Anything built on top will subside."

Anatoly inclined his head in agreement.

"But," Joel continued, "to get all the roots out it's going to disturb a large area of ground to quite a depth, causing another version of the same problem."

"You're right, but that's why we've moved where we're sinking pilings on that corner of the building, added the extra, and we're going further down with them."

Joel blinked. "Possibly my Russian is letting me down here..."

"Not at all. You speak it impressively well."

"Thank you...but have you just told me you've been redesigning the foundations yourselves as you go along?"

"If we didn't then, as you said, the building would subside in that corner."

"But you can't do that!"

"We had to. Like I just said. Like you just said."

"Without informing the architects? Anatoly you really..."

"No! Of course we spoke to the architects. They cleared it almost two months ago."

Just at that moment the vodka arrived.

"Nostrovia!" said Anatoly, clinking glasses with Joel before they both knocked the generous measures back.

"Tchhaa..." said Joel, wiping his eyes and coughing before trying again. "Two months ago. So that would be the previous architect, not Stern Johns Rubikov?"

"They didn't tell you?"

"No, they didn't tell us."

"Ah! So that must be why that girl they sent out last week got so upset."

"Presumably. And before we get on to what we do about this, can I also ask why all the holes are a smaller diameter than on the plans?"

"Eh? Oh, because of Russian drills."

Joel frowned. "Russian drills? What do you mean?"

Anatoly looked nonplussed for a second, then nodded. "In Russia we have different standard sizes. If we wanted a drill for the size your firm changed the holes to on the plans we'd have to bring one from Finland. That would be crazy, no?"

"So you just reduced all the hole sizes?"

"Yes, but we're going half a metre deeper to compensate."

Joel tried to think through explaining all of this to Stephen and found himself wading into mental quicksand.

"Joel listen." Anatoly was leaning in. "You've seen enough of the local area. There are concrete tower blocks everywhere and they don't fall down. We know how to build these things here. Don't worry, my friend!"

"That's easy for you to say! I'm going to have to do some fast talking here, but I think we may be able to smooth this out. Send me the latest version of these plans of yours. I'm going to call London and explain the reasons for the changes. Then we'll see if we can get something everybody agrees with before you place more steels or pour concrete. How does that sound?"

"Like a good idea Joel! I tell you, life would be a lot easier if everyone spoke Russian."

"Indeed. I won't be back at the site today, but can you check your email regularly for any questions and updated blueprints?"

Anatoly grinned. "Sure thing." Then he got up to leave, but paused and turned back to Joel, a newly-troubled expression on his face. "Please don't let this cause delay though. Those foundations are rubles and we need to plant them into the ground soon. As we say in Russia, money is like down, one puff and it's gone."

"Excellent work Joel! Excellent!"

"Thanks Stephen. And for trusting me with this too."

"Had a feeling about you Joel! When you get back we're going to have a chat about a position in my group. First, though, we'll have revised plans with those diameters and working round that bloody oak footprint with you by the end of the night. You'll make one hundred percent sure that's what everyone has and is going to use, right?"

"Definitely."

"And while you're there I also want you to use those sharp little eyes of yours for any and everything else, including confirming they're getting every root thicker than a drinking straw out along with all other traces of that infernal tree."

"Will do."

"Great. Okay, it's late where you are but go get yourself a well-deserved nightcap. On Team Latham we work hard and we party harder, so that's an order!"

"Copy that then, Stephen! Good night."

He hit the end call button, then sat there dazed. Before turning the computer off he flicked, out of habit, to email, where an extra glow to this surreal day was waiting. It was a first-ever message to him from Gemma. Sure, she was probably just fishing for gossip, but that was no kind of reason to refuse her suggestion they go get a drink together sometime soon.

He closed the laptop rather than reply too soon and eagerly. Joel stood up. Then, for the second time in a little over twenty-four hours, he toppled backwards onto his massive hotel bed with an ear-to-ear smile across his face.

The sun was shining again, Dimitri's grunted salutation was barely hostile, and a pair of brand-new boots in Joel's size sat outside the portacabin.

As soon as he walked on site Joel's eyes went straight to the oak, or rather where it had been. It was now nothing more than a short stump sticking out of churned ground sprayed with ripped leaves and shattered twigs. The carnage gave his good mood a tinge of regret around its edges.

Anatoly was bent over the new plans with Dimitri, and from what Joel could see the Stern Johns Rubikov changes were acceptable to both men.

Over the course of the morning the three extra Russian-drill-size borehole locations were marked out, and Joel spent most of his time answering emailed questions, confirming the occasional minor detail with Anatoly, and watching progress with the tree roots.

A little after lunchtime a two-hundred-and-seventy-degree arc around the forlorn stump had been dug out, cleared of roots, and compressor-hammered back into place. All that was left was the front of the tree, or at least what Joel thought of as the front based on those ghostly letters P.V.L.

Beep-beep-beep, grind grind growl. He'd been listening to it all day, making it strange when the engines went silent and the only sound left was shouting.

Moments later the door to the cabin crashed open and Anatoly was rushing towards the cluster of men by the tree. Discarding the mug of foul coffee he'd been sipping at, Joel followed him.

The centre of interest was hidden by one of the diggers, but as Joel rounded it Anatoly was there to block his path. "My friend it is better that you know nothing of this."

Joel looked the project manager in the eye. "I thought we'd established some trust yesterday?"

"We did, we did. You can go see if you must Joel, but my advice to you is walk away and forget you saw anything."

"Anatoly, my firm sent me out here to take note of everything I could." He moved decisively round towards the other side of the big, yellow machine.

"No good can come of this," murmured the Russian as Joel passed him.

The men were packed close together, all looking into the digger's half-raised shovel. Then Dimitri moved, leaving a large gap. Through it Joel spotted bones poking out of the soil. Somehow they had a peculiar magnetism about them.

From the hole a few metres away came noises of spades being used, then a collective gasp and the Russian for skull. The workers around the digger moved as one to this more dramatic attraction, and Joel found himself alone with the remains of some long-dead fellow human. He leant in closer.

They looked like a radius and an ulna, if his recollection of school biology was correct. He reached in and eased away some soil. Yes, there was the array of tiny bones that formed a hand. They were coiled around something. Joel brushed away more dirt and saw a small piece of what looked like tropical hardwood. The form was peculiar, squarish with four semicircles cut into it. A puzzle piece? There was something fascinating about it. Joel picked it up and wiped encrusted muck from its surface. Red glinted: rubies?

"Joel?"

His hand closed convulsively around the square of wood then fled to his pocket to conceal the evidence. Joel was amazed to find himself stealing from a corpse, but it was too late to reverse his action.

Anatoly came round from behind the digger.

"Ah, there you are. I wish you had taken my advice."

Joel looked back at him, puzzled. "But I'm not squeamish."

"Okay, a question for you: back in England what happens if you find a skeleton while you're digging foundations?"

Suddenly Joel grasped the other man's point. "You cease all work and notify the authorities."

"Yes. The same here. In theory."

The implication was clear. The advice had been pragmatic, but he hadn't taken it.

"Joel please believe me that no-one back in London wishes to know about this." Anatoly was rushing words out. "Do you know how many lives were lost in this area when the Nazis invaded? Two million. And Lenin, Stalin and their ilk added many more. Russia is soaked in blood and built on bones. If we stopped every time something like this came up we would never be able to build the future. Do you see?"

"But surely if that's the case the hold-up wouldn't be too bad? And what if someone reports this to the authorities like they did the oak? I don't see how I can avoid mentioning this."

"Ah Joel, you put me between the devil and the deep blue sea then. I hinted at this yesterday but I hoped I would not have to explain it. The financing for the project is on a knife edge. The two major backers controlling seventy percent are affected by EU sanctions over Crimea. At the moment they can pull out with only small losses, but once the foundations are poured one of the contractual project phases completes and they will be locked in much tighter. These works have to happen without delay."

Now Anatoly was watching him closely, and with an almost tender expression of concern on his face. "Joel, I like you. This is why I promise that revealing what you've seen here today to anyone at Stern Johns Rubikov will do irreparable harm to your career. You know the word discretion? Welcome to its ugly, real-life meaning."

Joel looked at the bones. "So you'll just put them back in the soil and cover them over?"

"Yes. Five thousand rubles and a little threat to each of the men on site today, two minutes with the digger, and this is finished. As long as you are discreet. Are you going to be discreet Joel? If you also need some rubles..."

"I don't need rubles, thanks." That was at least one thing he could decide; he'd taken more than enough that wasn't his already today. "As for being discreet, I don't believe I have much choice. I won't say anything."

The Russian nodded in relief. "Please trust me that the new plans will be followed and we will be careful to remove all the roots. My suggestion is you might enjoy the retail opportunities at the airport more than continuing to be here."

Joel nodded, heeding the advice this time.

Soon the two sat in silence driving the few minutes back to the hotel. Anatoly pulled up in front of it, they shook hands, and Joel walked to the lobby door. Again, there was all the gilt. He caught a glimpse of his new reflection, but this time he didn't feel like studying it further.

It was only back in his room that Joel remembered what he'd pocketed. He took it to the bathroom and carefully cleaned it. What emerged was dark-grained, beautifully-made and unfeasibly heavy. The face material was surely lignum vitae, one of the most expensive woods in the world. And what looked like a single piece of it was in fact a composite of many parts, their grains so perfectly matched that not a single one strayed by a fraction of a millimetre as they formed the bizarrely compelling shape leading inwards to the two rubies at the centre.

Snapping the spell, Joel turned the piece over and saw the back was finest ebony. Strangest of all, the edges were dotted with pinpricks of shining metal. They seemed to be the ends of wires that ran between the two layers of wood. But a metal that lasted decades underground without even tarnishing? Between that fact and the colour he guessed it must be platinum.

This was something - or a part of something - extraordinarily costly.

Exhaling tightly, Joel forced his conscience quiet, burying himself in the practical tasks of packing, checking out, and catching his plane back to London instead.

Only several hours into the westward flight did he allow his thoughts to return to Russia.

He'd performed beyond all expectations; Stephen had confirmed as much. An incredible opportunity had come his way and he'd grabbed it to fast forward his career.

So why did he feel diminished? He pondered this the whole way over Germany. Because that skeleton had opened his eyes to bigger pictures? Because discretion was just corruption by a nicer name? Because if he lived to a hundred Joel Elliott would always be subject to forces beyond any level of control he could hope to attain?

Perhaps, but he'd already had a fair idea of such things. He'd long since been schooled in compromise. He could do what was needed to avoid being tarred as someone insufficiently professional, someone unable to carry his share of life's often onerous load. Not discreet meant not reliable, meant not employable, meant not Team Latham.

And it was vital for him to be Team Latham. Even after the year-long internship that would now be his, he still needed the Master's degree component to qualify as an architect. He would then be nearly a hundred thousand pounds in debt and seeking an entry-level job in an extraordinarily competitive marketplace.

So no. That wasn't it. Choice was an essential prerequisite to suffering a guilty conscience.

Finally, as some nondescript part of the Benelux countries scrolled beneath him in the summer evening's murk, he worked it out: it was that place in the air above the island in the mire.

Its impossible sting had jolted some essential pillar of his understanding of the world. And the worst of it was everyone else had known. Their footprints had avoided it.

What instinct did they possess that he lacked? What did they perceive in that spot that he could not see? He'd always been one of the fastest in life, making it hateful to feel slow and stupid.

Nor would he be able to forget this sensation. Not so long as he kept the little square of dark wood. That souvenir of the whole damned experience stolen from the dead.

3.

London, August 2015.

Joel reached over to run his fingertips down Gemma's naked spine. "You have a lovely back."

"Mmm, I bet you say that to all the girls."

"Only the ones with lovely backs."

She gave the same throaty chuckle that had bewitched him the previous evening and well into the early hours. "Joel, would you be a darling and fix me a morning coffee? The good stuff's in my desk drawer. Where my thieving housemates can't steal it and replace it with instant granules, if at all."

He rolled reluctantly out of bed and went over, finding a half-full packet of grounds.

"Now, I'm afraid the kettle's in the kitchen, and finding a clean mug may take initiative or washing up, but I promise not to get dressed in the interim."

Joel grinned and scoured the floor for his t-shirt. "You make a compelling argument."

A glow of animal satisfaction had been lighting her face, but now it slid away like money from a bank balance. "Huh. Well apparently not all that fucking compelling."

That this subject would not come up again so soon had been a naïve hope. "So you didn't manage to drink those neurons to death last night then?"

"No I didn't. And for all your talent with looking calm and composed don't tell me you're alright with it either."

Joel sighed, yesterday's reality returning to pop the morning's pleasant spell. "True. But we always knew only one of us would get it. I thought it would be you actually."

Gemma sat up. "What on earth are you talking about? As well as being a much-needed diversity hire you're Stephen Latham's golden boy who, word has it, went off to Russia and single-handedly negotiated Stern Johns and fucking Rubikov out of a very sticky situation. I mostly fetched Starbucks."

"Yes, but you have THAT going for you." Joel indicated the long, languid line of Gemma's body under the sheet, "And I know the effect those miniskirts of yours had on me."

"And a first from Cambridge for which I sweated blood, thank you very much."

"And a first from Cambridge, but we all have good degrees.

My point is that in an office controlled by middle-aged men who spend all day working out how to erect things..."

"Oh very droll!"

"Thank you. That, well, I thought you were a shoe-in."

Gemma narrowed her eyes. "I still reckon you thought you'd get it, and by the way all the secretaries fancied the arse off you, but okay; let's say that I probably could have been in had I been prepared to put out. I wasn't though."

Joel raised the coffee packet to her in salute. "And thus the CAD monkey wins the day."

"Body odour, grotty little beard and all, yes. But hang on, we've not finished with Joel yet."

"We haven't? Good!" Joel tried on a lascivious grin.

"That topic we can return to, but what I mean is you were drafted into Team Latham and appeared to have ascended as if on shining wings from the stinking pits of interndom. What the hell went wrong?"

He'd been trying not to think about the anti-climax of the last three weeks, but Gemma was clearly determined and it was reawakened now anyway. "You have to keep this secret, okay?"

"We still have secrets from each other after last night? Darling I'm most disappointed."

"No, I'm being serious. Do you swear?"

"Fuckers. Will that do?"

Joel gave a sardonic laugh. "I like you Gemma. But I'm not saying a word unless this goes no further."

"Well for one, who would I tell since as of yesterday I'm an ex-intern? And two, as you're in the same boat why do you give a flying fuck?"

He sighed. "Because you never know if a route back opens up some day. All pretence aside, I'm desperate. I already owe so much and I'm still only half-qualified. And even if I ever get my year's experience and the Master's component there are just no jobs out there. AND even if there were there are one-thousand-plus unemployed architects per year for each of the last seven years of this economic downturn BUT most of them were paying three grand a year in fees rather than the nine you and I pay so they have lower debts and can afford to work for a lot less. Stern Johns Rubikov may be no kind of bridge to anywhere, but I still can't afford to burn it."

Gemma made a face. "Poor bunny," she teased, but her eyes on him were tender with generational understanding. "Do you have anything lined up?"

"Nope. I'll look for more architecture placements but the chances are slim-to-none until next summer. Temp work I guess. You?"

"It's going to have to be my dad's marketing agency, unfortunately. Nothing to do with my degree. No RIBA points. Inevitable familiarity with the nearest Starbucks."

"I don't suppose they need anyone else?"

"'Fraid not. They don't even need me, but you know, Daddy's the CFO. At least you living chez parents means you can save a bit. No hope in London otherwise."

"True. Although since Grandpa died and Nonna moved in I'm already sharing a room with my brother." Joel was starting to feel sick as the full collection of his worries was dragged to the surface. "And my oldest brother and his girlfriend were asking Mum last week about staying for a while when the baby comes."

"Yikes! Sounds grim. The future's grim Joel! Let's stop talking about it. Back to the mystery reason you're in this situation in the first place. I promise not to talk. Tell me."

Joel gave a resigned shrug. "Much like myself, there's no money. The project's dead."

"Really?!"

"You are not to gossip about this!"

"I already said I wouldn't. But what happened?"

"The foundations were construction phase one. Once that

was complete funding for phase two had to go into escrow, but it never arrived. Lawyers are involved and accusations are flying backwards and forwards, but it's all half-hearted because it's not so much that the investors won't pay as they can't. So that's that. I kept quiet for nothing and they chopped down the oak for no reason at all."

"Quiet about what? What oak? But that still doesn't explain why you were passed over for the internship. You did an amazing job and it's not your fault the rubles ran out."

Joel almost snarled at being forced to relive this. "Because, like I said, no-one needs any more architects. My Russian made me useful to Team-bloody-Latham, but when the project ended I wasn't anymore so he dropped me without a second thought. Olly did the smart thing by never trying to act like an architect. CAD modelling was the way to win. Doing every element of a skilled, technical job that should pay twenty pounds or so per hour. But he's on, what? Seventy-hour weeks for five hundred a month makes one pound seventy-five. Plus they have no obligation to keep him on after his year is up. That's what the people we're banking on to employ us want. I, on the other hand, tried to do the job I've been training for, which was the stupid play. Now does that explain why not me adequately?"

Gemma raised her hands, play-warding off his vehemence, and the sheet fell down to her waist. She caught his look. "I have to say you've made me feel more fucked than like fucking."

Joel laughed bitterly. "But what else do the young have these days? Would that coffee help?"

Gemma leaned forward to put her hands on the sides of his face. "So pretty even when you're in a grump! Well, interns fetch coffee and interns certainly get screwed. I'm sure you can do the math."

4.

Manchester, January 2016.

Joel awoke with the dazedness of a night spent in a tiny bedroom in which the window had been nailed shut. Worming his way across ancient, twanging springs to the front of his bed, he scrabbled in the orange-hued gloom for his phone.

8:26. Swearing and tugging on clothes, he was downstairs dressed and ready enough by 8:32, and now it was a case of waiting the designated hour until 9:30 to see if the agency would call with a job for the day. If they did he would have to leg it to the bus or search for an Uber to try and keep up the pretence that he had a car, as per contractual stipulation. If not: sorry, better luck tomorrow. Don't call us, we'll call you.

Or not. Yet again.

"How do they have the cheek to call this 'regular work'?" he complained to Big Kev, his landlord-cum-housemate, who was trying to extract a cup from the bottom of the half metre high pile of dirty crockery in the sink.

"Dunno. Suits me fine."

"Why?! You have to be up and ready every morning but then when they don't call you don't get paid and it's another day gone."

"I think it's only you does all that getting dressed stuff like they tell you. Anyway, it's a job so it keeps me parents off me back, and half the time you get to watch TV instead. What's not to like?"

"How about the lack of money at the end of the month, Kev? You know, for rent, food and making payments on our student loans."

"Oh, you took loans did you? That sucks."

"What do you mean 'did I'? Are you saying you didn't? How?!"

Big Kev chiselled with a knife at something stuck to the cup. "Dunno. I s'pose with the income from this place I've always had enough. And it's pretty social here in the house so I don't need to go out much. Have you seen the kettle?"

Joel let his gaze creep over the tiny, biohazard kitchen of twenty-two Westburn Road, Big Kev's illegally-divided and over-tenanted goldmine of a redbrick terraced house inherited from his grandparents.

"On the window sill. But watch out because I think someone was trying to cook eggs in it yesterday."

"Yeah, that were me. Didn't go well. You want a cuppa?"

"No thanks, I'll pass."

"You sure? Goes well with a nice morning of telly."

Outside drizzle was spraying the windows. Inside despondency lay in wait. There had been no architectural placements to be had after leaving Stern Johns Rubikov. Joel had found a series of temp jobs in London, each for a week or a few days, but his qualifications were a barrier to anything more stable: no-one would consider hiring him because they assumed he would leave for something better. Except there was no something better.

In early December his oldest brother John, complete with girlfriend and new-born baby, had moved air-quotes-temporarily into the Elliott family home. With Joel's parents in one bedroom, Nonna in another, and now John and his family in the third, the only option remaining for Joel, his older brother and younger sister was to install bunk beds and share the last bedroom. It had been a constant and vicious battle for space to the background music of a screaming infant who also made the whole house smell of regurgitated milk. Christmas had been far from festive.

Joel had been desperate to get out, and returning to Manchester seemed the best option. A university friend mentioned Big Kev had a room going cheap and could also hook him up with an agency job. Thus had read the brochure. The reality, however, didn't bear sustained contemplation.

His shoulders sagged. "What's on this morning then?"

"Antiques Hunt re-run. S'posed be a good 'un. Interested?"

Old people discussing old things. Joel really wasn't in the mood for that. "Maybe later. You start without me."

"Righto." Big Kev used the same knife as earlier to hack a lump of sugar out of a congealed packet into his cup, then stir. He scratched at an armpit before shuffling off in his slippers and dressing gown towards the foul sofa of the lounge.

There was neither a seat nor space for one in the kitchen, and soon posh English daytime TV chattering about porcelain figurines was wafting through loudly. Joel went back upstairs, held his breath against the stench of urine and mould as he passed the open door to the shared-between-six bathroom, and decided imprisoning himself in his room to brood was his least-worst option.

He stared at the walls and the walls stared impassively back.

Did returning, tail between his legs, to Bromley make more sense than staying here? His parents had been at pains to point out that space might be tight but it would always be his home too. Who was he kidding, though? The version of Joel living there would always be the person he was desperate to outgrow. Every time he resolved not to sink into the whole five-siblings squabbling, bickering, poking, teasing, overcrowded chaos...but unfailingly it had him again in no time flat. No, what he wanted was a new start. To move forwards.

In fact what he really needed was a lucky break. He would do anything for it. One bit of sunshine and good fortune that stuck. Hah! As if. And if he wanted that so badly why on earth try to find it in this grey city in England's north? Even northerners described the place as grim. But what was the alternative? He simply could not think of one.

'Please'. He almost spoke the word aloud.

But prayers were something this airless bedroom knew how to wring the hope out of. Mancunian to its woodchip-wallpapered core, it dealt only in shades of dissatisfaction. "If you really think you can do better elsewhere then leave," it seemed to say. And yet behind that contemptuous dismissal there seemed to come another voice offering something far more tempting. It was only the faintest of whispers inside a corner of Joel's mind, but it urged him...downstairs?

Given that was his only other option on a cold, sodden Manchester morning with no money, Joel chose to comply.

The programme on TV must have been filmed in the summer. Predominantly grey-haired people, dressed for a vicar's garden party, shivered around a large series of trestle tables. Behind them was a windswept grey castle, above which greyer clouds lurked ominously.

"Where's this from?"

"Oh, hiya Joel. Didn't hear you come in. Dunno. Scotland somewhere."

Hats held on by hands, the female presenter and a man in full kilt getup talked animatedly about a leather-and-brass thing for doing something to a horse in days of yore.

"Is there anything else on, maybe?"

"Oh no. This is me favourite. Plus they've got a special find coming at the end."

There was no use fighting Big Kev for control of the TV. If it came down to it - and it often did - it was his.

"A special find? How do you mean?"

"An antique that's really worth something. They do a teaser near the start but then they leave the reveal 'til the end. Some old battle-axe's got it. And a right foxy granddaughter I'd like to stick it to, know what I mean?"

"Invariably. Honestly though Kev, if you actually want to 'stick it' to a girl it'll serve you better never to use the phrase."

"Mebbe." Kev swivelled round, causing a high-plastic-content squeak from the cushions. "But easy for you to say. You know how to pick up the ladies."

"Picking up is another expression to avoid." Talking 'ladies' with Big Kev on a sofa that literally crawled beneath your touch while people brayed about antiques was making Joel wish he'd stayed upstairs. "It's also the wrong way to view it, men more or less having to prey on women, women having to sit around waiting for that to happen. Just think of it as two people who both feel like a bit of fun at the same time. Don't make it complicated and it won't be."

Kev shifted closer on the vile seating. "But that bird you had a picture of on your phone, I mean how do you even get up the nerve to go after a girl like that?"

"What, Gemma? We just worked at the same firm and left on the same day, had a few consolatory drinks and one thing led to another. Anyway we only saw each other for a couple of weeks. She could do better than me and we both knew it. Already has in fact."

Someone sensitive might have picked up on a touch of bitterness. "Oooh but ten-out-of-ten shaggable that! Right lucky bastard you are," said Kev.

"Showering and taking exercise can help attract women too," added Joel a little unkindly.

Kev gave a loud sigh that smelt slightly of soup. "Not sure I'd want to give up the bachelor lifestyle anyway." He gestured around. "It's just I get urges, y'know?"

Joel was on the point of making a run for it when Big Kev swung back towards the TV. "'Ere we go. Look."

The presenter was beaming. "Well I must say we've had the most marvellous day here at the Castle of Mey in beautiful, if a touch windy," the group surrounding her laughed appreciatively, "Caithness. But near the start of the programme I'm sure you remember Gordon Gilfeather's expert eagle eye spotting something rather interesting. Well we're not going to keep you in suspense any longer..." the onlookers smiled and chuckled during the lengthy pause which was clearly a timeworn ritual, "...and we're going to return to that right now."

A tall, thin old lady with a face like a hatchet was beckoned forward, an even taller young woman shuffling awkwardly behind her.

"Phwoar," said Big Kev.

"Really, her?" It always amazed Joel how little some men understood about the opposite sex. "Okay, granted, she has quite a nice face and figure, but look at the hair and the clothes Kev. Notice her eyes, the way they won't land on anything that looks back. She'd sink right into the grass there if she could. She's not even comfortable in her own skin. Beware of that type: never a moment's fun and she'll make life a misery for anyone she ever gets together with, trust me."

"Do nicely for me urges though."

"Ah look, here's the expert Kev. We should listen to the TV."

A portly, goatee-bearded man in tweed regalia and a monocle was filling the screen. "Thank you Susannah, and welcome again Elaine and Nat. And..." The camera zoomed out, "...this most interesting and exquisite piece that you've brought along to show us today."

The old woman nodded briskly.

"'Ow much, 'ow much? That's what she's thinking. I love this show!" Big Kev leant sideways to nudge Joel in the ribs with his elbow.

But Joel was barely aware. All his attention was focused on the object now visible on the table in front of the pair. It was a jigsaw puzzle, beautifully made in darkest wood. At its centre was an empty space where four keys reached inwards but found no locks in which to fit. Separate and alongside it sat a single piece that was a good but obviously inferior copy of the small strange square with its two red rubies that was hidden inside Joel's suitcase upstairs.

"Now Elaine. You have, I believe, Russian heritage in the family?" You could have fried something in Gordon Gilfeather's words as he rolled the R of Russian at her.

"Yes. My grandparents. They were from Petrograd."

"And might I ask your grandfather's name and, perchance, title?"

"Baron Leonid Nikolayevich Romanov."

"Ooooh," murmured the audience.

"Ah, Petrograd! Now, as I'm sure most of you at home already know, this great city stands at the gateway to the Baltic Sea. After spending just ten years going by that moniker it was known as Leningrad for the next sixty-five before finally, in 1991, reverting to its original name of St. Petersburg. And prior to communism it was, of course, the bejewelled capital of the Russian empire."

Murmurs and 'I told you so' nods from the crowd.

"And I'm sure equally well-known is Romanov, the familial name of the last Tsars."

The onlookers were eating out of the antiquarian's hand now, with the exception of the granddaughter, who continued to fidget uncomfortably, and Elaine, who looked impatient but prepared to hang on in there for the good stuff.

"Well, well, well! So Elaine, what can you tell me about this wonderful piece of craftsmanship?"

Elaine frowned. "It's a jigsaw puzzle."

Gordon held his sides and cast around in overdone mirth.

Joel, leaning all the way forward on the sofa, wanted to yell at him to get on with it.

"No, dear lady. Perhaps I mis-phrased my question. What I meant to ask was can you enlighten us as to its provenance?"

"We don't know much about that. It was something my grandfather had made just before he left Russia because of the revolution, but the centrepiece was wrong and he would go into an awful rage if the jigsaw was so much as mentioned."

"Hmm, yes. And indeed, sad to say, this one, markedly inferior piece that goes in the middle is clearly not the original. It has in fact swollen so that it no longer even fits in place. Do you know anything about the commissioning of the puzzle, or why your grandfather never possessed the true centrepiece?"

"No."

"Then," sighed Gordon happily, "I can see the onus falls upon myself to attempt to flesh things out. Well, I think where we shall start is by taking ourselves back to those times. The late eighteen and early nineteen hundreds were an era of great wealth in Europe, and that bred prodigious investigation. What we remember now are the advances of people like Darwin and Edison, but thinking about how those great minds transformed the prevailing narrative in fact tells us a lot about the preceding status quo.

"Mysticism abounded, and though we have come to see them in a much-reduced light through the lens of our technological age, in their day the theories and researches of such as Grigori Rasputin in Russia and Aleister Crowley here in Britain were treated with a seriousness equal to anything from the budding world of science. Such men were held by many to be visionaries, and their visions were often dark and diabolical!"

There was a hush under the scudding, Scottish summer clouds and the expert played it for every penny it was worth.

"The design of this piece - why, I feel a touch of the heebie-jeebies just focusing on it! - undoubtedly originates in that school of thought. The pattern that the jigsaw forms...I think the only way I can describe it is like an Escher drawing, appearing to extend almost into another dimension. Yes, the grain of this precious ironwood, which is also known as lignum vitae or pockholz, has some design which is clearly of the occult. Also - and I don't know if the cameras can pick this up - I believe these little metallic dots along the edges reveal a deeper layer beneath the wood that is a whole other design drawn in platinum thread. Why such expense when it is hidden from view between the two outer layers? And the extravagance of using ebony as nothing more than a backing board! This truly is a most magnificent and singular, if slightly sinister, creation."

Joel, now hooked despite his impatience, didn't need to look, nor be told. He had spent many hours studying his square of dark wood from every angle.

"C'mon, what's it worth, eh?" grunted Big Kev at the TV. For once Joel was in accord with his landlord: he badly wanted that question answered.

Gordon Gilfeather, however, cut to the chase for no man. "So we have a piece of exquisite craftsmanship, and I believe from that, the location of St. Petersburg, and the date of around nineteen-seventeen given by the revolution your grandfather was escaping, I can infer that the maker was none other than the renowned Pavel Vasilyev Lebedev. Indeed this may well be his final work, his pinnacle and coda."

P.V.L. Those initials from the tree! It was confirmation. Had that skeleton at the site been the puzzle maker's? But why had he been buried with the centrepiece when it was part of a valuable commission?

"Now Pavel," continued Gordon, "who is believed to have died mysteriously that same year, was never truly recognised in his lifetime. He made relatively few pieces and for the most part they were chess sets, crosses, a couple of other jigsaws - which were in vogue at the time - and assorted highly decorative bits of woodwork for the upper-middle classes. Sadly such opulence was little appreciated under the revolutionary communist rule that followed, and many of his works were damaged, lost or destroyed. Thus those which survive are rare indeed."

Eyes were lighting up in the audience; finally this was the good bit.

Gordon kept them waiting like one of those people who enjoys balancing biscuits on their dog's nose. "To monetary worth, then!" he boomed at last. "In recent years, I am happy to say, Soviet oligarchs have been getting very competitive at auction for the best late-empire works of Russian art and craft. Thus, a century after his demise, Pavel Vasilyev Lebedev has become not only well-known but also highly sought-after."

Elaine was leaning in, but Gordon held up two palms and assumed a sombre expression. "Alas, though, before we go further down the road of valuation I fear I must return to the issue of what is missing. We can only speculate whether the original might have been stolen for the two rubies I'm assuming were set into it, but, as we already know, where the crowning centrepiece should be we have only this crude approximation of the real thing."

He picked it up and the camera zoomed in. "As you can see, it's just a single layer of oak painted to look like ironwood. You'll also notice these red stones are merely cut glass. And this loss, I'm afraid, strips away most of the value because buyers in this particular market really do demand perfection." He shook his head sadly.

"Now Gordon," Susannah was wearing a patient smile. "I think you're going to have to put us out of our suspense here. I'm a trifle worried it's getting a bit much for a few of our audience!" She was right, some had turned very red. More genial chuckling, but with a hard undertone. All eyes in the crowd were on the scene like a tiding of magpies.

"Indeed Susannah! You must forgive my excess of enthusiasm. Well! In this incomplete state, were this remarkable jigsaw puzzle to be placed under the hammer, my estimate is that it would fetch in the region of ten to twelve thousand Sterling."

The gasp from the audience was a muted one: very good for an attic find, but hardly lottery jackpot territory. Elaine attempted a smile for the camera. Behind her the granddaughter, Nat, continued to look like she didn't want to be there. Joel felt violently deflated, and Big Kev gave literal form to that sentiment by releasing wind as he leant back on the sofa.

"But!" Gordon Gilfeather was looming in the camera again, index finger held high. "If you were somehow able to reunite this jigsaw puzzle with its lost centrepiece, then I feel certain that the auction would conclude at no less than a quarter of a million pounds!"

5.

Manchester, Scottish Highlands & Reay.

It was the break Joel had pleaded fate for.

Now he needed to exploit it.

"Think I'll head upstairs," he declared to Big Kev, voice barely under control as the Antiques Hunt credits rolled.

"Right y'are." Kev was already searching for something else to watch and appeared to notice no change in his tenant.

Bolting the door to his room, Joel went straight to his suitcase zip pocket for the centrepiece. That new voice in his head seemed to inhale in anticipation as the rubies glinted in the light of the bare bulb. Holding the little square gingerly in awe of its new-found worth, Joel gazed at it, its dark lines filling his mind with all the possibilities they would unlock.

Finally he set it to one side and opened up his laptop. Google found a headline from a newspaper called the John

O'Groat Journal: 'Reay Linked to Romanovs of Russia in Local Antique Find'. The article wasn't available online but he had the first few lines from the cached search result: 'Reay pensioner Elaine Sinclair and her granddaughter, recently returned local veterinarian Nat Sinclair, found themselves in for a grand surprise at the Castle of Mey when an old family heirloom turned out to be a valuable relic of imperial Russia. Unfortunately...'

It was enough for his purposes. 'Sinclair, Mrs. E.' and her address were listed in the phone directory for Reay, a tiny village at the eastern edge of the most northerly county in Britain, Caithness. Nat Sinclair turned up too. There was a photo of her and an older man presenting a dog to a blind person. She looked far happier in this context than on the antiques programme, and there was contact information for the vet's practice in Melvich she was listed as working at...

But no, the granddaughter was to be avoided. As he'd commented to Big Kev, there was an awkwardness there that was too hard to deal with. Old Elaine was the far better bet for his approach. Based on what he'd seen on TV she understood financial value. That, in the end, was what it always came down to.

The whole rest of the day, as gritty rain streaked his unopenable window to the wider world, he plotted. What he settled upon was to offer Elaine twenty-five thousand pounds for her incomplete jigsaw puzzle. It didn't seem cherished and she hadn't given the impression of being well-off. It was twice the estimate Gordon Gilfeather had given them, so he felt sure it would do the trick.

Of course money, or rather its lack, was the usual glaring problem. His strategy required laying his hands on twenty-five thousand pounds. Could he find an antiques dealer to fund the acquisition? Possibly, but he'd have to play that carefully. Any character willing to advance such a sum might scent blood and try to take over the whole scheme by parting Joel from his centrepiece.

Frowning, he pushed all this to one side for now. He would get an agreement for the purchase from Elaine first and worry about paying for it later. Given the worth of the completed puzzle he knew there would be a way, even if it meant rushing backwards and forwards between London and the other end of the country a few times.

His other fear had been that she might already have cashed in. Fortunately there were several websites covering Pavel Vasilyev Lebedev's work. They all contained details of the Antiques Hunt find but made no mention of any subsequent sale, so he was reassured; Elaine still had it. Even so, time had gone by and there was no more to waste. He concluded the best approach was to go unannounced and in person; be right there holding his centrepiece in front of the old lady to charm, cajole or whatever her. He could get everything signed and sealed quickly and cleanly. It would be a costly trip, but a worthwhile investment. Once he got his hands on that money all such worldly little problems would be behind him.

Still struggling to process that all of this was real, he decided to take the last concrete step he could today. He couldn't book anything yet, as his bank account balance was down near zero, but he could search for accommodation in Reay.

There were two options. The Reay Arms, a friendly-looking old inn, was feasible. The prices of the other were beyond astronomical. What a surprise, Joel thought, that a remote village of just a few hundred souls would also be home to 'The Champ Scotland International Golf Resort at Fresgoe Castle'.

Again he seemed to hear that faint whisper in his head, its curiosity urging him to the Castle's web page. Why not?

Reay, it turned out, was the ancestral hometown of Sir Charles Maxwell Patrick Campbell, and the golf resort was this great man's way of giving something back.

Everyone knew Campbell's name. The man behind it less so, but Joel had in fact researched him years ago for a school GCSE media studies project. The voice seemed very interested, so he trawled back over the details in his memory.

The second son of a self-made Birmingham press-baron, and needing braces to walk until middle childhood, Charles grew up derided by his father as a weakling. At Eton his academic results were poor, his face noted for its forgettability, and he was overshadowed in and on all fields by his older brother. He was also reminded frequently of his origins and place, often in ways that left bruises.

At twenty, and funded just enough to make him go away quietly, he started running town and county-level beauty pageants across the northwest, ultimately growing these into a nationwide 'adult entertainment' business in the late 1960s. It may have been a contentious industry, but it was a recession-proof one through economic downturns. Charles was already a rich man when, his brother having died in a boat explosion just months earlier, he took sole inheritance of his father's stable of local newspapers in 1978. His first act with the family business was to slash staff and overheads to increase profitability. His second was to break what was left apart and sell it piecemeal. The funds he raised went into property speculation. Also the 1980s high life, under the new nickname 'Champ', and toting a string of permed trophy wives and girlfriends who rarely lasted a year.

In the early 90s, legend has it based on a single Silicon Valley conversation about what the coming 'internet' would look like, he moved out of property and into media and tech. Broadening his original business into controlling stakes in several national tabloids, 'men's mags' and commercial TV production, Champ was ready with the content when online came calling, and now figured in 'Britain's Richest' lists.

In the opening years of the new millennium his sights

turned on what many believed was his lifelong target: the great bastions of professional journalism. One after another revered newspaper fell to his leveraged buyouts, and he amassed a 43% ownership of the UK press. A grubby outsider old money had held its nose at even as it trousered the cash, Campbell, now knighted, was the new establishment. Despite his official retirement in 2010 at age 65, rumour had it that a necessary pilgrimage of any would-be British Prime Minister was to Champ's yacht, thereupon to abase themselves, pledge allegiance, and seek anointment.

Joel's teacher had awarded him the worst mark he'd ever received for an essay. In response to the assertion that Champ Campbell's relentless acquisition of money and power was an inspiration, she'd written, in red pen, "5/10. This is a horrible human being. You need to learn to see the difference, Joel. Please."

The low grade and that patronising comment still irked the hell out of him to this day.

After a sleepless night where every slight sound was the denizens of South Manchester breaking into the house to make off with his treasure, Joel decided it was still less risky to leave it here while he went out. He'd been mugged a couple of times in his life and would not let today make three times unlucky. Working the plaster rose of his bedroom's ceiling light loose, he hid the piece inside then pushed everything back into place.

He took his laptop, mp3 player, headphones and a couple of architecture coursebooks to a pawnbroker's, and secured just enough cash to fund his journey. Returning home he rushed to retrieve the centrepiece before booking The Reay Arms and the last-minute deal he'd found on the overnight train to the far north. After killing the rest of the day locked inside his room, at just gone midnight he was waiting on the platform at Preston station as the long snake of the London to Inverness Caledonian Sleeper rumbled in.

He located his cabin and was relieved to find he had it to himself, but he still couldn't shake his paranoia about being parted from his puzzle piece. He'd made a protective case for it out of an old cassette box and some soft cloth, and he gripped this tight in his hand rather than leave it in his bag on the floor. Worried he might drop it during the night, he took off a sock, pulled it over his fist as it gripped the case, then lay on his side to pin that arm. Positioned thus, he eventually drifted off into a fitful doze.

He awoke as the train pulled out of the cavernous wind-tunnel of a station at Perth. He'd imagined that his first-ever morning in Scotland would begin with vistas of the snow-covered Cairngorm mountains, but as they left the town behind there was only darkness; a night-time like you never encountered amongst all England's people, buildings, cars and their various lights. He was travelling into an empty vastness, the chill of which seeped through the walls of the carriages as they rattled north.

Occasional knots of streetlamps came, paused, and then slid away as they stopped at small, granite stations. Dunkeld and Birnam, Pitlochry, Blair Atholl, Dalwhinnie, Newtonmore, Kingussie, now Aviemore. These names and the dim pre-dawn outlines of rugged ridges dispelled any notion of British singularity. He was now far, far away from London.

A steward knocked, seemed glad to see him awake and out of bed, and handed him a paper bag containing an oily muffin and a giant cup of tea. One hour left on this leg to Inverness, then two more to wait in the city followed by another four on the train yet further north to Thurso, where he could catch a bus to Reay. The distances up here were huge, and the means of crossing them were slow.

That was okay though. It gave him plenty of time to reconsider.

Maybe it was some strange effect of the Scottish air, but during the night his heart had taken against his head's carefully-constructed plan. Now he wanted nothing of that original scheme. Sure you could argue that it was just business and all the rest, but there was a wrongness to it.

He was embarrassed in fact. Embarrassed by how he'd lost himself in the face of temptation. Team Latham had used then discarded him, and to an extent – albeit an enjoyable one at the time – so had Gemma. He knew the sickening taste when you found out that future plans excluded you, and it wasn't something he wished on anyone else.

His fortunes had changed. This was a new start into a different version of himself, and the rules that person would live by were not yet fixed.

Outside snow-dusted countryside was appearing ghostlike as sunup neared. Ignoring a whispered snarl of contempt from that faint voice in his head, Joel decided to do this the decent way. He would simply show the centrepiece to Elaine as soon as he met her and propose that they split the sale profits fifty-fifty.

No. Fairer still, because she had forty-eight pieces to his one, Elaine would get the first twelve thousand – Gordon Gilfeather's upper valuation – and then everything above that, the higher price only his piece made possible, would be divided in two.

This revised proposal even solved the problem of needing cash up front. Elaine would welcome it and it was the moral choice. The one he could be sure would never return to haunt him. He hadn't been able to afford scruples back at the construction site in St. Petersburg, but now he could, and it felt freeing.

Nodding resolution as he exhaled, he calculated swiftly: half of two hundred and fifty minus twelve still equalled one hundred and nineteen thousand pounds. And Gilfeather had said 'no less than'. There would be auction house commission, but it still meant he would have the funding to complete the two years of his architecture Master's degree and emerge qualified with all loans cleared. That was enough. When you'd known the soul-sapping stress of falling behind the affluent in life's race of attrition, it was enough.

The sky darkened again outside and sleet shot suddenly from it to rattle against his window, but nothing could dim Joel's inner glow as the night train started its descent out of the mountains.

Hours later and the sun, harsh and headache-inducing, struggled to clear the southern horizon. It made the views from the Thurso train even more spectacular; wide, stark glens of scree and snow-frosted brown heather; small villages of stone cottages with bare grey trees huddled close around. Above it all shining white mountain tops rose into wisps of cloud and Joel felt a thrill at the sight. As they trekked yet further north, though, all gave way to a vast, dark bog rimmed by distant peaks. This Mordorish expanse was broken only by the giant forms of wind turbines, mile after mile of them. It was an unsettling juxtaposition, and from somewhere in that mire crept an inexplicable sense of foreboding. Even though it was barely four, the sun's low parabola wilted and twilight returned.

A delay on the train meant he missed his bus and had two hours to hang around the amber-lit streets of Thurso, mainland Britain's most northerly town. Eager to stretch his legs he walked, exploring stone-bordered roads, cold and unsoftened by vegetation. There was an ancient, ruined church amongst the close-packed houses. Then a grim harbour beyond which giant waves curled towards a falling-down castle across the river mouth. He turned the other way and went alongside a bleak beach. Its end, delineated by the spectral light of foaming surf, seemed unfeasibly distant.

He left plenty of margin to catch the next bus, and after a half hour grind through sparsely-populated countryside he at last arrived in Reay. Stepping out of the vehicle, Joel shivered as the wind nipped his now-sluggish body. He was happy to see The Reay Arms right next to the bus stop.

Having checked into his room, a seat by the fire and a pint of the amber ale regulars were drinking made a tempting prospect. He had only tonight and tomorrow here though, and a lot to arrange. Late and dark as it was, he resolved to stick to his plan and go straight to Elaine's house to introduce himself.

It was now bitterly cold on the long main street of Reay and he was still nagged by that bizarre uneasiness from earlier in the day. Sustenance, though, could be found in the tantalising closeness of one hundred and nineteen thousand glorious, life-enabling pounds mere footsteps away.

6.

A little way out of the village and isolated down a small lane, Joel found the two semi-detached one-and-a-half-storey cottages, the left of which was listed as Mrs. E. Sinclair's. Aware he might already be being watched, he walked confidently in through the gate and up to the door to rap the brass knocker. There was no sign of light from inside, nor sound. He knocked again, this time as loudly as he could. There was still no response.

In all his planning the one thing he'd stupidly never considered was that Elaine might not be at home. Was she just out for the evening or away for the whole weekend? Had he come all this way, wasting the last of his money, on a fool's errand? The sense of misgiving that had risen from that bog returned full-force; was this whole endeavour cursed?

Sucking in a deep breath, he forced himself calmer. Even if he couldn't seal it this weekend, the deal was still there to be done. And Elaine might just be napping or have the TV on old-person loud in a room at the back of the house. So get a grip Joel. He was about to knock for a desperate third time when the door of the adjacent house swung open and a figure leant out.

"Yes?"

Nat Sinclair, the awkward veterinarian granddaughter. In real life she was even taller, the equal of his own five foot eleven. Her expression was unreadable, glancing at him and then sliding away as if embarrassed. He would look a dark shade under the solitary streetlamp, but he saw no fear in her eyes as they flitted at the air around him like a bat. So what was it? Shoving those thoughts aside he summoned an easy smile designed to reassure.

"Hi. I was looking for Elaine."

"For Elaine?"

"Yes, Elaine Sinclair. This is her house isn't it?"

What was wrong with her? Her mouth had drawn tight and she seemed unable to answer this simple question. Sensing this was only going to go downhill, Joel switched to a hasty plan B. "But perhaps you can help me. You're Nat, right?"

She blinked a few times. "Yes. Why?"

Joel flashed his grin again. "My name's Joel Elliott. I saw you and Elaine on an Antiques Hunt re-run two days ago and I had to come in person. You see I have the lost piece of the jigsaw."

"Oh. Right." She seemed disappointed if anything.

This was like wading through treacle. "So, if we were to put my piece together with Elaine's rest of the puzzle," he explained slowly, trying hard not to sound sarcastic, "we'd all be in for a real windfall. A quarter of a million pounds, the expert said."

She just kept on not quite looking at him.

"So that's what I'd like to talk to Elaine about," he added, to try and appease the silence.

"Why didn't you call first?"

Joel shrugged boyishly, trying to lighten the heavy atmosphere. "I got carried away with enthusiasm, I guess. But as I'm here...?"

"Look, I can't do this now. I have to get ready. Are you around tomorrow?"

He considered asking for Elaine again, but it seemed like he was going to have to get past Nat first. "Sure. Tomorrow's fine."

"How about at eleven?" Now she just wanted to escape, delay this. Why, when so much money was at stake?! It would be enough for her to move south to the cities or whatever she wanted. Her whole attitude made no sense.

"Great. I'll come back then."

"Right you are." And her door closed and she was gone.

Joel recovered himself and walked out through the gate and up the lane back towards the main street. "What the...?!" he demanded of the uncaring sky as soon as he was out of earshot. The only reply he got was a sharp lick of icy drizzle.

After a meal of fish and chips back at The Reay Arms, and wanting a distraction from his vexation at Nat, Joel asked the landlord, "What is there to do in the evening, around here?"

"To do?"

"As in places to go, people to meet."

"Ah. That. Well you're in luck actually, we've a band on." He pointed at a poster sellotaped to the wall. On it the face of an angry-looking pale young man with a prodigious Adam's apple glared out above the caption 'Tonight Only – The Euan Pettifer Band'.

Joel considered it. "Okay. And is there anything else? You know, at all? Anywhere locally?"

The landlord thought about this. "No. No there's not."

"Right. I guess I'll need another pint then, please."

"Aye," affirmed the landlord, reaching for a glass.

The first of the musicians to arrive was a nondescript lad of around Joel's age alongside an older man with glasses and chaotic hair. Together they lugged a series of cases inside and began setting up a drum kit.

"I wanted him to take up the piccolo," the man quipped to Joel in passing, having noticed him watching. "Ah, here's Nat," he added, and moved off towards the door.

Of course it was the same Nat, now toting a bass guitar and amp. She spotted Joel, stopped dead momentarily, then dove into setting up her equipment and talking to the drummer.

Twenty-five minutes later, when the bar had filled up to the tune of nineteen people and a dog, Euan Pettifer and his guitar made their entrance. He went over to the other two, leaving a middle-aged woman - possibly his mother, based on their similar looks - to carry his amplifier in for him. The star of the show then spent an age faffing around with an array of floor pedals, but was eventually set up and ready to go.

There was a sharp squeal of microphone feedback. "Alright! We're the Euan Pettifer band, so. And a-one, two, three." The loud A-minor hammered a little out of time on a slightly mistuned guitar came as no surprise, but Joel groaned anyway. He rarely loathed anyone at first sight, but Euan had that certain something about him. Unfortunately there was clearly nowhere else to go in Reay and he would hear this as loud in his room upstairs, so it looked set to be a long evening. All he could do was force himself to pay attention. Talking about her band's music with Nat might be a way to break the ice, and heaven knew he was going to need one.

After a pair of frenetic dirges in the Scottish miserabilist tradition, Euan decided to connect with his audience. "Thank you, thank you, thank you, yeah. So as you all know, we've been a bit on hiatus while Nat was down in Edinburgh doing her studies. I've been using the time off to write some killer new material, and youse lucky bastards get to hear it here tonight at our official relaunch gig."

There was polite applause.

"Alright! So this is Tethered, our hit single. A hundred and twelve listens and counting on Spotify."

The drummer did a ba-da-boom comedy roll and got a glare for his troubles. Joel was now mildly drunk and would have been finding some ironic enjoyment in the whole show were it not for the imminence of more music. He listened through 'Tethered', in which Euan griped about one more part of the world that either didn't understand him or was holding him back – both, probably – but when the next song began Joel's resilience was failing.

"Pack of cigarettes, please." It was the man who'd come with the drummer.

"I thought you'd given up?" yelled the barman over the noise.

"You know how it goes. And I've really to smoke them out back have I?" the man shouted back even more loudly.

"'Fraid so. It's been the law for ages."

The man nodded, paid, and almost ran for the door. 'Good idea,' decided Joel, and followed him.

Outside there was a rime of ice forming on the black grit. The man turned and shot a worried glance at Joel before relaxing into a smile. "Sorry, thought you might have been someone I know."

Joel shrugged. "I promise I'm not."

"Do you smoke? Want these?" The man offered him the unopened packet of cigarettes.

"No. Thanks all the same."

"Me neither. Vile things."

"But you just bought them..."

The man closed his eyes as if in pain. "Please don't tell anyone in there, but I just couldn't take any more of the music."

"So that..." Joel, struggling not to laugh, forced himself to breathe, "...was your escape strategy?"

"Yes!" The man's face relaxed into a sheepish smile. "Jamie, the drummer, is my nephew. He's got no dad and neither he nor my sister drive, so they ask me. Once I'm there, however much I might want to, I can't just get up and leave."

"Sorry but I have to ask: why do they let them play here? They're kind of awful."

"Partly supporting something local, but also this is the only pub in Reay. Think captive audience and alcohol sales."

"Clever! But as designated driver you can't drink yourself into oblivion. That must be, well...their songs certainly make a lasting impression. Do you go to many gigs?"

Now both of them were grinning openly. "I think it's the sheer persistence that reaches the parts of me other bands mercifully leave well alone." The man leant in conspiratorially. "I was hoping they wouldn't restart, but Nat, that's Euan's girlfriend, came back and Euan roped Jamie in again. I was the one who got him into music so I can't stop supporting his playing. Make that kind of faux pas in Caithness and they never forget. Never! I can't afford that."

"I feel for you! But talking of feeling, my toes have gone numb. How long would you say we can last out here before hypothermia sets in?" Even as he asked this only part-jokingly through chattering teeth, Joel wondered if life as Euan's other half went some way to explaining Nat's disposition. Their music was joyless.

"I reckon it may already have started. I can't think why else I'd be giggling like a drunk."

"It could be worse."

"Do you mean sleeting rather than just threatening to?"

"You could be that poor dog. They have very good hearing."

Both succumbed to laughter now, and the man stuck out a hand. "I'm Derek."

Joel shook it. "Joel."

"And what brings you to Reay in warmest January, Joel?"

Joel, wanting zero mention of why he was really here, tried to distract with the first silly thing that came to mind. "Thought I'd come up and shoot eighteen holes at my old friend Champ Campbell's place, you know."

An instant lid clamped down on Derek's humour. "You are joking?" He scanned Joel's face and clothes – sadly all High Street – as if seeking clues.

"Yes," Joel assured him, also serious now. "You're not a fan then?"

"No I'm not a fan. Not when every project I do within two miles of that golf club gets hit by senseless planning objections. They never have a case, they just use the law to bully with. And I mean blatantly. Stymie the little people's plans with costs and delays so they give up, which puts everyone else off doing things they're perfectly legally entitled to do."

Joel raised his eyebrows at the tirade. "Sorry, I didn't know. Planning objections...are you an architect?" It was a surprising thought, because Derek, with his disordered curly hair, non-brand specs and rumpled shirt didn't look like one at all.

"I am, yes. I've a practice in Thurso but my family's from Achvarasdal a mile down the road so they all tend to come to me out here. Listen, it's me who should say sorry for just now. I had one of those problems I mentioned come in from the planners yesterday and I'm a bit on edge about it."

"There's no need to apologise," said Joel, relieved that the conversation hadn't returned to why he was in Reay. "I'm an architect too, as it happens."

"Oh?"

"Or trying to be anyway. I finished my Bachelor's last June but I need to get the RIBA experience year before I can do my Master's. Even with a first-class degree it's nigh on impossible to find a placement at the moment though." He shrugged. "What's it like working in a place like this?"

Derek was eyeing him with increased interest. "Mostly conservatories, extensions and garages, but they pay the bills and I'm my own boss so I can't complain. Plus you can pick up an old church manse with half an acre of garden for less than the price of a flat in Edinburgh. And I have. I may not get to do much interesting architecture, but I can afford to live in it up here. So which uni did you take your Bachelor's at?"

"Manchester. Do you know it?"

"I know its good reputation. So as it happens, Joel..."

At that moment the door behind them crashed open and someone staggered out to be noisily sick into a nearby patch of earth. Derek recognised the man and rushed over to check he was alright. Joel, meanwhile, realised he was shivering from the cold. Although it had been interesting, the way Derek had turned made him wonder if the guy was trying to pick him up. That was hassle he could do without. He also had to be prepared and in good shape for tomorrow, so it was time to beat a retreat.

"Are you okay there Derek?"

"Eh? Oh yes, Alan here'll be fine now that it's all out. Won't we Alan?" He patted the bent-over man on the back.

"Right. So it was nice to meet you, but I'm starting to feel that hypothermia coming on and I've an early start. I'm going to call it a night."

"Oh. Okay, only I was just going to ask..." Suddenly Alan convulsed again, and Derek was busy dancing his shoes clear.

Waving a hand in farewell, Joel nipped back into the warmth and awful noise. He felt like going straight upstairs to his room but instead found a hidden corner from which to observe Nat a little while longer, still seeking clues that would help him unravel her and get closer to Elaine and her jigsaw puzzle.

She played her bass guitar accurately enough, but without any sign of passion for the songs. Nor was there any musical exuberance, although that was unsurprising since Euan's guitar and vocal left no space for it. She looked mostly at her fretboard or the ceiling, hardly ever at her boyfriend standing in front of her. When she did it seemed almost as if she disliked the experience. Neither did Euan seem to know when her eyes were on him, for he missed every glance. On those few occasions he did turn his head back towards her, the movement seemed imbued with a mix of possessiveness, fear and resentment. It all looked like a train-wreck of a relationship to Joel, and he decided that he would learn nothing of use to him here.

Yet for a moment longer he watched on anyway, now imagining how her face, high-cheekboned porcelain flanked by curling trestles of rich, dark hair and eyes he couldn't catch the colour of, might look in animation or delight. Quite beautiful actually. And her long, lean body if not drawn into itself with some tension... He made himself stop. Any such train of thought was a hiding to nothing and he was losing focus on what mattered here, which was securing that money.

Frozen by his time outside and tired from his long journey, he went upstairs to his room. Sleep, though, seemed unlikely, for below the bare floorboards The Euan Pettifer Band continued into the night, ranting out their grievances against the universe in general.

7.

Upon waking it took Joel some moments to work out where he was. Head stuffy from one pint too many and last night's dinner heavy in his stomach, he pulled open the curtains and was lanced by the baleful glare of the rising sun.

Caithness by daylight was, if anything, bleaker than by dark. It felt huge because everything was low, making all horizons faraway. Flagstone walls chopped expanses of close-cropped grass into bare rectangles, and along the edge of a black, wet road, cement-coloured bungalows surrounded by gnarled shrubs seemed to hunker down into the ground for protection.

Nine o'clock exactly. Two hours until his meeting with Nat. He needed to be alert and on top of his game, so decided to go for a walk to clear his head. He put the puzzle piece in its case inside his jacket pocket, went downstairs, and on finding no-one around let himself out and into the street.

It had been years since he'd stood on a shore, so he decided to make for Sandside Beach, the spectacular bay he'd seen on the satellite map of Reay.

This proved easier said than done, though. A path running alongside a stream headed the right way, but after a few hundred metres it ended at a high fence topped with barbed wire. A sign read 'Private Property of Champ Scotland International Golf Resort at Fresgoe Castle – Access Strictly Prohibited. Trespassers WILL be Prosecuted'. Joel turned irritably round to tramp his way back to the road. In the easterly direction he'd taken there seemed no other obvious route towards the beach, only files of giant pylons that dragged cable webs from a distant cluster of industrial buildings around a huge sphere. And was that the tail of a jumbo jet in front of them? Reay just got stranger and stranger, and he resolved to research the place as soon as he had internet access.

Retracing his path down the road and back past The Reay Arms, he tried another track that ended at an identical fence. The sky had now clouded over and he was getting cold, but he was determined to make it to that shore.

Further west in an older, more attractive part of the village he spotted a lane signposted to Fresgoe Harbour. He followed it past a cluster of cottages nestling round a stream, and it was all quite pleasant until he reached the line of the golf course. If the earlier barriers had been unwelcoming, the sides of this road felt positively menacing. To his left and right ran even higher fencing marked with 'KEEP OUT' signs. Privacy screening had been attached to it, but through tiny, wind-made gaps Joel could glimpse immaculate greens and manicured bunkers. Behind them was a dense, dark stand of trees, beyond which rose the turreted tower of a neo-Gothic castle.

The long alley of fenced road was spanned by two concrete bridges in shallow arcs – for the golf buggies to pass overhead, Joel assumed. At both he saw signs of protests. There were ghosts of words: 'Scotland Right To Roam', spray-painted and then scrubbed out many times, and there were gouges in the undersides of the bridges where rectangular objects had been nailed into place and then ripped away. Security cameras on tall poles surveilled the scenes from all angles now. The road ran like this for a full half mile, and when the fences ended it was a profound relief.

A little further on he finally arrived at the beach. It was a watercolourist's delight, yellow-grey sand cut by three silver streams, beyond which the sea churned bare parchment. The slate line of the Orkney Islands sprawled along the north-easterly horizon, and to the left and right of the beach's curve brown rocks angled out of the water and into low cliffs. On the other side of the bay he now had a better view of the industrial complex he'd seen earlier. And it was indeed a massive jet plane parked there. He could even make out the giant, golden 'Champ' signature plastered across its fuselage. The Fresgoe Castle owner was in residence, it seemed.

Was he also responsible for those fences? The words of Joel's media studies teacher nagged at the back of his mind, especially 'horrible', because that was how it felt to pass between them. They spat contempt, and the awareness he would have to return to Reay that way was not pleasant.

With a soft hiss from the voice in his mind he pushed such thoughts away and turned to look inland towards the village where his fortune lay. Dunes bordered the beach, hardy grass topping the pale sand. The sky was vast and unending above the circle of low hills. It was all so austere, but Reay had an undeniable beauty to it. Only one element jarred at the sense of harmony; they were too homogenous, too lurid, those fairways of the golf course.

It was now that he noticed the darker mass of cloud rolling fast towards him, and the grey blurring beneath it. It was already gone ten and he could not risk being late to see Nat, so waiting this out was not an option. For that matter there was no shelter here anyway.

He started jogging back towards the village, and as the heavens opened he was near enough to run under the first of the golf course's bridges. It offered no real protection from the wind-whipped sleet though, so he hunched up and ploughed onwards.

He was freezing cold and soaked through when he made it back to The Reay Arms, but it was now twenty-to-eleven so there was only time to towel his hair dry and change into his other set of clothes before dashing out again.

Fortunately the weather left him alone for the walk to Elaine's cottage. It and Nat's next door were well-made, stone buildings on an attractive low rise next to a stream. He could also see that both were in need of maintenance. That was a good sign. They would agree to sell the puzzle. People with enough money didn't leave their houses in that state. One hand caressed the centrepiece's box in his pocket while the other knocked on Nat's door.

She opened it quickly, baggy knitted jumper hanging over worn jeans, long, chestnut hair a waterfall mess, and most of last night's mascara still in place. Her eyes, it turned out, were a deep green.

"Hi. You'd better come in then," she said cautiously in her lilting Scots accent.

Joel considered making small talk about the Euan Pettifer Band, but decided nothing positive lay there, so followed her in silence. The hallway was a narrow passage between lines of hanging waterproofs and piled-up animal medicine bags. It smelt of damp grass and sterilising liquid. Off it was a sparsely-furnished sitting room. Pulling over a hard chair for herself, she directed him towards a lone armchair by a wood-burning stove, for which he was glad because the cold seemed to have an iron grip on him. He tried to keep focused on his strategy for this meeting, but his mind was scattered and numb.

"So, you said you've the lost piece?"

"Yes." He reached into his pocket and brought out the case, then stopped himself. "I'm sorry but I can't open it yet. It's got too cold. If I don't let it warm up first the air in here could damage it." It made him sound like a con-artist, but he knew about wood and relative humidity and could take not the slightest chance when so much money was at stake.

Her eyes flicked to his, moving on before he could see them properly. Suddenly she sighed. "Listen, if you were expecting more enthusiasm it's because...well, you're not the first person to get in touch claiming to own this. While we're waiting, do you mind telling me how you come to have it?"

The heat from the fire was making his forehead sweat without touching the ice in his bones, and this was a question he'd hoped wouldn't come up. "It was...handed down to me. But is Elaine not coming today? The jigsaw's hers I believe."

She seemed not to guard her face from her thoughts at all. He watched her perceive the lie, the attempt to change the subject and his wish to sideline her. Clearer still was her disappointment, profound as if he'd let her down badly. She turned to stare out the window. "Gran died a week after they filmed that show. The jigsaw puzzle belongs to me now."

He bowed his head, accepting the reproof. "I'm sorry." She clearly had him pegged as just another in the line of con-artists she'd mentioned, but why did that wound him so? It wasn't her doubt about whether he had the true piece that worried him, for opening the case would answer that. It could only be that he didn't want to be this person she was seeing.

Deep inside him coursed an illogical ache to remedy this. Honesty? The unspun truth? It was a risk, but maybe it was the answer.

"I'm sorry." He said it again and meant it more. "For your loss and for being evasive there. What happened is I was sent to a Russian building site by a firm I interned for in London last summer. They were digging out an old oak tree and found bones beneath it. The piece was there in the soil amongst them, and...well...it wasn't anyone's and they were just going to bury everything again, and for some reason I took it before anyone else saw. I think the skeleton was the craftsman who made it,

Pavel Lebedev." He felt his head spin as he said this out loud; this weighty and immoral truth he'd kept bottled up for months revealed, just like that, to a perfect stranger. He looked up in time to catch her gaze sliding off him. Her suspicions had been at least partly alleviated, he thought.

"Thank you, Joel. So what are you proposing?"

He felt a rush of relief there was no allegation of theft from her ancestor, which would have been difficult to rebut. Instead he was free to launch into the spiel he'd rehearsed on the train...only now it felt presumptuous rather than generous and his tongue stumbled over the numbers.

She didn't show even a glimmer of excitement. "I don't know," she responded finally.

"It's negotiable. You do have forty-eight pieces to my one, so I could see my way clear to..."

"No. That's not what I mean. Since I was tiny I've never liked that thing. I don't trust it somehow. I'm aware it sounds ridiculous, but I'm not sure the pieces should be reunited."

That foreboding was back in his head again. Also the voice, its whisper fearful and angry now. Joel frowned through the fog: "But it's just a jigsaw."

Nat blew out a long breath. "I know, I know. It's not logical, but I just can't shake this weird terror of it."

For a moment her fear infected Joel, but he forced himself to think of the money, all that it would do. "Listen," the encouraging half-smile was one learnt from Stephen Latham, the intonation of the voice not unlike the one he'd been hearing these last couple of days. "How about we just put all the pieces out on the table and then take stock. Are you not at least that curious? I mean, really, what harm could assembling a jigsaw puzzle possibly do?"

Unhappy spasms worked their way across her face.

"I did come all this way."

"No-one asked you to. But fine, I can't come up with a

rational reason why not. I'll go and get it from next door."

"Do you want me to wait outside?" Joel offered it automatically: in Bromley or Manchester no white person would leave a dark-skinned stranger who'd cold-called alone with the run of the house.

Nat glanced back at him as if he was mad. "No, stay here. Aside from anything else you look like you need some warmth into you." Then she was gone, and he sank back into the chair gratefully, his body shuddering as he relaxed the hold he'd been exerting over it. He'd got far colder than he'd realised earlier and really did feel unwell.

The box Nat carried in and set on the coffee table was excellent woodwork. Must-smell from the faded red velvet tainted the air as she opened it, then Joel's eyes were snared by his piece's long-lost brethren and stopped registering anything else.

"This craftsmanship is incredible," he murmured. A quarter of a million pounds for a jigsaw puzzle had seemed absurd, but it made sense now. It was disturbing – much more so than had been obvious on TV – but also stunning.

Nat didn't say anything, just started removing the pieces in order from the box. Joel, almost hypnotised by their exquisiteness, leant forward and began to slot them together. Only after he'd completed a whole edge did it occur to him that he might be committing a violation by touching them, but despite her scowl she'd made no move to stop him. Silently, they continued to work like this until a seven-by-seven square sat in the centre of the table, that single, gaping void in its centre.

Now Joel's hand moved to the box in his pocket. It no longer felt cold, so he placed it on the table, eased its lid open and folded back the cloth inside. Nat sucked in a breath as she got a first look at the centrepiece.

Then there was an impulse in his head, a rush of images of wonderful money. Just as when he'd pocketed his piece in Russia, his hand seemed to move of its own accord, and in a single, fluid motion that was faster than Nat's gasped "Wait!" he'd pushed the last square into place.

The room distorted around the puzzle, three dimensions no longer enough to contain it. Everything bent into a warped hole, and then there was a shadow, the red rubies lighting up its approach, and it was all around him. Venomous blackness, swirling and growing darker. Freezing cold, a harsh sulphur tang in the air, wrongness. One of those dreams where you want to run but are rendered immobile; must speak but are struck dumb; have forgotten the motion of breathing and panic that you will not remember it in time. A colossal presence seemed to probe his being. It began to seep into his veins, only to snap back as his heart thundered defiance. His mind stumbled free for a moment and wailed at his frozen limbs to do something – anything – and he felt himself toppling forwards. Then her hand was on his chest to catch him and peace flooded into his head. There was a sudden crash, the oppressive shadow tore away, and he jerked back into ragged consciousness.

"Woah there! That's it. Relax. Breathe. In, out. Yes. Try to make it a little longer, a little deeper. Good. Good!"

He opened his eyes, and stared straight into the absolute caring of Nat Sinclair's soul. Her gaze shied immediately away and he almost cried out in anguish at its removal.

"Why did you not say you'd got this cold? That nothing jacket of yours is wet through." She was chastising him like a mother after a child's close call on a busy road. "Were you out in that sleet storm earlier? If you go walking in Caithness in January you take layers and you take gloves."

"I'm sorry."

Her nostrils were flared like a horse's, and Joel saw that the pieces of the puzzle lay strewn across the floor.

"I'm sorry," he gasped again. What for? Not wearing adequate clothing and getting sick? Fitting the centrepiece in place? Or for whatever it was that had entered the room when he did?

All of it. He regretted all of it. The greed that had brought him to the far north and everything he'd done once here. So much that had gone before too. His adherence to the Team Latham façade maxim; the whole notion of packaging and marketing yourself into someone else just so you could grab a sliver of life's pie. The monetising of all good fortune. The very ethos he'd been...what? Consciously living his life by?

"I'm sorry."

She didn't look at him. Certainly didn't offer any comforting, banal lie like 'No harm done.' Instead she reached for a nearby blanket and roughly tucked it in around him. It smelt of dog. "You got too cold and your body went into a kind of shock. I think you passed out for a moment. Sit and warm up here while I make you a cup of tea. Then I need to go out anyway in fifteen minutes or so. I'll drop you back at The Reay Arms. Don't exert yourself for the next couple of days, keep warm, and you'll be fine."

She stood up, looked around, and bent to retrieve his jigsaw piece with its two red eyes. She replaced it in its little box, then handed that to him. "I'm sorry but I'm not interested in selling, and I'd prefer you not to ask again."

He tried to meet her eyes, desperate to catch another glimpse of that truth inside her, but they evaded him with practised ease.

"I won't Nat. And it's me who should be sorry."

"Yes, you keep saying that." But she paused and eventually gave a single nod of acknowledgement. Then she was away to her kitchen, leaving him trying to collect the shards of what had happened into a coherent memory, and failing utterly.

8.

Wick.

After a short, shivering nap of simple fatigue, Joel checked out of The Reay Arms and caught his bus. If all had gone well he could have ditched his cheap flight south and stayed on here, but now he was desperate to get away as fast as he could.

Wick, the town in the east of Caithness with the county's tiny airport, was yet more grim, rain-lashed stone above which seagulls shrieked. He made his hunched way to the harbour area where there was a cheap guest house. Every room was available, so the landlady gave him a sea-view one in which the wind whined between the blasts of hailstones now rattling at the window. When she left he crawled fully-clothed under the covers and lay in a frozen half-fever.

What had happened in Nat's cottage? It felt like a nightmare, but had the durability of the real. Was it just an effect of losing consciousness? No, he couldn't believe that. There had been something demonic there in the room.

But then why hadn't Nat said anything?

At the thought of her he remembered his awakening. Her sheer, true concern. Her honesty of being. But how was it bearable to have yourself that visible? How could you endure in a society so based on pretensions and confidence tricks?

Or was that why she squirmed away from human connection? He tried to summon an image of those green eyes of hers in the hope of succour, but couldn't. Even in memory they were evasive.

Round and round such thoughts whirled as his body froze and sweated in fever. He was unmoored and could make no sense of anything anymore. Coughing and shaking, he pulled the bedding tighter around him, and eventually found the mercy of sleep.

The next morning he felt shattered but closer to himself. In his dreams he'd been trapped and hunted, so he forced himself up to walk those sensations out of his system.

Out in the grey street the storm had abated, but overturned wheelie bins and broken branches littering the roads testified to its ferocity. He found a place to buy breakfast, but it had no noticeable restorative effect. He walked some more, but began shivering again, so returned to the guest house to kill an hour wrapped in the blankets and staring out at the disturbed sea.

Arriving early at the airport for his flight south, he checked in and then went to sit in the tiny departures lounge. So this was it. The end of his mad, expensive little adventure. It had been all for nothing, and now he could only slink back to Manchester and Big Kev's, laptop pawned and scant hope of making rent at the end of the month.

Maybe he could sell that damned jigsaw piece, but to whom? Anyone who didn't know its potential value wouldn't pay much.

And anyone who did would try to reunite it again.

Not that. Of all possibilities, not that. His delirium had left him with a single word for what he'd felt: evil.

He'd never believed in pure evil, but the truth of what he'd experienced was undeniable. If you lived, as he tried to, by taking the world at face value, then you had to be prepared to alter your parameters. If not you were no better than any other blinkered bigot.

Evil did exist.

An evil going beyond the limits of his imagination.

Worst of all, he was convinced it was now here on Earth, and certain that he was in no small part to blame.

He'd been sitting there morosely for an hour or more when a figure leant over in front of him. "Joel? Fancy seeing you again. I'd say small world but that's Caithness all over."

Joel looked up. It took him a second to reorientate and a few more before he blinked in recognition. "Derek? Hi. Oh, and sorry for bailing on you the other night, but I was freezing and I've a dislike of vomit."

"Who hasn't? As it happens you missed two repeat performances so it was a wise choice. But listen, I'm very happy to run into you here. This may be a little out on a limb, but do you remember I wanted to ask you something?"

"Did you?" Joel hadn't actually forgotten.

"Yes. I'm in a bit of a pickle you see. My practice is small, just myself and an architectural technologist, Karina. She's due to go on maternity leave in a week's time. I'd found someone who was going to come up from Glasgow and cover, but they cancelled on me a few days ago. I've taken on way more projects than I can handle myself, but if I let any of them drop it'll wreck my reputation locally...all of this is another reason I was bit twitchy the other night. Again, my apologies."

"Please forget about it."

"I just want you to know I'm not normally like that."

"Really it's fine."

"Thanks. So anyway, there I was having a problematic night, but then it seemed the answer came out into the car park right after me."

Joel tried to focus. "Meaning me?"

"I reckon I'm a reasonable judge of the aura of competence. And Manchester's a top-rated uni and you said you got a first, which is very impressive. So yes, would you be interested? You did say you needed to get your practical experience year and it was difficult finding anything."

Joel blinked, wishing his head would clear. Was he being offered a work experience placement?! By rights he should be buzzing with energy at even a sniff of one...but the problem was with all prospects of a windfall from the jigsaw puzzle gone he'd lost the energy to keep running from fiscal reality.

"Derek, thanks. It's an amazing offer, but I'm flat broke and there are just no more loans to be had. I think I'll have to carry on with temp work and save up so I can try for an internship again in the summer. I'd certainly be interested if it was still available then, but I guess..."

Derek's eyebrows had risen almost to his hairline. "I'm sorry Joel, but did you think I was asking you to work for me without paying you?"

"Weren't you?"

"Of course not! What kind of cretin would do that?"

"All of them!" Joel didn't know whether to laugh or cry as good possibilities flooded back into his battered head. "So you mean an actual RIBA-qualifying job but with a salary?!" This was so far beyond improbable in 2016 that he hardly dared breathe in case he woke up still feverish in his guest house bed.

Derek held up his hands. "The money side isn't what you'll be used to down south. I can't go beyond eleven hundred a month. There's a small flat over the offices you can stay in though. I'm afraid it's cold and very basic, but you'd only need to cover the bills."

A tiny plane had landed during their conversation, and its huddle of travellers were now scurrying across the tarmac towards the safety of the building. "Good morning," a Highland-accented announcement rang out. "That's the plane in then. They'll just be a wee while getting everything ready, and we'll soon be starting the boarding for our midday service back down to Edinburgh."

"Joel I can see I'm springing this on you and you'll have to go for your flight. Look, how about you give me your number, take a couple of days to think it over, and then I'll phone you? I mean I'm also getting a bit ahead of myself here. I do need someone badly but we should do some form of interview process."

Now Joel felt an icy fear that this might also be taken away from him. "Please do Derek. Or could we talk on the plane?"

"I'd prefer not to," Derek said, grinning. "I'm only here to pick up my wife."

A crazy idea appeared in Joel's head. "But all being well you'd want me as soon as possible?"

"Yes. Although as I said..."

"I've all my project and course files here on my phone. We could make a start on that interview right now and if everything looks promising I could always just not get on this flight. What do you reckon?"

Derek blinked, ran a hand through his hair, then laughed. "I reckon you've passed the vital question about whether you can move clients to make decisions! Okay, show me some AutoCAD plans can you?"

Joel pulled up the portfolio of his best designs and opened one of a 'luxury beachside house' project he'd got a top grade for. He handed his phone across.

"Goodness me, this is better than I can draw!" Derek exclaimed. He started flipping through some of the other blueprints.

"What else does the role need? I can show you surveying spreadsheets and area and quantities calculations. Presumably the work's mostly small multi-element timber or block structures?"

"Yes. None of which is going to tax you, I can see." Derek was shaking his head. "Is this really the standard they're turning out architect graduates at now? Neither of my degrees covered the half of this." He gave Joel's phone back and looked him in the eye. "Do you genuinely want this job and can you commit to a year in Caithness?"

Joel was suddenly more nervous than even his Russia trip had made him. "Yes and yes. I promise I won't let you down Derek."

"Then when can you start?"

"I have no plans for tomorrow morning. Would that be too soon?"

Derek was grinning broadly. "It would not! You're sure about not getting on the plane? If so I can give you a ride back to Thurso, although I'm afraid the back seat pongs a bit of dog sick."

"It'd be perfect."

"I'll have to see about a bed for the night too. The flat would be too cold."

"Any temperature is just fine, really."

Derek thrust out a hand which Joel clasped. "Well then, welcome aboard!"

"I only just got off the damn plane; what are you talking about? And why do you look so smug?" A slim, blonde woman with a strident Islington accent was eyeing the pair of them.

"Janet! You're home!" Derek turned and grabbed her in a bear hug.

"It's been three days Derek. Who's your friend then?"

"This is Joel. He's my new architect's assistant. He's coming back to Thurso with us. He's going to start tomorrow morning."

Janet cocked an eyebrow. "Pleased to meet you, Joel."

"Likewise, Mrs..." He shrugged helplessly. "I'm sorry but I have no idea what Derek's surname is."

She glanced at her husband before turning back to Joel. "It's Dewar. Call me Janet. Do I hazard a guess you'll be staying at the flat tonight then?"

"I...well I think so. I mean if that's alright?" Joel looked at Derek for confirmation and his new boss nodded enthusiastically.

Janet pursed her lips and then frowned. "How can a man who designs houses for a living be so disorganised about practical matters? Derek, Joel is very obviously cold, tired and in need of feeding. It's raining outside, so the car, perhaps?"

Derek jumped. "Right! Pick you up at the door in a mo'." With a final grin he was dashing off, keys in hand.

Janet turned back to Joel. "I'm intrigued to hear the story behind all of this. London, right? Southeast of the Thames? Forgive my bluntness, but is this something that's been thought through properly? My husband is one of the genuinely nicest men you'll ever meet, but he is prone to making enthusiastic promises."

Joel, realising that this was an unexpected second part of his interview, pulled himself together and met Janet's gaze. "Yes, Bromley. I've just finished my bachelor's degree in Manchester. I've got the skills Derek needs, which he's verified from my portfolio, and I'm committed to a career in architecture. I need my RIBA experience and I'm happy to spend a year up here to get it. Tell me any and everything the role requires – both of you – and I'll put my all into delivering my side of what seems like a win-win arrangement. Does that help?"

Janet smiled and took his outstretched hand. "It does, thank you. Welcome to the practice Joel. Ah, here's Derek with the car. Come on then, let's get going. Thurso's a bit of a culture shock, but it has its charms."

"So sleep well, and if there's anything you need just give me a call, okay?" Derek stood in the flat's tiny hallway looking almost apologetic.

"I will. And see you downstairs at 9:30am."

"Whenever you like. There's no rush."

Joel was feeling restored after a hearty meal with Janet and Derek in their beautiful old house out at Westfield in the countryside. "Honestly Derek I couldn't be happier with how this crazy day's turned out. I'll be there at 9:30 ready to get started. I'm looking forward to it like you wouldn't believe, and thank you once again for everything."

"All of which validates my hiring you like this Joel! Okay, I'll leave you in peace now. You've got the cereals and orange juice for breakfast. Do you need anything else?"

"No, Janet stuffed me like a turkey. I only need my bed thanks."

"Righto. Well, see you in the morning."

"See you in the morning."

Then Derek was gone and Joel had an actual flat to himself. Front door, lounge, kitchen, bedroom and bathroom. He would be three or four years into his professional career before he could dream of this anywhere in London. Somehow his escapade north had gained a silver lining. Tomorrow he would be both back on his career track and earning a salary, a wonderful conjunction that had seemed impossibly far away these last six months.

He drifted to the bathroom – his own bathroom! – and brushed his teeth. Then to the bedroom, and it was all he could do to pull on pyjamas before crashing into bed.

3:33am. All the threes. His body was knackered so why couldn't he sleep? Those Reay memories still lurked but the day's good fortune had stilled them for now. What, then?

There didn't seem to be any specific reason.

After twenty or so minutes of tossing and turning he got up and went to the kitchen for some water. As he passed the lounge on his way back he glanced at the television. Realising he had no housemates to worry about waking, he went in and turned it on. Faced with a choice between infomercials and news he chose news.

The main headline on the 4am bulletin was an apparent cull of editors and managers right across Champ Campbell's stable of newspapers and TV companies. A bleary-eyed woman in awkward Liberal clothing analysed this as an aggressive move by Campbell to retake day-to-day control of his empire for some nefarious purpose. She was adamant this was a flagrant breach of competition guidelines that threatened democracy, and she got so heated that the BBC presenter had to interject, saying they were trying to wake up someone with an opposing viewpoint to maintain impartiality.

Ten minutes of it had the desired effect of making Joel's eyes glaze over. Returning to bed, he sought out the last vestiges of warmth under the duvet, which he pulled tight around him like a cocoon against the world outside.

9.

Thurso, February 2016.

When they went in detail through what Derek needed from him, three quarters of Joel's job was variations on the same, relatively simple themes. It also helped that Joel's computer skills were better than those of his new boss. Aside from a few omissions and mistakes that Derek laughingly dismissed as why RIBA insisted on a year in practice, Joel quickly got a handle on the work and had his praises sung to him on a daily basis.

Feeling established, he paid Big Kev some extra over the

rent arrears to mail his few possessions up, and his parents couriered a big parcel of his stuff from their attic. Even if it in no way felt like home, having his things in one place meant this was where he lived now.

That was a strange thought, but then Thurso was a strange town. Or at least unlike any he'd encountered further south. On his first Saturday he'd gone to buy something to read but forgotten his wallet. Embarrassed at the till, he'd been about to replace the book. "No no. Just take it and drop the money in the next time you're passing," the shopkeeper said. In response to his puzzled frown, she'd added, "That's yourself working at the architect's, isn't it?"

In the weeks since a couple of people had stopped him in the streets to talk; people he didn't know but who seemed to know him. Trying to enter into the community spirit, he'd let an old lady know she'd forgotten to lock her car, but received only a baffled look for his troubles. He'd later learned from Derek that many people never locked anything here.

This was an alien concept to him. Also one at odds with the sudden, new direction of the world in general in 2016. Having not much to do after work, Joel was spending a lot of time watching television and reading the internet. It was like lower case had vanished overnight from everyone's lexicon. Whether the topic was economics, immigration or society, and whether it was a TV studio, press article or a conversation on the street, there was an underlying tension. This year had the feeling of a Friday evening argument in a nightclub about a girl that was about to kick off.

Many commentators traced this sea change back to the altered tone of Charles Campbell's empire, but an equal number of newspapers and experts made angry rebuttal that Champ was the target of a corrupt elite who resented challenge or exposure. What Joel couldn't help noticing was that the rebutting newspapers were ones Campbell owned, and most of the experts in one way or another on his payroll.

Odder still was how all the capital-letters squawking seemed divorced from truth and irrelevant to people's real concerns, like living their lives and paying their debts. Three times a week Joel would decide to quit social media and watching news and go do something healthy instead. Then, in some tired or bored moment, it would be too easy to tap on an app.

At the end of his third week Janet asked if she could pop by the flat for a quick chat.

"Morning Joel. Hope you're not finding it too cold?"

"I'm learning to appreciate fleece jackets."

She laughed. "Wish I could tell you it gets better. Not to put you off, but even summer here's mostly grey and ghastly."

Joel smiled. "Don't worry. I'd go live in Antarctica for the opportunity I've got with Derek."

"He's delighted with you. Has he said?"

"Yes. Actually I wish he'd stop saying it quite so much. It's almost getting awkward!"

Janet laughed again. "Okay. Well there's not going to be a suitable segue, best to launch right in. Looks like you're going to be quite some while in Thurso, Joel, so I wanted to warn you to be careful here."

Joel was surprised by this, as Thurso seemed the opposite of dangerous. "I grew up in South London and lived in a dodgy part of Manchester while I was studying. I really don't feel unsafe here."

"Oh no, I don't mean anything like that. You see Thurso's a small town much like any other, but the big difference is there's nothing else near it. You have to go one-hundred-and-twenty miles to Inverness to find anywhere larger. Everyone knows everything about everybody and very little changes. Net effect is that any and every choice you make here will stick to you."

Now Joel caught her drift. "And to Derek and you by association?"

She shrugged. "To an extent. And in his business that does matter. You're an attractive young man Joel, and you'll want to socialise...I feel like some dreadful old Austen aunt telling you all of this. Do you mind?"

"Ever since the train journey up here I've been aware of how different it is. I'm glad of the advice, Janet. Please believe me that my priority is to succeed with Derek and I'll avoid anything that could jeopardise that."

"Nicely said. Listen, I'm not proposing you live like a monk. In your case, yes, you might get an occasional sniff of racial prejudice, and sounding English can be a real problem with some people too, but there's a lot that's fantastic about Caithness and its people. Just take it slowly and carefully with your associations and keep your wits about you, because you don't get a second chance to make a first impression in the far north."

Joel nodded. "I understand. And thanks. As I said, I appreciate the heads-up."

"Good-o. It'll work out fine for you here, you'll see. Who knows, you might never leave!"

"We'll maybe not go that far! But if it's not rude to ask, how did you end up in Thurso yourself?"

"Hah! Fell in love with a scruffy young architect who was failing to find work in the city and pining for home. Twenty-six years and counting."

"It must have been a big change. Any regrets about leaving London?"

"Let's think: dismal shopping, takes an age and a half to get to anywhere else, bloody freezing three quarters of the year especially in our old manse, bugger all will grow in the garden, and voracious insects everywhere in the autumn. But you know where you stand with people here, not busy everywhere like the south, lovely big house, and our two children have grown up to be admirable human beings if I say so myself. So on balance, no. Listen, must dash now to beat the Post Office queue, but I'm glad we did this."

'Live like a monk.'

It was a surprisingly interesting idea. Monasteries provided a rigid set of safety rails to tempt the directionless. He wasn't that, but what had happened the previous month in Reay had broken some surety in him. The same surety damaged by that bizarre stab in St. Petersburg.

As he'd told Janet, his goal up here was his job. The chance to learn and to earn and to never again have to rely on handouts from fate; handouts which could have a flip side, like that centrepiece.

How he regretted the way he'd completed Nat's puzzle. How he wished he could undo it. But as that was impossible he at least wanted to avoid further embarrassment.

So could he narrow his world to his profession? One year dedicated to work, then leave for his Master's degree with his experience in the bank and some money saved?

Just do the months; no trying to build a life here.

Simplicity and focus. Serenity even.

He liked the idea. He would try this.

Maybe it would even help him sleep. Quiet the nightmares of a dark shadow emerging from a suddenly-opened tunnel into somewhere human minds fell apart. They'd started in his first week at the flat, and were getting worse.

He'd considered trying to free himself by flinging the puzzle piece into the Pentland Firth, but he was morbidly convinced of its durability. It would wash up somewhere and be found. No, theft had made him its custodian, and he would just have to suffer the unwelcome dreams and memories attached to its presence.

Or was even that pretence and conceit?

Probably so. For he did not believe discarding the centrepiece could solve anything. Joel's grim suspicion was that it had already achieved its Earthly purpose via his hand.

10.

Thurso, June 2016.

Joel arrived at the Olrig St. Gardens tennis courts early. Anastasia wasn't there yet and he wasn't sure if this was a good or bad sign.

Not that this was a date, he reminded himself sternly. Live like a monk, remember? That mantra was just about holding. He was here only because he'd signed up for a league and her name and this time had been texted to him by the organiser. The days were long now, the sun in the sky for nineteen hours, and after almost five months of too much computer and television he badly needed exercise.

Still, Anastasia... It was a name you felt certain had an attractive girl on the other end of it, and with summer arriving Joel was feeling undeniably lonesome in that direction.

But no, damn it! Janet's warning had been spot-on. Yes, there was that safe, trusting side to the far north, but there was also a quiet watchfulness that took its time to decide. Even after five months of good work for a local business he was still being assessed by this place. A wrong move – making a move on the wrong person – could mess up the good deal he had going. He'd recently initiated small payments against a couple of his nastier loans, but the tiny dent he was making over the interest charges only emphasised the colossal nature of the burden he'd taken on by studying for a career. He needed to complete his year in Thurso.

It was five past the hour now, and when he saw a car pull up across the street and Nat clatter out he knew instantly: Anastasia. So attention-grabbing with its five syllables. Not something she'd be at all happy to wear. No-one christened their child Nat – an insect's name – but it wasn't like their conversation had got near such idle pleasantries as what it was short for.

He'd seen her around town twice. Once on the opposite side of the riverbank walking the other way, and again at the supermarket checkout as he came in. If she'd spotted him either time she'd given no sign. Neither had he made any attempt to go over or hail her from afar.

Whilst a part of him couldn't forget her gaze, any interaction between them would have the subtext of that day at her house and the jigsaw puzzle. Janet had hit the nail on the head about the permanent nature of first impressions in Caithness, and he knew he'd blown this one irretrievably and shamefully.

She'd noticed him and his tennis racquet now, made the connection. She ducked her head and hunched even further into herself, but kept on walking towards him. He felt it irritate him, the way she somehow introduced difficulty to the situation before she'd even uttered a word. Like she'd planned this but now didn't want to be here and almost resented Joel's presence as a result.

"Anastasia?"

"No, Nat. They wrote it down wrong. Hi again, then. I hear you're doing well up here." She dumped the bag she was carrying, and a line of blue and gold 'Say NO to Brexit on 23rd June' flyers slithered out. Squatting down to retrieve them, she held one out to him.

"I'm okay thanks. I'm probably not even registered to vote here."

She blinked rapidly. "You don't think this is important?" Her tone seemed accusatory.

"I don't think it makes any difference," he replied stiffly. "It's just politicians and noise. Nothing will really change whichever way the whole referendum thing goes."

"No, everything will! This is about co-operation and reason versus lies, division, ignorance and delusion. How can you not care which side of that wins out?" She clearly cared a lot, and he seemed to make a convenient target for her frustration.

Which, Joel realised, he resented. "Nice as such lofty concepts are, remember the UK has to pay for them with thirty million pounds of its citizens' money to the EU every day," he said sarcastically, recalling some headline he'd seen in a newspaper somewhere.

"Oh come on, that number's wilfully ignoring all context. And really, just money? Is that all you think is at stake here?"

For a split second he thought she would throw his avarice from January at him to support her point. She didn't, but he could see the memory of it written on her face and wanted to shout at her that that wasn't the real him...or if it was then only because it had to be.

"Well maybe some people don't get the luxury of ignoring the money side of things. In case it gives your low opinion of me some context, I always studied and did well in school. Never been in any trouble. At sixteen I decided I wanted to be an architect – people need houses, right? So I got top grades and into a good university and kept working hard. I do that, live frugally, and what do I have to show for it? I'm fifty-three thousand pounds in debt and still have to complete two more years of training to get certified. When and if I do, what few good graduate jobs there are out there go to people with connections and influence whose parents can subsidise them through unpaid internships. I might seem obsessed with money to you, but I can't afford not to be. I'd class a society that does this to its young as a broken one. Therefore why should I bother voting to maintain the status quo?"

She contorted her face, but not in apology. "I'm not saying things are perfect or fair right now, just that they can get a lot worse."

"I'm not sure how."

"It's what these Brexit con-artists are learning from that foul man Campbell..."

"Champ Campbell?"

Her face had turned dark. "He's never been a champion of anything except himself so I won't use that nickname. Somehow he's...I don't know...it's like he's broken the universal agreement that truth matters. Yes that's it! In every one of his newspapers and TV stations since he retook control, in insidious ways which pander to each specific audience's prejudices, his lies encourage and validate people's selfish grudges and frustrations, their worst and most irrational impulses to divide up and fight amongst ourselves. And our society seems to have no defences against it. It's as if the world's gone wrong all of a sudden. Like a healthy body struck down by a disease it has no immune response for. It terrifies me."

Joel felt what she said resonate, but his temper was still up and he did not want to get drawn in. In fact it had been a long week, and if there was no Anastasia to be enjoyed he at least wanted a game of tennis to get brain and body in sync. He let his expression communicate this.

She saw and gave a self-aware grimace. "Please can I just try and explain why I can't let this go? I heard yesterday from a Polish couple I became friends with when I was in Edinburgh. They'd set up this lovely little café and I used to have breakfast there. Polite, intelligent, speak English perfectly. I don't doubt they pay all their taxes and so on. They emailed to say they were selling up and wanted to let their customers know why. Two times in the last month their front window's been smashed. The second time people broke in and defecated all over the counter-top. They also spray-painted swastikas on the walls with the caption 'Fuck off Pole scum.' That's how it can get worse: following so-called leaders down that road. Normalising blind hatred of anyone different. So yes I resist, because as I see it what is society if not the continual struggle against prejudice and division and the sowers of those things? Surely you, of all people up here, can understand?"

It was an implication Joel resented, that the targets of racism had a greater responsibility to get involved in fixing the problem. "I'm sorry to hear about your friends. Of course I don't condone any of that...but listen, as time's ticking on maybe we can just play our match now. Enjoy today's rare nice weather, you know?"

She glanced properly at him just for a split second, but it was enough to show deep disappointment. "Fine. You serve first then," she said neutrally.

Stung and vexed, Joel walked round to his side of the net, swinging his arm to loosen it. There'd been a park with tennis courts near his family home and he was decent at the game. Nat, on the other hand, stood too far forward in her sagging tracksuit, hair blowing across her eyes and racquet held too tightly. He resisted the urge to hit his first serve as hard as he could, instead sending it at medium pace down the centre. He was mightily surprised when she whacked it back clean past him, the topspin dropping the ball inside the line.

'Okay then!' he thought. His next one was full power and had some slice on it. She netted the return, but only just. Joel took the game, but each point was close and he could feel his adrenaline rising.

Nat's serve was almost as fast his and she was capable of some nasty hook on the forehand side. He got to all of them but only one of his returns went in and she won to love. He was swatting rather than swinging and it carried over into his next service game, which he lost after a deuce.

She took the first set six-three, but in the second his strength and fitness began to tell. Renewed confidence relaxing him, his technique started to lose its rust. He won that set six-two, broke her serve at the start of the deciding third, and was relishing polishing her off as comprehensively as he could.

His first serve of the next game was a mediocre one, but rather than hit a hard forehand for an edge going into the rally, she lofted a lob skywards like a beginner. 'Hah!' he thought, feeling wolfish as he moved forward for the smash. But the ball was moving strangely; as it rose it encountered some sort of sea breeze and began to accelerate sideways, so much so that when it came down again it was going almost perpendicular to the court and his whole body was angled the wrong way. He lunged at it, off-balance, and achieved nothing more than clipping the ball with the frame of his racquet.

Seven more times over the next five games she hit the same shot, and seven more times he couldn't find a way to deal with it. It made the decisive difference, getting her points when she needed them and shredding his rhythm. She took the six games without reply to win the set and the match.

"Well played," said Joel through gritted teeth as they walked back to the net. "That's a tricky little shot you have there. Shouldn't work really."

"And yet it does." She was, as ever, not quite looking at him. "I was in a tennis club here through my teens. That wind up there's always blowing, out the north and nasty. If you forget, even for a moment, someone who wants to bring you low can exploit it. And then everything just falls to pieces, doesn't it?" She hoisted her bag, nodded to him, and then walked off back towards her car.

Joel glared after her. Of all the arrogant, presumptuous,

naïve... He snorted and shook his head clear. She might be those things, but she was also right, damn it. And he did know what she was upset about better than most. He resolved that he would in fact register to vote against Brexit, but hell would have to freeze over before he would ever admit to her that he'd done so.

As no-one was waiting for the court, he grabbed his racquet and went back on. Lofting the ball high in the air he tried and tried again to understand the wind that blew up there. Each time it eluded him. After ten frustrating minutes all he had was a headache from staring up into the flaming sun and a muscle cramp that ran through his shoulder and up his neck.

"Screw this," he muttered, and gathered up his things to stomp the short distance back to his flat. Once there he turned on the TV by default, saw a news channel come up, and switched it off again. The one thing he wanted no more of today was worldliness.

11.

London, December 2016.

Breath misting in the frigid air, Joel walked along the gritted station platform to board the six a.m. train. He was returning to the family home in Bromley for two weeks over the holidays, his first time back in England in almost eleven months.

The guard's whistle blew, the train clunked into motion, and soon Thurso's lights were receding behind him. How well 2016 had turned out after an awful start. He'd now clocked up enough architecture practice to satisfy RIBA. He'd done well at his job too. Derek still told him often, but so did the recent expressions on clients' faces: having Joel work on something for them was no longer being fobbed off with second-best.

He would even begin 2017 owing less than the year before,

a first in his adult lifetime.

So why this continuing malaise?

He recognised it was there. It must be obvious too. Why else would Janet, who knew he wasn't religious, have suggested he join her and Derek at church a couple of months back? Was it his whole tread carefully vow of abstinence thing? Perhaps, but in truth that hadn't hindered him at all for the last four or five months. He worked; he shopped for food; he cooked uninspired little meals then sat in the flat watching TV or playing Xbox; he ran; he played in a squash league; he went to the pub once most weeks, where he was on casual bantering terms with a few familiar faces. It wasn't exactly monkish, but it had become habit.

He'd already signed a six-month contract extension with Derek that would take him to the summer. He might treat himself to a proper holiday somewhere warm then, and in the autumn he would start his Master's.

Everything was well on track and he could afford to take the brakes off a bit.

If he could just remember how.

The train joined up with the Wick carriages at Georgemas Junction, then rattled out into that vast bogland whose foreboding he'd never quite shaken off. Joel settled in his seat to sleep, his last waking thought that over Christmas he would reconnect with his old self and soak up some of the South.

Thirteen long hours later, nearing London, and the high-wire tension was what he noticed the most. Had it always been this bad? He remembered people under pressure and frustrated by issues, sure, but not the mixture of furious, bewildered and afraid that he was picking up on everywhere in this train.

He tuned back into the conversation of the pair of thirty-something professionals in the seats in front. Since getting on at Crewe they'd been seething about the US presidency being won by the candidate with four million fewer votes, the Brexit referendum vote to leave, and the snap UK general election called for January. It went beyond disappointment that their side had lost. It was visceral and existential. Just like Nat's outburst at the tennis court all those months ago had been.

"...Exactly! I mean it's blindingly obvious they'll have to have another vote," the man was saying.

"Ideally one enshrined in law and with the consequences spelt out, not just a load of hyperbole," the woman agreed, nodding.

"It'll happen, I'm sure of it. Hopefully the left takes it up as their top priority for the election."

"I fear they won't. They seem to be eyeing mass nationalisation in pursuit of some sort of socialist utopian dream, in which case being free of EU law actually helps them."

"But no-one's going to vote for that!"

"No, which is why everyone's predicting a landslide for the right. And that's the whole reason this election was called of course; an opportunistic power grab."

"Yeah, as if anyone was buying all that 'fresh mandate' guff. Well at least that repellent Geoffrey Petard and his retired-sergeant-major blazers and false blokeyness won't be there this time. I can't stand him."

"He's surely got all he wanted..." there it was in the woman's voice, that fear beyond difference of opinion, "...and yet the Just Brits Party are actually fielding candidates in every seat. They're getting a lot of positive press too."

"But why?!" Now the man was raising his voice at the woman he was agreeing with. "The whole raison d'etre of that bunch of toxic fascists was getting a Brexit referendum. What purpose can they have now?! They should just go away and let this country see sense again. No, what has to happen is..."

Joel made himself stop listening. Rewriting the rule book after the game was the preserve of despots, so you could hardly call it up for the fight against despotism.

He'd voted against Brexit himself and losing was unpleasant, but however rational the arguments, it served no purpose to rail against lost causes like these two in the seats in front. Like Nat. Growing up with non-white skin had taught him that the best tactic for any minority – even a 48% one – was to keep your head down and stay quiet. The world was what it was. Why keep on talking and make yourself a target for those who held power?

Frustrated by his failures to get all such thoughts out of his head, he forced his attention back to the girl sitting by the window across the aisle. He'd looked up to catch her assessing him during their hour-long delay in a Midlands siding, and she'd returned his smile before letting her veil of blonde hair hang forward to cover her profile. They were separated by hefty older people occupying the two seats in between, but Joel knew it would be easy enough to engineer his exit from the carriage to coincide with hers. Say hi. Perhaps get to talking, suggest a drink after such a long, gruelling journey. Laugh over the delay and the crapness of England.

He'd begun learning such rituals at around age fourteen and was a decent player of them. Or at least he had been. He supposed he still knew the moves well enough, but he'd lost the desire to make them.

Instead he was looking forward to seeing his family. The thought of constrictive living and sibling wars for the next ten days didn't daunt him as before. Maybe it was because he now had his own flat. All that space, which was in fact rather lonely much of the time.

He'd brought Caithness gifts for each Elliott, unique little bits of art-and-craft selected to delight his kin. He imagined their faces when they opened them. Anticipated the time spent together. He would maybe mention to his parents that they'd done well by him, thank them for it all. Perhaps say to his sister she was bright and attractive and sweet rather than a self-absorbed bathroom-hog. Even not resent John for squeezing him out of the house. Instead tell him he would be a good dad. Play peek-a-boo with the baby. Let his other two older brothers win on the occasional computer game once in a while.

Why all these mushy thoughts instead of flirting with a pretty girl who'd been sitting right there for the last four hours?! She looked nice too. Kind. But casual encounters didn't entice him anymore. He'd lost his path to the type of happiness found there. This girl would never look at him the way he wanted.

And how did he know that?

Because...well, now someone had, hadn't they.

Just once, but it had apparently been enough to flip his world upside down. How galling then, how cruel, that the someone in question was on the other side of a completely burnt bridge: Nat Sinclair.

"Good evening ladies and gentlemen," began a passenger announcement. "We apologise for the delay to this service, which was due to the unforeseeability of wet leaves on the line. We will be arriving at London Euston in around ten minutes, and remind anyone who has a voucher for a free coffee or tea that the catering service on this train is now closed."

Joel stared out at the passing black wall of a tunnel. Reflected in the window he could see the definition of his cheekbones and jaw, his complexion ghostly from living in Thurso. The eyes were too dark to see though. Their truth hidden; his...what? Strong feelings? For Nat?!

Even if you ignored the unpleasant fact of her boyfriend, it was insane. Okay, a few days after that tennis match in which she'd deliberately humiliated him, he'd looked back and been able to smile ruefully. She'd 'telt' him – as they were fond of saying in Caithness – with some panache. Dwelling on the encounter he'd realised how fine and athletic a body she had. At least as far as he could see beneath her bad clothes. And true, her face below her thoughtless haircut was Norse and beautiful, if only she could leave it still long enough to be studied properly. It had strength, but also the capacity for softness, tenderness...

No! He almost snarled at his reflection to get a grip on this. There was no hope there. It had been almost six months without so much as a sight of her in town. His thoughts returning to her as they kept doing was futility itself.

And both times they'd met some weird soup of dislocation from being around her had drowned him instantly and made him not himself. She turned him erratic and clumsy, stripped away his hard-won skill of composure. Why? Why?! Well he'd told Big Kev that she wasn't comfortable in her own skin and damn it but he saw no reason to retract that comment. It was understatement if anything.

Where did that awkwardness of hers even come from? Was there some reason behind it? Was it one that could be got past? Was it inevitable that she would make life hell for anyone she ever got together with, as he'd glibly decreed before avarice had consumed him at the sight of the quarter-million-pound space his centrepiece could plug?

Which was exactly why none of this crazy train-of-thought mattered anyway: his completion of the jigsaw puzzle overriding her objection. That terrible first Caithness impression that could never be repealed. The doorway for evil it had opened.

Did she get the nightmares too? He kept a little child's plug-in night light in the room now. Often woke in a cold sweat and almost screaming if he forgot to turn it on.

That was another reason why he wanted so badly to be home. On a thin air-mattress, three-to-a-room in the crowded

Elliott family home, he could hope to sleep soundly for the first time in months.

The train slowed to a halt beneath the dim lights of a grim and endless roof. Joel stayed in his seat whilst the rest of the carriage's occupants joined the scrum for the exits. He didn't look to see if the girl across the aisle waited for him. If she wanted to meet anyone tonight she should find someone who might bring her a little cheer.

Finally he rose and made his way out with the last few stragglers. As he trudged down the long, sparsely-lit concrete walkway, faster footsteps came from behind him. He glanced sideways to accidentally lock gazes with a well-dressed, elderly man in a turban. "Merry Christmas," the man said in an educated English accent, smiling.

"You too," replied Joel, before sinking back into his thoughts. He felt as half-lost in London as he did in Caithness now; a stranger everywhere.

"Hey! Hey, fuckin' Paki. Yeah I'm talking to you!"

The raw aggression snapped Joel back into the moment. Two white lads, maybe late teens, branded sportswear and tattoos, were crowding alongside the man in the turban up ahead. "Why don't you take your shit-stink back to your own fuckin' country, yeah?"

In Joel's experience this kind of thing normally circled like hyenas, slinking away from challenge. But now it was bold. The difference was there in the aura of the aggressors. They seemed to feel enabled in what they were doing. Authorised even.

It was exactly what Nat had been so angry about.

Joel's response was instant, speeding up towards the three. "I...I'm English. I...I was born here."

"Like fuck you was towelhead," spat one of the lads.

"Mohamed," shouted the other. They'd whipped themselves into a frenzy now, cavorting around him like territorial baboons. Joel moved deliberately alongside their target and they took a step back.

"This ain't no business of yours, bro," one snarled.

Joel didn't even look at him, just at the man. "Is everything okay here?"

"Fuckin' Paki-lover," one of the youths replied before the man could say anything. "We'll get your type too."

A portly man in a fluorescent stationmaster's uniform was approaching and it seemed to break the spell. After a final volley of curses the two aggressors skittered off in the opposite direction, pausing once to turn and make crude gestures.

The man in the turban released a shuddering breath and turned to Joel. "Thank you so much. Most people wouldn't have helped."

"Really?"

The man's eyebrows rose. "Absolutely. Not these days. Have you been away somewhere this last year?"

"I guess I have. But listen, do you want me to walk with you?"

"No, it's fine. The main concourse is just up ahead. I wish to thank you once again. I believe if you hadn't come they would have attacked me."

"Please forget it, and enjoy the holidays."

The man placed his hands together, gave a little bow, and then hurried on his way. A short while later the man in the yellow safety jacket finally arrived.

"What were all that about then?" he wheezed.

"Those two lads were threatening that man. If you have any CCTV footage maybe you can get it to the police?"

The man eyed him quizzically. "Don't think they'll be bothered by a bit of joshing like that and no harm done." He paused, trying to catch his breath. "An' anyway, I mean it's just what you get, in't it?"

Joel turned full towards him. "What?"

"Y'know. When there's so many of 'em about. Muslims an' that, trying to change 'ow we treats our women. Like them Just Brits posters 'ad all them photos of. No offence, like. I'm just sayin'."

How did you reply to that? From an official?! Joel made no attempt, just shook his head angrily and strode off towards the main concourse to catch his connection.

12.

Thurso & Reay, February 2017.

"You know Dot Andrews, Joel."

"Sorry Derek, I'm not sure who she is."

"Came north from Somerset for her husband's Dounreay job in the 80s? Lives out on the hill above Reay? Retired here and has no intention of ever returning south even though she's been widowed for a couple of years now?"

"It doesn't ring any bells I'm afraid. When did I meet her?"

Derek thought. "You probably haven't, but I'm sure someone must have mentioned her."

"Could we just assume I don't know anything about her?"

"This is exactly what Janet was like for her first five years here! Anyway, Dot's going to be your first solo client."

"Seriously? Do you think I'm ready for that?" Joel was being disingenuous, because he did feel ready for this and he'd been itching for it to happen.

"I think you were ready several months ago but I shamelessly kept you on all the work I don't like doing. So the first thing you'll need to know is she's hopeless at thinking spatially. No idea at all. What she needs is a relatively simple conservatory extension, but you'll have to talk her down from the barn-sized structure she's got it into her head she wants. Use all your wiles. You'd better go well inside regulations too, because the conservatory's going to have a view down over the golf course and they'll be all over the planning application looking for even the tiniest flaw."

Joel knew the Fresgoe Castle people by reputation now, enough to make him nervous. "I'm really keen, but are you sure this is the right project for me to take my first lead on?"

Derek made one of his theatrically ambiguous gestures. "To be honest it's also out of necessity. She thought I'd agreed to do the job but all I said was I'd chat over some of the options with her. With the Ormlie project it'll be seven months before I've got any space in my diary to do a costed plan. Especially for her in fact, because nice as she is she's one of these older, single people who assume everyone has all the time in the world."

Joel nodded, understanding. "But she's local so you also daren't let her down?"

"Exactly! You're learning Joel, you're learning Caithness! Listen, you'll be fine. Oh, and watch out because she'll try to ply you with endless cups of tea. Go easy; having to use a client's bathroom is never a good look."

Now Derek turned thoughtful. "Joel, even if maternity leave laws mean we shouldn't say it out loud, I think we're all aware Karina's probably not coming back. You've done brilliantly this last year. Remember that if you stayed on longer than the summer we could work out a schedule compatible with doing your Master's remotely from up here..."

"I promise you I'm thinking about it Derek." Variations on this idea had been coming up at least once a week for the past month. "It's just such a commitment. To be honest I have this...I don't know if I'd call it a worry or a premonition: that if I stay here too long I might never leave."

"I know, I know. You must take your time. But listen, on

an unrelated topic, now that you're going to sites solo you'll be needing your own transport."

Joel spread his hands helplessly, but before he could explain why a car was financially beyond his means, Derek was swinging a key in front of him.

"Your company vehicle, all insured and ready to go. Also personal use so long as I don't officially know about it. It's nothing flash. The opposite in fact. Owned by one elderly, atrocious, recently declared ex-driver who's used it all of once a week for the last eight years. I pounced the same day I went round to measure up for converting the garage."

"You're serious? Really?"

Peter nodded, a glint in his eye. "It's more than merited Joel."

Even if there was some ulterior motive of trying to get him to stay on, it was genuine appreciation. The kind of thing that lit a glow deep inside you, and something he'd never encountered in his various jobs 'down south'.

He rumbled over the cattle grid, nervous for his new little car, and down the track to Dot's bungalow, where she was waiting at the door. As she welcomed him and ushered him into a brown lounge, Joel found himself uncomfortable at the idea of cajoling and charming this old lady to get her to be sensible about the plans for her conservatory.

Happily though, Derek turned out to be wrong. All Dot needed was someone who took the time to explain things fully and visually. When they set up her dining chairs with a plastic tablecloth strung between them to simulate a wall and went back inside the lounge to look out, she realised her sketched diagram wasn't the room she wanted after all.

"Making it smaller will bring down the cost, make it warmer, and I think frame that glorious view of the beach and the sea even better," Joel assured her. "It also reduces any possible friction from the golf course. Keep it modest and well within the sizes allowed and they'll have no grounds to object."

Her enthused nodding stopped and her face turned mutinous. "It's disgusting is what it is. Reay used to be such a nice place before that vile man bought the castle and the club. My Frank used to love playing down there on a Sunday back when the course was still open to the public. Stolen from the community, it has been. And for the likes of that ghastly Geoffrey Petard to swan around on. Can you believe his Just Brits rabble got seventeen seats in parliament? He's staying there all special-guest-of-the-owner right now you know. And as if that's not enough Campbell and his henchmen try to bully those of us who've lived here for years. They pick baseless fights and then bleed their opponents dry by outspending them on professional fees and with perpetual appeals."

Joel made a helpless gesture. "It's wrong, I completely agree. It could well be a complication for your extension though, I'm afraid."

She wielded the teapot yet again and Joel didn't dare refuse, even though he could feel his bladder nearing capacity.

"I know you're just doing your job properly Joel, but I hate it. Hate it! If you want proof of how awful they are then just look at what they've done to Jimmy. Go on then. Look!"

Not sure at what or why, he did as directed and leant forward to peer into the brass telescope that was focused on a small stone house right on the edge of the golf course.

"Six generations that croft's been in Jimmy Bain's family. They used to have a track down to the beach and they'd bring back seaweed to wash in the stream and fertilise the vegetables with. The old owners of the castle didn't mind the path crossing their land, but nothing was ever written down. As soon as that Campbell man came here they were onto Jimmy. Tried charm at first, they did. An invite to the castle and 'maybe you'd find it easier in a nice, modern bungalow nearer town, Jimmy? Think of the jobs for the young folk locally. It's just we do need your bit of land, you see'. Pressured him with big numbers on contracts suddenly waved under his nose. 'This offer's only good for today, Jimmy. You won't get another one like this. Want a pen?' Reckoned without the Highland stubbornness though, so they did. He's such a stubborn man, that Jimmy. So very stubborn."

She seemed to lose her place, but Joel was now intrigued. "So what happened? Obviously he didn't sell."

"No. Told them thank you but he wasn't interested. Well they didn't like that. Tried for compulsory purchase order from the council. I mean for a private golf club! Isn't that absurd and an abuse?"

"Yes, it is," agreed Joel wholeheartedly.

"You're quite right. Next they cut off his track to the beach with one of those hideous big fences. It was eight months after Frank had died and I tried to help Jimmy with that. I wrote an objection letter for him, but they just hired two slimy solicitors who went to great lengths saying there was no proof of maintenance, even if there had been a track there was never a permanent right conferred, and finally that the existence of a track would jeopardise the whole project and all the investment it was going to bring to the local community. Hint hint."

Joel bent back to the telescope. "And now there's no track."

"And now there's no track. You're not drinking your tea. Is it warm enough? Should I make a fresh pot?"

"I'm fine, honestly. But what is that next to the croft, that massive wall thing?"

"It's a massive wall, exactly like you said. That was their next move, build that monstrosity. Apparently that foul Campbell directed things personally. Painted it and put in mature trees on their side, left concrete blocks like a prison on Jimmy's.

They claimed it was necessary for health and safety, something to stop golf balls flying into the property and potentially injuring someone."

"Is that true? Even so it seems far too big, and surely you'd just use fencing instead?"

"Of course it's not true! That wall had one purpose only, which was to take away the view of the sea Jimmy had from his house between those two big dunes. Now is that not just the most spiteful, vindictive, petty thing you've ever heard of?"

Although neither could think of much to say for several moments after that, the whole exchange seemed to pull Dot into a focused and pragmatic mood. In a productive next forty minutes they went through all the parameters and she agreed to a sensible conservatory proposal that Joel could take away to draw up and quote for. Derek was going to be delighted.

It cost Joel two more cups of tea, though. As the cattle grid on the lane out shook his body he realised making it back to Thurso was going to be touch-and-go. Even the attempt would be risky: the Caithness landscape provided no cover whatsoever, and he knew that the last thing any incomer should allow was to get themselves grouped with 'that North Coast 500 crowd' by toileting at the roadside. Seeing The Reay Arms up ahead, he decided to stop.

He pushed open the door. "Aye aye," said the landlord in recognition, as if it hadn't been just one night more than a year ago.

Joel barely noticed. His full attention was on the floor in front of him, where Nat Sinclair was gazing into the eyes of a prone, ancient collie the exact way she'd gazed that one time into his.

She glanced up at him, tensed, then refocused on the dog.

"Okay Kelpie. Relax...relax...that's it. The massage helped didn't it? The pain's better now, isn't it? So we're going to try that again, and this time it'll be okay, I promise. I'm not going to touch you, just be here in case. That way you'll know you can do it."

The dog looked at Nat and whined softly, its eyes wet and wide. Standing behind it an old man, white-bearded and weathered like a stump, wrung his hands nervously. "Come on old girl. You can do it," he murmured.

Trembling and shaking and almost impossibly slowly, the dog's hind legs levered it upright.

"That's it," Nat enthused. "That's it Kelpie. Good girl! Good girl!"

This dog's frolicking days were long gone, but she still made a game effort and was clearly overjoyed, whimpering happily and trying to lick the old man and Nat.

She ruffled the collie's fur. "That's it. Calm now, that's it. You're up now, but you're not a puppy anymore, remember?" The look on Nat's face! This was what made a pretty blonde stranger on a train irrelevant.

"Will she be alright now Nat? Will she make it home, or..."

She was standing now, then stooping again to be level with the old man. "You'd best go right away Jimmy, and straight there, but she'll be fine. It's only getting to her feet that's the problem. Try to watch her so she doesn't plonk herself down too hard. Put a blanket over her back legs when she's in her bed for the night, and it'll help if you can massage her like I did to warm up the muscles before she tries to stand."

"Right, right. And the tablets? She doesn't like them, you know, but I hide them in her food. Should I give her an extra one, maybe?"

"No, don't. One a day is the right dose for her and more will harm rather than help. She's getting on Jimmy, and it's a cold month. Keep those muscles warm and no sudden movements, same as works for you and me."

He nodded, relieved but sad. Joel could see the desperate hope for Nat to work an age-reversing miracle all concerned knew to be impossible. "And what is it I owe you now?"

She laughed. Was that the first time he'd ever heard her laugh? It was. She had a warm, kind, rich laugh.

"Away with you. I'll take a bag of tatties if you've them to spare in July, but don't try waving that wallet of yours around in here."

"You're an angel Nat, you know that?"

She reddened. "I'm just a vet, Jimmy. Off with you now, before poor Kelpie gets too tired standing there."

"Aye aye. 'Course. Come on then old girl, let's be away home. Thanks again Nat."

"Call if you need, remember. Day or night."

Jimmy and Kelpie shuffled their way out the door, then it finally felt okay for Joel to speak. "Hi Nat. I was just passing and needed to...thought I'd stop. How are you?"

The same infernal hesitancy and shifting! But then she sighed and seemed to relax a little. "Bruised and stiff, as you ask."

His brow knotted in instant concern. "Why, what happened?" Euan Pettifer? The caress of the tormented poet boyfriend's fists?

Her eyebrow raised quizzically at his look. "A cow. A one-year-old heifer to be precise. She chose three in the morning to go into early labour and then the calf was twisted round. Neil, that's my boss, couldn't get in there so he called me because I've got long, thin arms."

What fortune Joel hadn't voiced his peculiar first thought! Why had it sprung to mind? That awful song probably. He made himself focus. "By 'in there', do you mean...?"

"Well obviously. How else would you go about it?"

"I don't know. I've never even seen a real cow up close."

She shook her head. "That's so strange. Anyway, I'll get a cup of tea as I'm here. I guess you can join me, if you want..."

"No!"

She looked stunned, and he backtracked hastily. "I don't mean I don't want to join you. I just can't face another cup of tea. I've been at a client's house and I've had about a gallon of the stuff...actually you'll have to excuse me for a second. Please let me get your tea, and I'll have a half of brown ale if you don't mind ordering. I'll be right back."

"Dot Andrews? Will you be doing her conservatory?" she asked as he returned from the bathroom and sat down at her table. "Did that psychopathic cat of hers have a go at you?"

Three months into the job Joel had questioned Derek about client confidentiality and been told 'You can try if you want.'

"Yes. Dot that is. I didn't see a cat. Was that Jimmy Bain with the dog?"

A knowing and slightly sad smile flickered over her face. "It was. Dot mentioned him then?"

"We were talking about avoiding planning objections from the golf club and she told me what they did to him. Was it as bad as she says?"

Nat's face drew tight. "Worse, if anything. The problem is that in the council down in Inverness they only care about attracting money to the area. Not about the people who already live here and the character of the place. That's why we have a golf course that excludes the local community and destroys the dune system. And all these wind farms ruining Reay."

"No, that's the pylons." Joel said it without thinking, only belatedly realising who he was being confrontational with.

"The pylons?"

"Yes," he replied as mildly as he could. But he did know his area history now, and had researched that mysterious dome building he'd seen from the beach. "Dounreay was a fast breeder nuclear reactor delivering two hundred and fifty megawatts. There was no use for all that up here, so they had to put in infrastructure to get it down to Edinburgh and Glasgow. At say five pylons per mile that's well over a thousand of them. Even ignoring the massive cost of the steelwork and cabling, that's over a thousand land purchases, a thousand planning applications plus handling objections, a thousand access tracks needing land easements. You don't do all of that again unless you absolutely have to. It makes economic and environmental sense to re-use a grid connection like the old Dounreay one to get green energy to where it's needed. The turbines do stick out like a sore thumb, but I'm afraid with the wind resource and the sparse population up here...well, if you accept that such things have to go somewhere then it makes a lot of sense to site them here."

She studied him, which was exhilarating but also worrying, because he had no idea how she was going to respond.

"How have I never thought of some of this?" she said finally. "It's actually democratic I suppose. Euan's going to hate that."

Joel felt his skin prickle at the mention of Euan, and he moved to change the subject. "So why did you decide to be a vet? Does anyone truly dream of inserting themselves into a cow at three in the morning?"

He only spotted the double-entendre as it came out, but it made her snort with laughter, choking on her sip of tea. "I don't know. Maybe it's because animals only shit on you literally, unlike people. Obviously I'm joking."

He wondered if that was true or not, but inevitably she had the shutters down before he could try to read her.

"What about you Joel? How come you stayed up here to

work? I don't mean to be rude, but you didn't seem the type."

Didn't. Interesting. Did she know that past tense was getting more and more appropriate? "It was a salaried job that also got me professional experience, and in the current climate you don't turn that down. True, it's extensions and garages and conservatories, and I'm mostly just doing drawings and legwork for Derek, but I enjoy it. I used to want to work on high-profile commercial developments and suchlike, but I'm not sure anymore."

"That's intriguing. Can I ask why?"

He'd been trying to answer that too, and finally, here in The Reay Arms he thought he'd grasped it. "Maybe it's proximity to the human side. Like with Jimmy and his dog just now; you were helping the dog but you were helping him at least as much. A conservatory might seem a very basic structure, but it changes that homeowner's life. And up here you're always seeing those people again. There's a good half-dozen already, stop me in the street every month or two and tell me how they love their new room so much and they can sit in the warm sun, or now there's space for all the family at the dining table. I'm rambling here, but do you know what I mean?"

And there it was again, a brief window into the true, wonderful Nat through those green eyes, leaving him almost gasping for it to be returned.

"I do," she said, but now she was shifting uncomfortably. "Look Joel, this isn't my place, but you seem..."

'What?' thought Joel as she stuttered to a halt. 'What?!' He found himself thrown by her. Just when he thought he had a handle on her he was somehow out of his depth again. It was a sensation he hated.

"Be careful seeing Freya Patterson, okay?"

It was an unexpected smack across the face. He'd finally been enjoying a proper conversation with this woman who'd been too much on his mind, but now she was telling him off.

"Excuse me?"

He'd met Freya on the train coming back after Christmas. She was twenty-eight to his twenty-three and recently divorced, but gym-bunny attractive and good fun. She'd made the first move and he'd decided to go along with it. It was nothing for the longer term but both of them knew that so no-one was going to get hurt...all of which was beside the point. What the hell business of Nat's was it if he and Freya enjoyed time together? He let his expression make that thought abundantly clear.

"Look forget I mentioned it. Sorry."

"Well that doesn't work, does it? How do you even know?"

She was squirming like an eel now, but also irritated at his naivety it seemed. "This is Caithness. Everyone knows everything about everybody here. Surely someone's told you that by now? I do small animal work in a vet's surgery so gossip gets to me even when I really don't want it. I was just trying to give you a friendly warning, okay?"

"A warning? I think I'm capable of deciding if Freya's good for me or not."

"Not about Freya. Her ex-husband, Calum. He takes badly to her getting involved with anyone."

"I can't believe I'm hearing this, and least of all from you! Ex-husband, you just said it. What business of his is it who Freya sees now they're separated?"

"None. None at all. You're right!"

He could see that on one level she just wanted out of this argument, but some bloody-minded stubbornness wouldn't let her quit until she'd made her point.

"It's just Calum and his friends are rough people, and maybe you're out alone in the dark on the country roads driving to see clients. I don't want you to get hurt. You look different and you're an incomer and they might well think that gives them license. Especially these days, you know?"

It brought back a jarring memory of the aggression he'd

witnessed in Euston station, the sensation of violent darkness alive in the world. He pushed past those thoughts irritably. "License for what exactly? This is the kind of resentful, controlling...well I suppose I shouldn't be surprised. You are together with Euan Pettifer after all."

"And just what do you mean by that?" She was staring at him now, her face a mix of indignation and some sort of insecurity.

"That song Tethered. It's about you, you know."

She shook her head. "Don't be ridiculous. It's about Caithness. Not that I agree with it."

"I'm cursed with an ability to remember songs and it's about you. Why else would the first letters of the verse lines spell out your name? Couldn't resist that nasty little bit of what he thinks is cleverness could he?"

Even as he said it his anger popped and daylight flooded back into his mind. He'd tried to wound her and now had no idea why. "Look I'm sorry, Nat. I'm sorry. I'm wrong, okay? Please just forget I said it."

But, like the slotting of that final jigsaw puzzle piece into place, this wasn't something that could be taken back. He saw her lips move slightly as she thought her way through the spittle-flecked lyrics.

Not going anywhere anytime soon.
Always I'm made out to look like the fool.
Tethered, I'm tethered. Tethered by you.

Needle is spiking the air from my lungs.
After my oxygen life blood comes.
Tethered, I'm tethered. Tethered by you.

Ooohhh, ooooh, tethered.

Now that you've claimed me how can I fly free?
Airborne and beautiful as I was made to be.
Tethered, I'm tethered. Tethered by you.

Ooohhh, oooooh, tethered.

NAT, NAT, NAT. It was an anti-love letter. And she'd stood there onstage singing chorus backup to his misogyny. Had he taken pleasure in engineering that? Had his bulging Adam's apple throbbed in delight at her secret humiliation?

Nat jerked upright, her chair tipping over backwards to crash onto the floor. Joel saw tears streaming down her face before her hair fell across to cover it, then she'd slammed through the door and all that was left was the gust of icy air that had come in to take her place.

The landlord walked over to Joel's table and reached for his still half-full glass.

"I'm not..." Joel stopped speaking, awakening to the context.

"Oh but you are finished here, laddie."

Joel stood and walked stiffly out and to his car.

All the way back to Thurso, in the close winter gloom, he found himself tense and apprehensive at the lights of other road users. In the back of his mind was that thirteen-month-old scar from the shadow, feeding away on both this new fear and the fight he'd never wanted with Nat.

Back in the flat he listlessly ate takeaway chips he'd bought. They slid down like greasy lead into his belly.

What had come over him? Why the hell had he deliberately hurt her? He'd been determined to grow into something better here, but he was making a lousy job of that.

And with the woman whose good opinion mattered the most to him. It had been going decently; what had possessed him?!

Eventually he resorted to the TV to drown himself out, and was surprised to see a twilit Caithness landscape appear on screen. At the bottom of a steep ravine lights shone on a racing green sportscar, smashed to pieces. After a few minutes of helicopter footage the studio presenter appeared on screen.

"To recap today's tragic events from the far north of Scotland: Geoffrey Petard, leader of the Just Brits party that is currently in talks over a 'Brexit coalition government' to provide a working majority in parliament, was killed when his Triumph Spitfire plunged over the cliffs of Berriedale Braes in the county of Caithness. He had been returning from a golfing break at the Reay castle of media magnate Sir Charles Campbell...and in fact Sir Charles has just released a statement, which reads:

'I am profoundly shocked by the death of Geoffrey Petard, one of this country's true political visionaries and my loyal friend. That Remainer terrorists have resorted to murder appals me. Through my newspapers I will be offering a one million pound reward for information that brings these criminals to justice. I now consider myself personally involved in the fight to deliver Brexit for the people of Great Britain, and I will not rest until this is achieved. They won't take it away from us.'

"Er...now, we should make clear that although police are treating Mr. Petard's death as suspicious, having apparently found the remains of what appears to be an explosive device attached to the car's braking system, foul play has not been confirmed and nor have any suspects been identified. Viewers should wait for the full facts to be firmly established before coming to any conclusions about this tragic death."

Due warning against the ideas already planted given, the scene cut back to Berriedale Braes, where people in high-vis clothing moved slowly around the hillside. Joel watched on in a form of shock, Nat's warning about the dangers of Caithness roads suddenly feeling very close to home.

13.

Reay, March 2017.

Joel parked the car, took a deep breath, and walked through the gate and up to knock at the door before he had a chance to talk himself out of this.

She must have seen him coming because she answered quickly.

"Nat, I deserve it if you want to slam the door in my face, but I wanted to say I'm sorry. It was horrible of me. I don't know why I did it or what I was thinking."

She was less evasive, somehow not apologising for the space she took up in the world this morning. He watched with bated breath as she considered his words.

"You told the truth. And you were right about not giving in to the likes of Calum too."

Joel shook his head. "But I understand that better now. I talked about your warning with Derek and he backed it up. One thing is what's right, the other is pragmatism and whether I want to get drawn into a pointless fight in which there are only losers."

"Maybe, but I still think if anyone should be apologising it's me. So I'm sorry. And in fact while we're at it that's also for my smug little game with you on the tennis court last summer. I suppose I'd been reading too much angry news and I vented that unfairly on you."

Joel almost shuddered with relief. "Thank you Nat. Listen, if I tell you something that will make you smile can I ask you for a favour?"

She tilted her head. "I guess."

"I did register to vote against Brexit."

She laughed. "That does make me smile. What's your favour then?"

"Come with me to The Reay Arms for a coffee. I've been scared to go back since...well, you know, the last time. It's just I'm going to be around here quite a lot with work and it's the only place to get a drink for miles."

"Okay." She pulled a disbelieving face. "But I don't think you've any need to be worried about going there if you want to."

"Uh-uh." Joel was wagging his finger in contradictory fashion, and made himself stop. "Nat Sinclair is one of their own and Joel Elliott most certainly is not. If we go in there the landlord's going to glance straight at you for approval for me. I'll bet you."

She smiled again. "Okay. If you're right then drinks are on me. I'll get my coat."

"You see?"

She sat down at the table. "Fair enough, he did. Not that losing the bet matters as I never pay for drinks here anyway."

He looked at her quizzically.

"Because I come here to help Jimmy and Kelpie when they need it."

"Are Jimmy and the landlord related?"

"No," she said, as if that idea was absurd.

They lapsed into silence for a moment, until she broke it with a snort. "Do you know Euan and I were together since we were fifteen? We were the only two in our school year from this area so I'd get on the bus here and he'd sit next to me when he got on at Shebster. He dressed like a Goth and wrote poetry...don't ask!"

Were together. She'd said were.

"I guess that resonated at that time in my life. We kind of became girlfriend and boyfriend, as you do. Then came the band, which I learned the bass for, and somehow everyone started assuming we were this joined-at-the-hip couple, and that seemed to be that."

Joel blinked in disbelief. "Hang on...please tell me you're not saying you stayed with him just because it was too socially awkward to break up?! What about when you were away at university?"

"If it's alright with you I'm not going to think about that first question. As for uni, he never went himself but he would come down and stay in my room for long periods when I was getting my BVMS at the Royal Dick."

"The Royal Dick?"

"The school of veterinary studies at Edinburgh Uni. That might be why I never socialised all that much down there. To be honest he maybe poisoned my view of student life a bit...do you also remember the second song in our set, 'Both Yer Faces Are Snide'?"

Joel did, and winced.

"Right. Well I had the job at Melvich waiting and I always wanted to come home and work here anyway. Then things just sort of fell back into their old places, and..." Her words stuttered out, hands round her cup for warmth. "What's so strange is I'm single for the first time in ten years but I've never felt less alone. I was certain I'd be judged harshly for splitting up with him but everyone's been just brilliant, really supportive. In fact the general consensus has been 'what took you so long?', so if I wasn't getting you this coffee because you won the bet, Joel, it would have been by way of thanks. I'd actually been meaning to come and see you in Thurso to say as much, but I couldn't get up the nerve."

Joel, melting, met her soul-bared gaze for what seemed an aeon before she dropped her head, but still smiling.

"You know it's ironic." 'Why are you doing this, Joel?', a part of his mind asked.

"What is?"

"Tethered."

She frowned. "I'm not sure I agree."

"It applies much better to Euan holding you back. Do you think on some level he knew that?"

She was deep in reflection now. "I'm painfully aware how he must come across, but there's more to him than that. At least there used to be anyway. In answer to your question, it's possible. Either way I'm never going back to find out."

It was all Joel could do not to punch the air in celebration. "I saw him across the street in Thurso you know. It's what prompted me to come today after three weeks of dithering. Jamie told Derek that...well, Euan's saying you assaulted him."

"He's what?! I did no such thing!"

"But he has a broken collarbone. His whole shoulder's in plaster and his arm's stuck out like a teapot handle." Joel managed not to grin at the memory, just.

"What? Really? Oh no! How haven't I heard this? But listen...okay, what happened was I didn't see or talk to him for ten days or so after...you know when. Then we had a band rehearsal booked. I went there having persuaded myself it was all a misunderstanding about that song. I came in late and he and Jamie were already set up. He looked over and made one of his typical sarcastic comments; nothing particularly relevant, but in that moment I just knew you were right about Tethered. I admit there were accusations – enough that Jamie ran off outside with his ears red – and I did get angry, and, okay, I did brandish my bass like a club and he might have thought I was about to hit him with it...I would never have done it by the way."

"I might have in your place."

"No, you see he's very bony and I'm fond of that guitar."

Joel gave up fighting down a smile. "So what happened?"

"He scuddered away backwards, got his feet tangled in his guitar lead and fell over, which must be how he got injured. I didn't stay any longer. Just shouted something to the effect of we were finished then marched straight out. Or as much as that's possible whilst lugging a bass rig."

Now they were both starting to laugh. Then, suddenly, there was a growing roar all around and The Reay Arms itself seemed to shake.

"What was that?" Joel gasped when it receded, thinking it couldn't have been an earthquake because then they wouldn't have built a nuclear power station in this area.

Her eyes were shuttered again, her face drawn and scowling. "That'll be the new leader of the Just-fascist-Brits Party, Charles Campbell, landing his Boeing 747 on the old Dounreay airstrip. He leased it and got it extended so he can fly in for visits. You'll hear the helicopter going over to the castle soon. Everyone in Reay hates that sound."

They sat in silence for a few moments and her face grew tighter still. "I hate feeling hate. I've tried to see that man from any other angle but I just can't. I loathe him. I loathe what he's doing. The lies. The demonising. Blatantly using his newspapers to warp opinion and promote himself as the solution to fake problems no-one had before. He's...you see? I can't stop myself! I'm so sorry Joel, it's not fair of me to rant at you about it all. It's not fair of me to expect you to share..."

"It seems to me the mainstream right saw Just Brits as a threat in our first-past-the-post electoral system. The Brexit referendum was never about leaving the EU. It was a supposedly-harmless promise that would steal Petard's thunder, stem the leakage of votes and retain their grip on power. But the gamble backfired when Leave won, in no small part due to relentless propaganda in Campbell's near half of the UK media."

She was still, regarding him.

"Pandora's Box was opened," he continued. "Arguably by Campbell's hand. Why did the government call an early general election? Because via skewed reporting and manipulated polls the Campbell press hoodwinked a vain Prime Minister into thinking she could effortlessly reap a huge majority. Instead it was a hung parliament leaving Just Brits' seventeen MPs as kingmakers. Then Petard conveniently dies and, despite not being an MP, Campbell is welcomed with open arms as the new leader of the party. His first act is to pull out of coalition talks, causing next week's emergency general election. He labels Remainers as murderers and accuses all the mainstream parties of treacherous plotting to reverse the Brexit vote. Those are absurd and obvious lies, but with his media empire behind Just Brits they're rising and rising in the polls. As you said, they've shunned truth entirely. Their tactics, to use an architectural metaphor, drill holes in the creaking timbers of democratic society and stuff termite eggs inside. That's our shared heritage, our hard-won checks and balances against extremism. And yet the majority of the country seems not to SEE or not to CARE." He fell silent and, biting his lip, sat looking at her.

She exhaled a long breath. "I couldn't have expressed it better. So you've become politically engaged? I'm glad."

"I'm not. It's miserable. Every newspaper I read makes me by turns furious and depressed. But I saw something in London at Christmastime similar to those Polish friends of yours, and since then I haven't been able to lose my awareness of what's happening."

Nat was nodding. "And you see hatred stoked everywhere and you see it growing and you wonder where it ends? What's the point at which the resistance of truth and shared morality and law and order and the common good kicks in? And the scary thing is maybe it never does."

"Exactly," confirmed Joel morosely.

Things between them had been going so well until Champ Campbell's flypast. But even then he and Nat had found themselves newly aligned. Would only that their shared feelings weren't fear and futility, anger and loss. A sense of rapid decay being confirmed on a daily basis. It was like trying to bond over a mutual loved one's devastating illness. In it could be found no joy, no hope.

14.

Thurso, April 2017.

Joel's feet dodged peatwater-brown puddles as they pounded through the mud. The winters were long here, and spring came late and slowly, but at last the branches in the town's single area of trees were hazed with green and the light was losing its near-horizon harshness. When you found shelter from the elements in Caithness life was quick to emerge. On today's run he'd seen eight seals on the rocks below the Victoria Walks, and was now on his favourite part to finish, three quarters of a mile up the river Thurso and the same back on the other side.

It was cold and grey and there were few people out, but fingertips aside he was feeling warm. Approaching the cemetery footbridge, he noticed a tall, slender figure up ahead on the other side of the rushing water. Nat!

She had been constantly on his mind. Even during the collective national shock of Charles Campbell's Just Brits winning three-hundred-and-sixty-three seats in the election to make him Prime Minister, Joel's first thought had been for Nat. It was insane because they'd met all of four times – three of which had ended badly – but could what he felt for her, the knot-twisting new sensation dismantling him, be love?

Since that chance meeting in The Reay Arms he'd been too scared of making a wrong move to make any move at all. Despite having no pretext to be in Reay, he'd almost driven out to her house twice in the last week alone, but then bottled out. He'd acquired her phone number via Derek, but then not known how to use it. There were practicalities and they couldn't simply be waved away. Nat had only just broken up with a boyfriend of ten years. Also she was never going to leave Caithness. The relationship he imagined with her wouldn't be the days, weeks or months kind, so it would mean him settling in the remotest north of the country. For all its space and wildness, for all the warmth, trust and humour he'd found in the people he'd met here, was that an idea he could embrace?

He'd never been so lacking in decisiveness or confidence in his whole life before. Why, with something he wanted so much, this hideous, clammy-handed, debilitating nervousness?

Because this mattered more, yes. But above all because he knew he'd already betrayed her. Which was perhaps why Nat – assuming he wasn't deluded and she felt something similar – hadn't contacted him either.

That Saturday morning fifteen months ago could not be erased. The making of the puzzle and the shadow he'd seen come out of it. At some point some conversation would lead back to why he did it, why he placed the centrepiece over her gasped objection. And what could he reply? I was thinking only about the money. I was working out how to persuade you into the sale. I was prepared to trick you any way I could to get what I wanted. I was all about me and happy to discard you as collateral damage.

Leopards didn't change their spots, so how could she ever trust him knowing he had that inside?

And yet he wanted to protest that in that moment it hadn't been him. It felt like some...thing had seen his selfish thoughts, seized upon them, and in doing so gained enough control to move his hand and, too fast for her to prevent it, slotted in that last piece and...and...and what? What?!

It drove him crazy that he had could not get recall. Every time he thought about it, which was too often, there was only a hazy blur of invasive evil, his heart fighting back, Nat breaking the puzzle and her soul shining out of her gaze as he came round.

But it hadn't ended there. Not only did a scar remain in his own mind, that shadow's evil now seemed everywhere in the wider world and growing stronger. It was the multiplying wrongness they both saw all around.

Was that illogical? Egocentric? Yes, but he believed it nonetheless. It wasn't mere coincidence. What he and Nat so hated was all his fault.

For a second or two his breathing became gasps and then almost sobs, and his legs barely retained the power to keep running.

But getting overwhelmed wouldn't help. If he was in any way right about what he'd done then he had a responsibility to try and remedy it. Manage and maybe, just maybe, there could be a chance of that future he yearned for with Nat...

But he had no idea where to start.

Unless she turned around they would meet at the bridge. He sped up, wanting to hasten it, then slowed, not wanting to arrive panting and sweaty, then returned to his normal pace because he knew Nat saw past such trivialities. As he went up the steps she was already a quarter of the way across. He slowed to a walk and they met in the middle.

Watching him, she was all awkwardness again. 'I don't bite,' he felt like exclaiming, but thinking back over their encounters he wasn't sure he could make that claim.

"How are you Nat? I was meaning to call actually."

She was scraping wind-messed hair out of her eyes. "Derek said you'd be running this way. Tell me to butt out by all means, but I'm afraid this is the same warning as that time in The Reay Arms, just more urgent."

The good adrenaline from his run fizzled out instantly. "It's okay Nat. Like I said, I know better now. Please tell me."

She sighed with relief. "This is from someone reliable. Calum was talking about you to Shane Oag in the pub and money changed hands. They're not close, so I think there's only the one explanation for that."

Joel knew Shane Oag's name: six-foot-four at least, and infamous as the town nut-job in a town with more than its share of nut-jobs. He was a perennial fixture in the John O'Groat Journal Sheriff Court section, and had already had a couple of short stints for assault to acquaint himself with the inside of Porterfield Prison in Inverness.

Joel could feel his stomach tightening. "What would...what kind of thing are we talking about here?"

"I don't know. I've always steered well clear of all that crowd. Most likely an 'accident' of some kind waiting for you, though. Possibly quite serious because Shane's a thug and doesn't understand moderation."

Joel swore, a mix of frustration and fear. "I don't want to get involved in anything like that. But Nat, giving in to this is wrong. How do I not take at least some stand for..." he didn't want to say another woman's name to Nat, but couldn't think how to avoid it, "for Freya's rights in all this?"

Was this stupid? Beyond some physical fun she'd turned out to be depressingly shallow, and he was pretty sure she'd only wanted him for an exotic tryst to gossip about and was now getting bored. His own feelings for her had ebbed away completely. In fact he hadn't even seen her in almost three weeks, and as for sex, which seemed the extent of their mutual interest, you had to go all the way back to a week before his trip out to Reay to apologise to Nat.

She was going right back to her old armoury of tics. "I'm sorry to be the one to tell you, but she's gone back to Calum. She's been at his house since the weekend before last."

"Oh." All he felt was relief.

Conversation ground to a halt for a while, leaving only the churn of the river below the bridge and the two of them watching it. They might have been looking for salmon, were it not the wrong season.

Joel rolled his shoulders to try and relax them. "I guess that frees me of any moral obligations. Which just leaves Shane Oag. Do you have any suggestions?"

Why did she seem to be getting even more nervous? The difficult part was over, surely? "You know how Derek and Janet's daughter's finishing uni in June and has been asking about using the flat?"

Joel hadn't been aware of that – how did Nat know so much more about his life than he did?! – but it explained Derek's vague mention of another contract extension with a big raise but 'changes in the job perks'. Joel had thought he'd meant the car.

"I had some idea."

"Listen, Calum's just being all alpha ape now he's got Freya back. He and Shane don't have attention spans to speak of. Get out of town for a bit and this will all blow over. And as you'll be needing a new place soon anyway..."

Her discomfort was now so pronounced that he couldn't help but smile at it. She noticed and closed her eyes, shaking her head even as she managed a self-aware grimace-cum-smile back. That part of her that stood in her own way was weakening, perhaps? "You probably don't want to be in Reay, and tell me if this is a stupid idea, but I've Gran's house just sitting there empty. It's a year and a half since she died now and it's high time I did something with the place. So you could stay there. If you want." Biting her lip, she glanced over at him.

"Nat that's...that's an amazing offer. I mean great, but I'm not sure I can afford the rent on a whole cottage. I'll have to talk to Derek about salary first and see..."

"I don't want any money. You can pay your bills, but otherwise...well, you could help me clear the place out a bit."

"Seriously?"

"You're...okay, look, you're the one person up here who doesn't know my whole family history. I have to face doing this, and that will make everything so much easier."

"Wow! They're beautiful buildings. Do you really own both of them?" He was babbling, unable to process this turn of events.

"I do. Joel, sorry, but is that a yes?"

"Yes. Definitely! It's an amazing offer Nat, just quite a lot to take in. So...when should we do it?"

Now there was a shadow of fear in her eyes again. "I suggest today, right now if you can. Between your car and mine we should be able to get everything in, shouldn't we?"

Premonitions of Shane Oag's silverback form lumbering towards him on a deserted street, Joel nodded. "Okay then. Let's go. And Nat...?"

"Yes?"

"Thank you. For all of it."

15.

Reay & John O'Groats, June 2017.

Reay made even Thurso seem chock-full of big-city attractions, which afforded Joel time to fix the many little things around Elaine's cottage that needed it. He was enjoying that, not least because beneath all the dusty chintz this was a well-built house in a wonderful spot.

He glanced out the kitchen window as Nat walked past on her way to his door, a beaming smile on her face. That was a welcome sight! They'd taken a walk to the beach together the previous day, but she'd ended up incensed by the addition of a vicious razor wire to the top of the giant fences separating the golf course from the road. It had spoiled another promising moment, kept everything between them in the same state of uncertain flux.

She'd said she wanted him to help clear out the cottage, but she'd resisted his every attempt to start on it. As a result he was still, seven weeks into this tiptoeing tentative tenancy, camping out amongst old-lady clutter. He and Nat were both working long and different hours at their jobs, so rarely bumped into each other by accident. It was easy to hide behind that. And they had been, stalling any kind of progress. She seemed to have gone that bit distant and uncertain again. Was she just giving him space or did she regret asking him to stay here? He wasn't sure. Maybe she'd just done it out of some misconceived sense of obligation and now wished she could take it back. He'd certainly noticed it cause her discomfort to see him moving around in Elaine's home and amongst her things. As a result, and grateful as he was, he felt tense and observed like a child in a cluttered antiques shop. He was back to having no idea where he stood with her, and asking for clarification carried too many risks.

The rat-tat-tat of the knocker echoed through the house, and he wondered how quickly he should answer it. That wasn't healthy, even having to consider such things.

"Morning Nat. You're up early."

"Do you want to see orca, Joel?" Her eyes were shining and she was practically bouncing. "I just got word there's a pod near John O'Groats and we can get a reservation on the boat."

Joel's single experience afloat had been in a plastic dinghy on a duck pond some fifteen years ago, ending with his brother pushing him over the side. "As in out on the water among them?"

"Yes!"

"Is that not kind of dangerous?"

"It's fine. They're highly intelligent mammals that present no danger to humans."

"But they eat seals, don't they? And people are a very similar size and lousy swimmers. Couldn't we just look for them from the shore?"

Nat shook her head exasperatedly. "They know the difference Joel. Will you trust me on this?"

To that question, he realised, he could only answer "Yes."

Her face lit up again. "I'll reserve the places and we'll go in about an hour then. This is going to amaze you!"

She'd neither slowed nor smiled as they passed the SPCA animal rescue centre, where she volunteered, and she'd taken the infamous Forss Hill bend at a speed that had him gripping the armrest on her passenger door.

"Nat?"

"Uh-huh?"

"I'm assuming it was the checkpoint got under your skin. How about you have a free pass to rant the entire way to Thurso and then it's forgotten and we try to enjoy our day?"

She growled, but her expression melted a fraction. "I do not see why everyone going in and out of Reay on a public road has to submit to a car search just because that odious man is coming to his castle."

"He is the Prime Minister. I guess they have to protect him."

"From fictitious Remainer assassination plots? If he genuinely believed a word of that bilge his papers print he'd stay barricaded in Downing Street. But then he can't not be here next week, can he?"

Joel held his breath, guessing what was coming next.

"Not when that nauseating golf tournament nonsense of his is on."

Joel had learned months ago that the worst topic to bring up anywhere within a five-mile radius of Reay was the Champ Invitational Charity Golf Cup. He already knew most of the details via Derek, Dot and the landlord of The Reay Arms, but had promised Nat her rant.

"So get this, every year at the start of July they hold a tournament here. In theory it's for charity, but it's actually one huge, revolting ego trip where all the worst hunting-and-fishing types in the Highlands plus a load more from London fawn in front of Campbell on his stupid little fish-crate-podium throne. Do you know who sponsors it? His own companies, for the tax loss. And do you know what they spent a good half of this so-called charitable donation on last year?" She glared across at him.

"No idea," he said untruthfully.

"A massive portrait of him to hang in the castle's dining room. I mean come on! And then there are the ex-pro fees taken out as costs too."

Joel had also heard about this but wasn't about to say so.

"They get paid to come and play the tournament so long as they lose to Campbell. Then it's line up in front of the cameras and all that 'He's a master of his own course', 'I tried my best but Champ edged me out at the end there', 'I reckon Champ could have gone pro you know, if he hadn't decided there were bigger bucks in business.' Ha ha ha, backslaps and champagne all round as the envelopes of cash are trousered. You once asked me why I'm a vet, remember? Well you'd never see animals putting on such a repellent show. I think he genuinely believes he wins on merit too. How is such delusion even possible?"

"But if people are spending money to enter, surely some of them must be trying to win?" Joel ventured, because he was genuinely curious about this point.

She shook her head. "Most are just buying their name into his good books to seek favour, so they all make damned sure to lose. Of course there are plenty who'd happily pay to put a dent in Campbell's ego, and there'll be many more now he's PM, but his minions check everyone out thoroughly before they let them enter. Trust me, you don't get in at that club if you're any kind of threat. You need to be reliably sycophantic and giving him something he wants."

She lapsed into silence, and they came over the hill and saw Thurso and its surroundings spread out before them.

Joel tried on a grin. "So is the poison drawn? Can we now look forward to enjoying the day surrounded by deadly marine predators?"

She laughed then looked over at him, calmer now and serious. "You're good at handling people, aren't you Joel?"

That made him focus. Was she raising the ghost of their awful first meeting? Was this her trying to chip away at its insurmountable barrier between them?

He took his time before answering. "Yes Nat, I suppose I am. I hope it's something I'm learning how to use more wisely. The idea of going out on the sea near killer whales scares me, frankly, but I trust you that it'll be okay. You know you can trust me too, even if that wasn't always the case before?"

She looked at him again, and he had the oddest feeling: he'd seen her true person in those eyes a number of times now, but he realised this was the first time Joel Elliott might be properly visible to her in return.

She blinked a few times, then focused on her driving all the way through the town centre and out onto the Castletown road. He was equally quiet, his head spinning with revelation.

"I do," she said suddenly, as the squat little Harold's Tower mausoleum topped the horizon looking north to Thurso Bay and the Orkneys. "I do know that."

The John O'Groats boat was a lot smaller and lower in the water than Joel had expected. He did have faith in Nat though, despite the danger signals going off in his brain.

"Aye aye."

"How are you Morag?"

The easy Caithness greeting for a warm friendship of long standing. Odd, therefore, that the boatwoman, who Nat had explained was a marine biologist by training, didn't look happy to see them.

Morag and the unspeaking first mate distributed life jackets to the waiting group: Nat, Joel, and a party of nature spotters from Wick. Then the boat's engine whirred into life and they slipped away from the jetty with surprising speed.

Gulls wheeled and dived frenetically, scouring the water and finding something they liked in it. Salt spray licked Joel's face as they bumped over waves towards the deserted island of Stroma. Nat pointed out puffins perched on the cliffs, but she was frowning and partly elsewhere.

"I didn't think they'd be over here. Not with this," Morag announced, before swinging the boat to starboard with surprising firmness.

Nat was scowling now, and several times Joel saw her look questioningly at Morag, whose own weather-beaten face was set like an angry cliff. The boatwoman caught one of her glances and shook her head, her eyes indicating the group from Wick.

They moved round the headland to where two rock islands

reared from the sea like colossal fangs. An older man amongst the group regaled the others with a Viking legend that these, Duncansby Stacks, formed the gateway to Hell. It certainly looked the part, the palette of the cliffs and the churning sea all dark with portent.

"This is wrong," Nat muttered. Joel looked at her, but she was staring down into the sea rather than at the stacks.

Suddenly, no more than ten or so metres from them, a giant fin ripped through the water. Then another, and soon there were seven of them, and one had lifted its head to eye the boat.

The Wick party were delighted, all cameras snapping and expostulations of wonder. Morag looked grim though, Nat too. And then even to Joel, after a quick succession of shock, fear, awe and elation had run through him, things somehow started to feel off. He knew nothing about orca, but London had taught him the revulsion of breathing polluted air into healthy lungs. That was the impression he got from these creatures. It was more than that, though: these whales were disturbed like Joel was by what he'd witnessed in Euston station. He couldn't have explained how he knew this, just that in his heart he was sure.

The pod stayed around the boat for two minutes or so and then submerged, their fins only reappearing briefly some distance to the east. The show over, the boatwoman returned them to the harbour.

Nat was all over the place, unreadable but with no remnant of the morning's anticipation. "Can we wait? I want to talk to Morag."

The Wick group made a beeline for the cafe, and the first mate was busy stowing lifejackets. Nat went to speak to her friend, but she shook her head. "Not here."

They followed her a short distance away, to where a gathering wind would disperse speech before it reached other ears, and then Nat could restrain herself no longer.

"What was that in the water Morag? Why did the orca hate

it?"

Morag was in a quandary. She seemed about to talk, but then clammed up, shaking her head angrily.

"You can trust Joel," Nat said.

"Aye. That's not the problem."

"What is it Morag? Please. I'm enough of a vet to know there was something very wrong."

Morag screwed her face up a time or two more, but then relented. "It's been classified as a military secret, okay? So don't you repeat it to a soul or they'll work it back to me."

Nat and Joel both nodded mutely.

"We found the first of it yesterday evening. The gulls were all over it, and the orca seemed almost like they'd been driven here trying to escape it. They were showing aggressive behaviour not normal for this season and I'd swear they were trying to communicate distress. Well I took a piece of what was floating all around in the water to report, but right away, from the skin colour, I had a guess what it was."

Morag fell silent, shaking her head and then spitting off to one side, as if trying to clear a foul taste from her mouth.

"What Morag? What was it?"

"Burnt blue whale flesh."

Nat stared at her incredulously.

"Just fifteen minutes after I put an analysis request into the system they called me back to blether about the Official Secrets Act at me. But I know Alasdair who was handling things, and so I got the story. Your man from Reay, Campbell..."

"He's not our man from Reay, Morag."

"Aye. Well they had him visit a navy destroyer that's up in Fair Isle waters on manoeuvres. It seems they sighted the whale and Campbell came up with the idea of setting himself up at one of the ship's cannons loaded with explosive shells."

Nat looked sickened.

Morag spat again. "And your man blew that magnificent

beastie up for nothing more than a laugh, and the bits have been washing down through the Pentland Firth. They whacked the highest military classification on all of it, so I suppose I'm committing treason or something by saying any of this, but I tell you I'm just that bloody furious."

Making a choked noise, Nat lunged forward and hugged Morag.

Tears started to run down the seawoman's granite face. "Ach Nat, you know I've always loved taking the boat out here so much. Showing people this beautiful wee bit of coast and its ecosystem. And they do all care for it better from then on, you know? It gives you hope. But it'll never be the same again. The gulls will pick the sea clear soon enough because those flying garbage cans'll eat anything, but I'll never forget this stuff floating here nor that it was my own species that did it. This place is defiled for me now, and it's fair ripping my heart in two."

Eventually Nat let her go, her forehead moving forwards to touch the other woman's, a tender form of Scottish kiss. "I'm so sorry Morag," she said. "If you open yourself to love you open yourself to hurt too. I'm afraid that's just how life goes."

16.

Reay, August 2017.

Everything was wreathed in thick mist. For the previous four days it had been such a heatwave, by Caithness standards, that Joel had even got to see Nat's legs. But now this; something they called the haar.

The gatepost was no more than a pale shadow, all beyond it departed. Everything was still and the birds had fallen quiet. It felt as though a shroud had been placed over the earth for the dead to rise.

Moving away from the kitchen window, he bumped the rickety side table with his hip and muttered an oath as the tall vase on it teetered, his hand catching it just in time. He was living with a ghost here in this very house: Elaine.

It was all as she'd left it on the morning she'd gone to the hospital, a bad flu becoming pneumonia that would put her in the mortuary a week later. That left Nat, at just twenty-six, owning two houses, and yet all she did was stay in one like a short-let tenant and leave the other for bordering on two years as this museum.

And to what? It wasn't as though happiness or love shone out of these rooms Elaine had lived in. Everything was stark and stiff. Nothing spoke of the soul of the house's former owner, nor of her relationship with her granddaughter.

Knowing that Nat had no plans for this Bank Holiday Monday, he decided enough was enough. He pulled on his shoes and walked round to knock on her door.

She took a while to appear. "Hi."

"Morning neighbour. Have you noticed by now that I'm not someone who enjoys being in debt?"

"Do you mean based on your diatribes about student loans? Yes, there's been the odd indication."

"Good. So almost four months ago I moved in here with the promise of helping you clear out this house. I've offered you money instead but you keep saying no. Rent is due. Today."

She twisted uncomfortably. "You're fine. No. There's no rush. Another time, okay?"

"No Nat, I'm just not accepting that again. It needs doing and this day's no use for anything else. Come on."

"No Joel. Really, I don't want to."

He and Nat had been spending a fair bit of time in each other's company, but since the day with the orcas things had stuck in a pattern of staying safe. He wanted to tear down that barrier, even if it ended up breaking what they had.

"Then how about you tell me what to keep, anywhere you don't want me to look, and I'll deal with the rest?"

"No. No." She shook her head. "It's something I need to do."

"Then when, Nat?"

He knew she couldn't answer that. He also had an idea for how to force her into action, even though it was high risk. Would it be 'handling' her? Yes, absolutely. But in the same way he'd seen her handle Jimmy and his dog Kelpie in The Reay Arms again the other night; justifiable because sometimes you wanted to help and you knew better.

"It feels claustrophobic you see, almost a bit macabre. Living amongst someone else's stuff, I mean. I saw Shane Oag's off to prison again so there's no worries there anymore, and I've been wondering if it would be better if I found a place back in Thurso."

Her eyes opened in shock, and he couldn't help feeling secret elation at being wanted by her.

"I...well. Okay Joel. If that's what you prefer."

"It's not what I prefer Nat! I love being here. I love...please just let me help you Nat. I promised."

They stood there for what seemed an age, bone-grey mist swirling around them on her doorstep. Finally she relented.

"Okay. You're right. Come in for a tea first though."

"No. No more prevarication. It's better if we just get started."

"It's not. I said it would be easier doing this with someone who doesn't know my family history. Well you'll find documents and photographs and so on. I'd rather you heard things from me first. Then I promise we'll make a start."

So he followed her into her kitchen. This was the only room in her house he'd been in since moving to Reay. She seemed to use it as a dining and living room despite having the separate lounge he remembered from that first visit here. He sat silently at the table as she brewed up.

"Let's start with what you've already heard." She handed him his drink and sat where she had the option of her eyes being either visible to him or not. "My great-great-grandfather, Baron Leonid Nikolayevich Romanov, was a minor noble at the imperial court in St. Petersburg. His wife Fyodora was much younger, seventeen to his fifty-one when they married in nineteen-sixteen. They fled Russia to London when the revolution came, and their only child was born there, a girl called Nadia. Leonid died in nineteen-nineteen and Fyodora, now living on the charity of relatives, came to Reay as something between a companion and a servant for a lady who was convalescing at Fresgoe Castle. While here she met and married Arthur Mackay, the estate gamekeeper.

"Nadia was...probably these days she'd have been diagnosed schizophrenic. She spent periods in the Craig Dunain asylum down in Inverness, but I think that only made things worse. She took to wandering at night, and got pregnant by an unknown man. In nineteen-forty she gave birth to Elaine, my grandmother, and died in the process. Fyodora passed away the same year of a wasting disease, and that left Arthur, now in his sixties, responsible for a little baby girl who wasn't even his own blood. He was dutiful about it, but reading between the lines of what Gran said it was far from an ideal situation." Nat took a long sip from her mug.

"The illegitimacy mattered back then, but I think Gran was quite a looker in her youth, and that helped."

Joel had seen Elaine's wedding photo on the dresser and concurred, but he made no comment.

"She married Derek Sinclair, a local farmer who owned these two cottages, in nineteen-sixty-six. Again there was just the one child, Mary. My dear mother Mary."

It was the first time Joel had ever heard anything like this bitter sarcasm enter her voice. He kept still, face neutral.

"Well let's get straight on to the next scandal shall we? Mary was a dreamer and lapped up her exotic Russian ancestry. This is why I was named Anastasia by the way, which, as you know, I hate. She had the knack for attracting men, and much to Gran's fury she'd a string of companions all over Thurso. My father was – still is presumably – an American. He was a marine commander stationed at the old US communications site in Forss. I was born in ninety-one, and by that time he had shipped out home as they wound the base down. I guess promises had been made because Mary was expecting him to bring her over when he got set up there. It didn't happen though, so when I was less than a year old she took herself off across the Atlantic to look for him. Found him too, and the wife and three kids that had been there the whole damn time. After that you'd expect she'd come back to her infant daughter, right?"

Joel inclined his head cautiously.

"Well not in our happy little family. No, instead she chose to join a cult over there. Finding herself, until glorious leader found a younger, lower-maintenance devotee to play with. Then she acted up, was cast out, but kept on living the same train wreck. I met her just the once I can remember, in London when I was fifteen. She decided she wanted to get me drunk, share a mother-daughter bonding experience with me. In the end all we experienced was getting thrown out of several pubs and her being cautioned for insulting a police officer. She said she had a good job lined up as a waitress in some seedy-sounding bar. Said it paid plenty of easy money and I could work there too in a couple of years and we could be gal pals just like Thelma and Louise. She tried to persuade me to go with her there and then. I didn't, obviously. Nor have I any idea what's become of her since. Gran and the Reay postwoman were very diligent about intercepting and destroying her occasional letters after that."

Nat seemed to be flagging, but Joel wanted her to get through to the end of this. He sensed that the missing details for finally understanding her better were coming out.

"So Elaine brought you up?"

"Yes," Nat sighed. "She used to apologise to me sometimes. Said she hadn't been cut out to be a mother the first time round, and then just when she was done with it I got dumped on her and she had to begin all over again. Told me that was why she got so furious. Actually she did well enough, even after Granddad passed away when I was seven. She was harsh and unyielding but mostly fair. I was quiet and studious, kept myself to myself. It's easily done out here in Reay, and she encouraged it. I moved into this cottage when I was sixteen and we got on reasonably well after that. Made decent-enough neighbours."

Now Nat's silence felt final. Joel didn't know whether to stay frozen or go over and hug her. Hold her tight so the wondrous warmth of skin-to-skin human contact could bring her in from so long in so much cold. In the end he couldn't move. He had never yet touched her; if he did it could not be associated with only consolation.

She forced a sudden smile. "So now you know."

"Oh Nat... But you turned out well in spite of it all."

"Yeah, right. Being a vet I get daily reminders of how innate character is in every foal or litter of puppies. Familial genetics can't be fought."

She said this with utter resignation, and Joel blinked in sudden realisation. Did she believe herself doomed? It was the opposite of the self-made philosophy he'd once espoused, and equally stupid and self-defeating.

"I'm serious Nat. I think you're a wonderful person."

She flushed scarlet. "I'm not sure about that. Incidentally Joel, do you understand now why I get annoyed when you complain about your big, happy, obviously loving even if you only ever got hand-me-down clothes growing up family? I'm jealous."

It eased the tension and he laughed. "But you know I gripe about them much less than I used to. My parents and sister are even planning to come up for a visit. If I've ever got a spare room for them, that is."

"Oh very nicely brought back to the topic at hand!" She smiled and shrugged herself free from the shadows of the past. "Finally spilling the Sinclair secrets is quite liberating actually. Now tell me: how much of all that did you know already?"

"Literally none of it. Not a whisper from anyone. I guess I'm still too much the incomer here."

"Less and less every day though. Come on then, let's go clear out. As you were right to say, it's more than time."

17.

"Here you are. I knew Granddad had them somewhere." Nat handed Joel a musty leather pouch which unrolled to reveal a set of piano tools.

"Are you sure it's okay for me to try tuning it?"

Nat glanced over at the Kaps-of-Dresden upright that had been liberated from its piles of books in the corner of the lounge. "Be my guest. That applies to everything you want to fix, by the way. I have noticed all the things that have started working or stopped squeaking outside both houses these last couple of months. I'm very grateful. I'm not sure you'll get anywhere with that piano though. It's ancient and I don't think anyone's touched the poor thing since I used to practice scales on it a dozen years ago." Nat's enthusiasm for their task had a brittle air and was clearly on the wane.

"It's got an iron frame and looks well-built so it may surprise you. The good ones last."

She gave him a tired smile. "Joel, listen, I also want to say thanks for this morning's kick up the arse."

"Anytime Nat. How are you doing?"

"Far better than I expected. Lots of memories, but they have fewer teeth than I feared."

Joel stood up and stretched. "I'm glad." He looked round at the piles of stuff, excavated and sorted according to new criteria, principal among which was 'take to charity shop'. "We've done well. Shall we finish that last cupboard and then call it a day?"

"Carry on if you feel up to it, but I should just go and check on Jimmy and Kelpie. It's not going to be long, sadly. When I get back I'm making dinner for us both. No arguments please; your kitchen's complete chaos now."

"Sounds good. So what's in here?" Joel bent down again and opened a small trunk that had been at the bottom of the pile in the dresser. Inside was a collection of dusty, marbled-buckram-bound notebooks. "These look really old."

"They are. That's where...it was."

He knew she meant the jigsaw puzzle.

"Those are his diaries," she continued. "The baron's. Of course we never had any idea what's written in them. I doubt we'd want to know anyway, as he seems to have been a horrible man."

Joel picked one up and leafed through a couple of pages. Amongst the spidery scrawl were sketches, complex diagrams. He scanned further, feeling his pulse quicken. References to a portal. To a voice that whispered from beyond it.

"Nat, can I take a proper look through some of these?"

She glanced at the page he had open. "Oh, you found the drawings. I suppose we will have to talk about it someday, won't we?"

She'd broken down barriers with all she'd told him this

morning, and here he saw a chance to tackle that remaining wall between them. If he could just understand what had happened when he'd completed the puzzle.

"Nat, I don't want to put the pieces together and sell it anymore. You know that, don't you?"

"Yes, or you wouldn't be living here. Look if you want. I don't think those diaries will tell you much though, not without being able to read the words."

"I can read the words. Have I never said that I speak Russian?"

She looked surprised. "No. Well aren't you a man of hidden talents. I'm not sure you'll like what you find, but see you at dinnertime, okay?"

Some hours later she knocked on his door. "Come on Joel. What's keeping you? I sent a message to your phone ages ago. Food's on the table." Then her eyes widened as she took in his face. "What is it? What's wrong?"

"We have to talk about the jigsaw puzzle. Now. What have I done keeping quiet for so long?! I have an idea of what it is, but it's..." His words ran out.

She moved closer, concern etched on her face. "What?"

"Nat, if this is real it's horrific. I don't want to believe it, but...somehow...I don't know...it explains everything that's been in my mind. But it's terrible."

"Tell me."

"I don't know how to. It's too much."

She pulled up a chair next to where he sat at the table, diaries scattered around him. "I am the baron's only living descendant. If there is a burden here then it's at least mine to share, Joel. So tell me."

Horror was constricting his throat. "Promise you'll try not

to hate me for this."

"Tell me."

Joel gestured to the pile of seven notebooks to his left. "That's his research. I've only skimmed it, but Nat, he was a fanatic. I should never have put that piece in place! We have to talk about what each of us saw and felt. I think I've done something so terrible."

"Okay, okay. We will Joel. Be rational though. You were feverish that day. I can see it made a strong impression, but let's look at it calmly and see if there's actual evidence for anything."

"But that's the worst part. I don't think it can all be just coincidence."

"What do you mean?" For all her talk of being scientific, she was catching his terror.

"This is going to sicken you."

"Tell me, Joel. You have to tell me."

He closed his eyes and sighed. "I translated three entries that...that, give an overview I suppose. But you're going to hate..."

She gave him a hard look until he picked up the last of the diaries, his translation sandwiched between its pages, and handed it over.

London, May the 12th, 1919.

Another enquiry begets but one more thieving and mediocre craftsman who cares little about his work and more about swindling the patron commissioning it. And Fyodora's odious cousin will not advance me even a twentieth of the price.

How I curse Lebedev. What did he do with it? Where did he go? That sneaking apprentice must have known what he gave to that idiot Ivan. Was he the thief? Did he take my centrepiece to steal its rubies? For cheap vodka and whoring? It makes me livid and my cough grows worse.

And are not the English working classes equally detestable? A mere six months after the end of glorious war and they have fallen back into idle sloth, immediate gratification and coarse gossip about their betters. And they have the nerve to demand yet greater rights! It is insufferable. This is the poison in mankind's veins.

Why do the great now hold their tongues? Why do they cease to lead, to make fight? Where has resolve gone? They are betrayers. All human progress, all of it, emerges from the fulcrum of conflict. Conflict led by noble generals with great and competing visions of the future. How else should we find our way? Not by pandering to the witless whims of the footsoldier. Not from commanders concerned by ants when they should stride like colossi. With focus, in a quarter century we might build a bomb that can flatten an entire city. All it requires is purifying hardship.

But pah, I cannot allow myself to be brought low by mere lack of money. I who have noble breeding, honour, discernment and the design for the key to change history. I have considered sharing what I know for the general good, but it is mine. I will find a way to have a new centrepiece made. I must. I was weak to impregnate Fyodora with that brat but she will still suffice for a sacrifice. The brat too, should its puny life have value to The Master. I will be His Host. He will heal my body using His power. My wisdom concerning this world will be at His service. We will spread the fear and the hatred and the order of master and servant necessary to make mankind great again.

She dropped the diary back on the table as if it was diseased. "Nice to get to know one's ancestors better isn't it?" Her expression was stony and marred with self-doubt.

"I'm sorry. You needed to know the nature of all this. Now another from six years earlier. It's the best indicator I've found of what the jigsaw puzzle is." Joel handed her the second journal.

Constantinople, 2nd of November 1913.

This is it, the missing piece! The necromancer's tomb in Heliopolis has revealed the secrets I had hoped for and I close upon the completion of my life's work! What is in Femi's photographs is incredible. One thousand five hundred years ago they heard His same voice. Their carvings would never have worked to open The Portal. No, the pattern lacks all of the necessary spiral detail I discovered from the Baghdad scrolls, but the overall layout is there and, most importantly, the complete second layer. Beatrice thought she had the design but it is all my achievement, mine. The conductive circuit needs to be in direct contact with the pattern — how did I not see this before? Platinum will be superior to the gold the Egyptians used, and now I understand the symmetry of the linkages. Two jewels will be needed for the vortex points. I shall consult a watchmaker about frequencies, but rubies I fancy. And I know now why my previous attempt at building The Portal failed, even if it did do something permanent to the air. These two foci are how the morphic resonance may build to connect the dimensions, as I discerned from the Kyoto writings. I have put the clues together and soon The Master's long days of waiting shall be done. And none too soon, for the hold of the Tsars on their empire grows weak. The design still requires refinement, but then I will commission the making of it. A jigsaw puzzle I think, for disguise and portability. Wrought of the finest hardwoods. My family fortune dwindles but will still suffice. Finding a capable craftsman may prove burdensome, but I see it now. It comes near!

"So he believed the puzzle was some sort of gateway between dimensions that would let this The Master cross to Earth?"

"Yes. And finally this one, which is his real starting point and also mentions what will happen if The Master crosses over. I should warn you that he..."

"Don't. Let me read it."

Grimacing, Joel slid a third volume over to Nat, who lifted it with an expression of determined distaste.

St. Petersburg, 4th of January 1906.

Forty years I have existed upon this Earth, and ever without a clear purpose until this very morning. She had been ejected from the palace after trying to gain an audience with the filthy so-called holy man Rasputin, and people were holding their noses and avoiding her as a madwoman. I should have done likewise had she not shouted that name The Master that I have encountered more and more as I delve into the occult. I demanded to know where she had heard it. She was at first hostile, but my offer of a warm fire, bread and wine tempted her. I took her to the apartment on Nevsky Prospekt. When she removed her hood I saw both her advanced age and her disease. She asked if I could secure a meeting with Rasputin, claiming that he would see the power of what she knew and use his influence to have a key of some kind made. I was minded to eject her at this point, but she began on her story and it intrigued me.

She was now penniless, but her husband had been a rich Frenchman whose obsession with the Marquis de Sade led him into the study of human pain. He seems to have been more a thug than a scholar, but the wife he took – this same Beatrice – had similar interests and far greater intellect. Her great-grandfather had been guillotined in the dreadful revolution and the family cast into poverty, and she desired revenge. Studying her husband's collection of demonic works she espied a pattern. Despite the disadvantage of being female, she was able to use his wealth to acquire the darkest writings from across the French and other empires, and from these, through all the mad drivel and illiterate superstition, she picked out a consistent and aeons-old voice: The Master. I knew a little of what she spoke and was rapt.

"The horde cannot rule," she declared. "That is the preserve of nobility and all others are but wheat in the field to be scythed and ground for bread. The Master knows how to restore this rightful order. He is immortal, infinitely perceptive and entirely capable of the necessary savagery. For that is the only language the peasantry truly understands, is it not sir?" she enquired of me. I readily inclined my head in concord. "His voice has spoken to those disposed to listen throughout human history, but it is only I who have joined those fragments together. We must build a particular bridge that He may cross over. This bridge is no great iron span to cross a river, rather it is a small thing but covering incredible distances, like the telephone invention of Bell. My design, assembled from a hundred or more scraps scattered across the globe, needs only to be constructed. I require merely the patronage to hire a craftsman. Then when He arrives He shall take a *sacrifice for strength, having only shadowy form here. That shedding of a life will empower Him to take a Host. A willing Host mind, for an unwilling one would reduce his force. This chosen Host's tongue – my tongue – shall gain the power to convert and to steer and to divide and to conquer. All the world shall hark to it, even as they understand not why. He is almighty and none shall be able to resist Him. He will bring the glory of hatred, the rod of righteous fear, the pure sanctity of war. You must help, good sir. Look, it is all here. I have catalogued it, all of it. Look!"*

Was it wrong of me to strangle her as I did then? But I could not take the risk of what she possessed falling into other hands, you see. Instantly upon hearing it I knew this to be my destiny. In the texts she showed me I felt a presence that called to me. Really it is her fault for writing everything down so comprehensively. In revealing her every secret thus she rendered herself superfluous. She was not worthy. No. And she was ill anyway; she admitted as much herself. I gave her a quick and merciful exit, in fact. Furthermore having to rewrite her many journals in my own hand will be most laborious for me, as will the disposal of her corpse. But I am The Master's chosen Host, not her. Through my hand shall He do His work.

"So he was a murderer as well." Nat, looking repulsed, slid the baron's diary further away from her on the table. "But Joel do you really believe all this Master and key stuff?"

"It finally explains things for me. When I put that centrepiece into position I saw a kind of tunnel open above the jigsaw puzzle. A shadow came through and I felt a blackness invade me. Something tried to possess me. It almost did but my heart fought back at the last. I wasn't willing. It was evil, utterly evil. Then there was a crash, which I think was you sweeping the jigsaw onto the floor, breaking it apart. Didn't you see that shadow too? Wasn't that why you broke the puzzle?"

Nat was staring at him, the total, honest Nat that he so craved, but now with fear and loathing distorting everything. "I did feel something...and yes, it was evil. Evil as I've never believed in nor encountered before. There's no other word for it. I thought I glimpsed a distortion in the air and a kind of dark shape too, but I wasn't sure and anyway I was focused on you because you were convulsing. I pushed the jigsaw onto the floor because I wanted to break it, and that seemed to drive whatever it was away."

"Was there anything else? Anything at all? I have to try and understand what happened. I need to know what I did. I need the nightmares to stop."

"I just don't know. It's all such a blur. I don't even know what we were doing assembling it like that, so complacently. When you put the centrepiece in it was so fast. I shouted at you to stop but you didn't hear and..."

"You shouted 'wait'. I heard and I did it anyway. I'm so sorry Nat. It was unforgivable of me."

She paused, considering him. "Perhaps. But that's not for you to decide, is it? Then, well only what I already said. Except for one thing: in the instant I reached down to break the puzzle I think I heard – or rather I sort of felt – an echo of my own shout. A command or a plea to stop. But with all that was going on I don't have clear recall about it, and believe me I've tried."

Joel just sat there, overwhelmed by a wave of relief at having all this out in the open, and a tsunami of despair at what it might mean.

Then Nat was standing, her face ashen as she grabbed the second of the two diaries he'd given her and reread his translation. "There, I thought so. The baron said his attempt at making a portal did something permanent to the air."

She grabbed Joel's arm, tugging at him to follow her. Bemused, he did so. They went outside, through the haar murk and into her house, down the corridor to the lounge. Its outer edges had been raided for furniture and the dust of a year or more's disuse lay thick on all that had been left behind.

"Does it explain this Joel? I've thought I was going mad. Where we assembled the puzzle the air stabbed me and I haven't dared go near it since. I use the kitchen for everything instead now. Do you see anything there?"

Nothing was visible but he was sure he felt the scar hanging in the room's centre. It was longer and deeper than the one he'd encountered. It must have really caused her pain.

"There was the same thing in Russia near where I found the centrepiece. All the footprints went round it. I thought it was superstitious nonsense and put my hand there. It hurt like hell."

"That's it exactly, like hell."

Hell. Hell, except on Earth. "Oh Nat, I think this must all be real. What have I done?"

18.

For the next four days of the week they mutually avoided the topic as impossible and everything was stuck and wrong. Numbers slipped from Joel's head at work, Derek even having to point out mistakes. Nat was scratched and bitten by normally placid patients, lost a golden retriever puppy under anaesthesia as she tried to repair the damage a car had done. The haar stuck too, against all precedent and nature, and to the consternation of all who engaged in comment on the weather, which in Caithness was everyone.

By Saturday morning Joel was going stir crazy, and rose determined to break the cycle. Outside was sunshine, finally; blue sky rinsed clean of the mists. He opened the window and inhaled.

He could not remain petrified into inaction. He would not let things stagnate any longer, not in his own head nor between he and Nat. He pushed open his front door and stepped out at the same moment she did from the adjoining house. She was intense like someone going into battle. He knew he must be wearing a similar expression.

"What can I do about this, Nat?"

She breathed deeply from the wonderfully clear air. "We," she corrected. "What can we do. Hope is what we need, so I'm thinking literally: Ben Hope at last. Burn this out of us or into something useful with hard exercise and a view of the world from above. Can you be ready to go in fifteen minutes?"

Ben Hope; most northerly of the Munros, the mountains of Scotland standing over three thousand feet tall. He'd seen its spectacular peak on the horizon plenty of times and they'd mentioned climbing it someday. He nodded agreement.

They said little on the drive there. Nat parked, and they strode out amongst the scrub of heather. As they worked their way higher, setting a hard pace, the view began to open up around them. Even at the end of summer the land's dominant colour was a hardy brown. Sheltered crevices around the foot of the mountain were mottled with touches of green, and then higher up all gave way to grey rock. The wide glen below was the end of 'the flow country', streams and rivers cutting stark silver paths through the dark peat.

By unspoken agreement they neither paused nor talked until they stood at the mountain's summit. Then for a while they simply gazed at the whole north-western tip of Scotland spread out below them.

"I can't get it out of my head." It was Joel who broke the windswept silence. "I keep telling myself it could all be delusions and coincidence, but I just don't believe it."

"I don't either. I've found out something Joel."

He looked at her, the feeling like when the phone rings at three in the morning and you recognise a family number.

"Yesterday I had the idea of calling an acquaintance at Wick hospital to check the register of deaths that day."

"Was there one?" Every bone in Joel's head felt tense.

"Yes. A club caddy at the golf course in Reay. Cause of

death unclear, but as there was no suspicion of foul play and he had a medical history it just went down as a suspected stroke. Time of death less than an hour after we..."

"After I. Not we. You had no part in what was done Nat."

"Of course I did! I could have just said no. I could have followed my intuition and left that puzzle where it was in the cupboard. I could have sent you on your way. Instead I...I was intrigued. So don't pretend I wasn't involved."

"If you must. But it was me that completed it, and you were trying to stop me."

"Far too little and far too late. And does that even matter Joel, really? The point is that here and now you and I are in this together. We believe this because of what we felt that day, but no-one else will ever accept it based on our say-so. So it's only us, but it's us."

Joel stared out at all the space. "Okay," he agreed at last.

"Okay. While that death falls short of proof, it corroborates things. It fits with what the baron wrote about a sacrifice, a human life being needed to give his Master strength."

"Did he...who was he? The caddie I mean."

"An older man living in Thurso. He wasn't married and had no kids."

"Not that that makes it any better."

"No."

Joel sighed, the stiff breeze giving it flight. "So if this Master thing somehow came through some sort of portal the puzzle opens and the baron was right about a sacrifice...does that mean there's a host? Is it in someone in Reay now? Possessing them, like I think it tried to possess me?"

"We have to assume it's possible. As I see it, if we've got this wrong then it doesn't matter what we try to do about it, it's just our madness and the rest of the world remains as it was. However if we're right then we have to try and rectify things. Do you agree?"

"Yes. That makes sense. How, though? I mean I've been thinking of nothing else all week but I've not a clue where to start."

"I have, but I don't think you'll like it." She was exuding a strength of purpose now.

"If I can't think of any alternative then I don't have that luxury. What?"

"We remake the puzzle."

Was she serious? Joel studied her, the face that he found more and more beautiful as she hid herself from him less and less. Her long, vibrant, healthy body. Those eyes, in which he'd seen – and hungered every day to see again – true generosity of soul.

She continued analysing, oblivious to his thoughts. "It's whatever I felt or heard telling me to stop when we made the puzzle. At first I thought it meant finishing the jigsaw and the warning just came too late. Now I believe it wanted me not to break the puzzle, not to close the portal that had been opened."

"You're sure?"

"Of course I'm not sure! Might we let more evil through? Yes. If this is all true then that has to be a possibility. I don't know, and I'm scared stiff, and...aaargh!"

Joel closed his eyes, nodding at how exactly she'd summed up his own thoughts of the past few days. "Ignoring your head, what does your heart say, Nat? I trust your heart completely."

She grimaced, not liking the burden he was putting on her. Neither did she shirk it though. That was the stuff she was made of, this one. "I don't think what I heard was evil. I'm not sure that means it's good, but it didn't seem out-and-out evil like that shadow. Also my distinct impression was it was potent and perceptive, to the point that it knew all that was in my head. That's why I believe it couldn't have been so behind events as to warn about something that was already happening, the completion of the puzzle."

"And it was only you who heard it."

She looked quizzically at him. "What do you mean?"

"You had no thought of completing the puzzle, that was my intention. If we can put the whole sanity of hearing voices in the head to one side, whatever spoke to just you did so because of what was in only your mind, which was to break the puzzle."

"Good point." She nodded, her gaze now cast far out over the land below. "So we remake it?"

"Yes, Nat."

Suddenly a thrilling sensation surged through Joel's body. He snatched his attention back from the panorama, realising that she had taken his hand in hers. They were touching for the first time. She must have felt the same thing because she was looking wide-eyed at him. They pulled closer to each other and then he was aware only of the warmth of her body and her hair flicking the left side of his face as the wind played with it. He desired her more than ever, but this embrace wasn't sexual. It was sheer relief. The secrets between them were out. The barriers had gone, and the air was clear.

Finally they drew apart and stood looking at each other. Nat's eyes were glorious as they studied his face.

"We'd better be off down the mountain. I have no idea what we're going to do next, but at least we're in it together and it's honest now. Maybe that will be enough."

And so they set off walking.

This mountain was named Hope, and that had been found here. Ahead of Joel paths which for the last eighteen months had led only into endless blackness now seemed pinpricked by lights. For all that the route they illuminated was terrifying, it was also wondrous to finally see.

19.

The Sunday late-summer sun was already high overhead when Joel knocked on Nat's door, the centrepiece nestled in his hand like a dormant viper.

The remaking of the puzzle had not been a task suited to yesterday's evening. They'd got home after climbing the mountain, shared some food, but then gone quietly to their respective cottages and thoughts.

Joel's had involved turning that embrace over and over in his mind. Where might it lead? For answers he knew he would have to wait. Some resolution of their shared task would be required before there could be space for love.

And yet, love. He'd been ignorant of it, but he felt he was growing up. Once you knew what you were looking for you saw it everywhere, invisible threads that joined people together into humanity.

In his family all the jostling and bickering now paled by comparison with the love. He'd in some ways resented his parents for the profligacy of bringing five children into the world when all they could provide was a cramped four-bed semi and the cheapest clothes. He was ashamed of that judgement and others like it now. He wouldn't dwell on it though, let it fester and erect barriers. Everyone concerned remained present in the world, so he was blessed with the chance to make good.

How must it feel to not have that path to redemption? How must it feel to be Nat? She had two houses and probably even money in the bank, but beyond some second cousins in Halkirk and a mother and father somewhere across the Atlantic who'd abandoned her, she was alone in the world.

Even as that thought formed he knew it to be incorrect: she had the whole of Reay. It was clear as day to him but he was convinced she only half-saw it. How else could she have thought they'd judge her harshly for breaking up with Euan? She had earned their love by giving back to her adopted kin wholeheartedly. And earned love was the very best kind there was.

She opened the door. "Morning." Smile, flash of awkwardness, half-smile, gaze slides away, cloud of responsibility. Today all that was fair enough.

"Are you ready for this?"

"Not really. I haven't changed my mind though."

"Me neither. Where are we doing it? The kitchen?"

"No. I can't afford to lose another room. We'll use the far side of the lounge."

Skirting the place by the fire where the scar split the air, they pulled the table over and sat down. As they took out their respective pieces Joel had a flash of déjà vu and shuddered instinctively. Then he set himself to once more joining the pieces as she removed them from the box.

Finally there was only the hole in the middle awaiting the four locks of the red-eyed centrepiece to complete the baron's key. He noticed his fingers trembling as he reached for it.

"No," said Nat softly. "This was my idea so if it goes wrong I want it to be my doing." She took his hand and gently moved it away. There was the same spark as yesterday's touch.

Picking up his piece she glanced one last time at him, offering the veto he hadn't allowed her. He didn't react so she moved it above its hole and let go, snatching her hand back.

Nothing happened.

Looking closer, Joel spotted that the piece hadn't quite sunk into its place. Fearful of touching it, he nudged the table to help it fall.

Now there was alignment but still there was nothing. Or perhaps the faintest sense of something, a call from across a winter field in a high wind? No. He was imagining things.

Nat was studying him. "Anything?"

"No."

"Me neither."

"At least the shadow, the evil, isn't there."

They looked between the pieces and each other. That it could be assembled as uneventfully as any other jigsaw puzzle was the one possibility they hadn't considered.

"Nat. When you felt something before, when exactly was it?"

She frowned in recall. "In the instant I swept the jigsaw off the table I think."

"That was the only time you touched the puzzle. Maybe we have to be in physical contact with it?"

To Joel it felt like checking if electric wires were live by touching them. Nat, someone who sliced with good intent into flesh for a living, looked equally hesitant.

"Together?"

She nodded. Their right hands intertwined over the puzzle, ten fingertips aligned like a piano octave minus the B and E.

As soon as they made contact with the dark wood Joel felt thoughts flood into his mind. They were so tangible that he wondered if he was hearing them out loud. He glanced at Nat and was certain she was experiencing the same thing. The sequence lasted for perhaps a minute or two, and then there was silence again. Simultaneously, they lifted their hands clear of the puzzle.

"I felt it!" He exclaimed. "Did you also get that..."

"Wait!"

This time he heeded that command from her.

"Joel we have to separately write out what each of us got. It's the way to confirm that this is real. That we're not mad."

He nodded, seeing the sense of her idea. She stood, dashed to the hallway and returned to thrust a pad and pen at him. "Don't say anything. Don't even look at me. Write everything down. When you're done come and find me in the kitchen. If

I'm not finished wait in the hall."

Then she was gone and he could turn his full attention to what had appeared in his head. The ordered train of thoughts was still crystal clear, and he began to write.

The puzzle utilises a harmonic resonance between matched patterns to create a connection across space and time, opening a kind of wormhole.

Something entered our world through it.

It has planned and coveted this for millennia. It projected the design to devil-worshippers to get them to make the key.

Earth has a uniquely strong life force but also a weakness which is its tendency towards aggression and conflict.

The shadow amplifies this to feed on the breakdown of societies.

It thrives on negative emotions and can manipulate whole populations to succumb to them and produce more and more. We won't understand how it does this so will struggle to resist it.

It is insatiable. It may end humanity.

He re-read the words like you would an exam paper. Yes, he had it all, and felt sick with fear. He stood and walked silently to stand outside the kitchen. When the sound of Nat's pen scratching ceased he went in. She turned to look at him, then held out her piece of paper. He took it, handing over his. Hers read:

There's an exact complement to the puzzle somewhere else far away in the universe and the completed jigsaw formed a bridge between the two.

A creature crossed over.

It has been trying to get here for thousands of years, whispering plans for this end of the portal to occultist ears on Earth.

Life on Earth abounds as nowhere else, but it is flawed by an innate aggressiveness and recourse to conflict.

It is a parasite. A foul deadly parasite we can't fight. It will exploit our weaknesses to make us fall into paranoia and hatred and violence and it

will feast on all that. We won't even know that it's doing this.
It will never stop. It could destroy humanity.

Joel looked up to see Nat watching him.

"It's the same," she said.

"Yes. Except you found exactly the right word: parasite."

"I'm a vet. We know the devastation parasites cause. So this...it's proof?"

"Yes. Only to us though. No-one else would ever believe we wrote these two pages independently."

"No-one else would believe any of this. At least we know though...but what do we know? All I got was the problem, not any kind of solution to it. You?"

"The same."

"Then how does this help us?"

"I'm not sure it does, Nat. I think we just have to hope that we get more from...from whatever put those ideas into our heads. Unless you can think of anything better?"

She shook her head. "Curling up in a ball under the table and sobbing maybe. What that presence in the puzzle was I've no idea, but it knows more than we do. So that's my best plan too: we keep trying the jigsaw in case it comes back."

20.

Monday: Joel went to knock on Nat's door but it was already wide open, letting air into the house.

"Morning. How did you sleep? Did you sleep?" she called from inside.

"I haven't been sleeping well for the last year and a half anyway. You?"

"I spent the first half of the night unable to believe yesterday was real, then the second half scared that I do believe it. So as you'd expect."

"What do you reckon it was we got all that from?"

"Something that understands what we're up against. Beyond that I've no clue, and I've decided it's better not to even think about it."

"Me too. And any ideas what we can do about this, assuming it is all true?"

"Zero. You?"

"Nothing. It feels impossible."

"The puzzle again, then?"

Together they went to her lounge, linked their fingers and touched the dark wood hoping for guidance. For a full half hour they sat expectantly, but nothing answered. In the end they had to give up and attempt their usual workdays as if the bottom hadn't fallen out of their universe.

Tuesday: "I've had an idea. A name, but I don't want to say." Nat, filtering coffee, looked even paler than usual.

"I have one too, after we were talking about sacrifices and hosts last night."

"Write it down again. That way we know we're not influencing each other."

Charles Campbell

...read Nat's scrawl.

Champ Campbell

...was lettered in Joel's neat handwriting.

"I was hoping I was wrong." She shook her head. "It all fits too well though. The caddie's death was the sacrifice, which places...it at the golf club. The hospital was told he was out on the links, but even the ambulance staff got no clue of who he was caddying for. Why not? Was it Campbell? We know he was at the castle: he flew out of Reay in his jumbo jet the next day. If the parasite needs a host who can enable the dissemination of anger and hate, the assumption has to be it can assess that capability. Campbell...well look at his newspapers and TV stations and their character. Did it find him? I can't imagine anyone better suited for its needs. Anyone worse."

Joel let out a ragged breath. "Yes. Unfortunately I can add to it. I can't be sure, but I wonder if I was steered towards completing the puzzle and Campbell."

He fell silent, but Nat waited him out.

"Even back on the building site in St. Petersburg, when I took the centrepiece from a skeleton and put it in my pocket. Please believe me that was out of character. Then it was like a voice urged me to the TV just when Antiques Hunt was on. If I hadn't gone downstairs then I'd never have known about the puzzle. And then when I was looking for a place to stay I read the Fresgoe Castle website for no clear reason and even recalled a whole essay I'd written for school media studies about Campbell. I'm not denying my complicity, but it was like I was acting as a conduit. I know it sounds ridiculous, but..."

"I think we can accept that, given the context. A conduit for what, Joel?"

"I have no idea beyond evil. Remember what you said that time on the tennis court? 'Like a healthy body struck down by a disease it has no immune response for'. The message we got from the puzzle said we wouldn't understand it, but perhaps it understands us. If you're right and it can assess a person's capability to do its dirty work there's no doubt Campbell would attract it."

Nat was nodding, but Joel pushed on before she could speak.

"And his retaking control of his empire was the first night I was in the flat in Thurso. That was all of about forty hours after I completed the puzzle and let that thing into this world right next to his golf course. Since then the world's gone into a nosedive to the extent we've got Campbell and his Just Brits running the UK and equally appalling people popping up as presidents all over the globe. It don't believe it's coincidence."

"I agree completely, but please stop saying it was only you Joel. Also, killing something as magnificent as a blue whale just for fun? If that's not proof of some inhuman evil in him then I don't know what is. What do we do about it though? What on earth can we do?"

"I have no clue. At least we've identified a target."

"A target...to do what to?"

"I don't know. That's what I'd love some guidance about."

"Well whatever it is he's the hardest target in the country. He's the Prime Minister."

"I know. I guess we just go and try the puzzle again."

There was still nothing. Even the bite of rendered air or that dark shadow appearing would almost have been preferable.

Wednesday: they held their fingers on the puzzle and waited. It remained devoid of anything. Resignation was seeping more and more into the vacuum.

"How's your morning looking Nat?"

"Small animal surgery and I'm expecting a couple of the regulars. Like that."

"Chocolate isn't good for dogs and the necessity of keeping guinea pig cages clean?"

"And a parrot needing his claws trimmed if I'm unlucky. You?"

"Garage conversion to draw up. Literally you could not utilise this space any less effectively, but the client's right even when they're wrong."

"Best get to it then. There's nothing going to happen here

so I don't want to think or talk about it anymore."

"Exactly. See you this evening."

Thursday: "Coffee before we try today? Eke out the forlorn hope for a few more minutes?"

"I won't thanks. I'm due at Dot's for signoff on the plans to go out to tender, so I'll need all my capacity."

Nat smiled, a rarity this week. "This will be the first time one of your own designs gets built won't it?"

"It will. I'm a little nervous, but she was so good about listening and taking everything on board. It's going to be an ideal addition that changes the nature of the whole house and she'll love it."

"You'll never want for a cup of tea in Reay again!"

Joel laughed. "Like you. Are you on farm calls today?"

"I am." Her face grew keen, already relishing the solitary drives deep into the countryside.

"Shall we go get you-know-what out the way then?"

"Let's."

And again, aside from the small joy of linking fingers with Nat, there was nothing there.

Friday: both bone-tired upon waking, they tried the puzzle first thing to no avail, then rushed off to complete their employed weeks. Routine in the mortal world didn't just cease, after all.

When Joel got home at six Nat came out to meet him. "I feel like a zombie. We can't go on like this, drifting forwards in a muddle of dashed hopes and brittle pretending. I've got a bottle of wine. It's where I figure on looking for answers tonight. Will you join me?"

"Gladly. I've lost sight of where my bad dreams end and this last week begins. My head's completely scrambled. Do you want to come round to mine where there's a lounge and we don't have to look at that puzzle?"

"Good idea. I'll be over in a bit."

Ten minutes later Nat handed Joel a full glass. "You'll need it. I intend to get half-baked and grim."

"I'm already living there."

Nat downed an impressive gulp from her own glass. "Please understand I'm not proposing this as a plan. Even if I did we'd never manage it. I'm just trying to understand what we'd need to do if it's us all on our own with this."

"You've landed on the idea of killing the host, haven't you? Killing Campbell."

Nat writhed as if she was trying to shrug herself out of her own skin. "Yes. I can't believe I'm saying it, but yes."

Joel reached over and took her hand, startling her and making her focus on him. "I know. I know exactly. I have no clue if assassinating Campbell would even serve to banish the thing, but it's academic because it's impossible. There's no way we can get near him. There's a vast queue of cranks and foreign agents with the same idea, which is why there's such a sophisticated security operation all around him. Our chances would be zero."

"Could you though Joel? Could you commit murder?"

He exhaled heavily. "My grandad passing away and seeing those bones in Russia are the closest I've ever got to death. I don't feel I have it in me to kill someone, but look at the things normal people do in war. So I don't know. Could you?"

Nat's face was pained in contemplation. "I'd have to say no. I can put down animals when it eases their suffering, but...I was asked to destroy this dog once. It had mauled someone and had that crazy look a badly mistreated animal gets. The thing is it clearly didn't want to die. I accepted the rationale for killing it, but when it came to it I just couldn't do it. Neil drove out and did it instead." She took another gulp of her wine. "But as you said it's all academic. That's why I've been wondering whether we should just give up and accept this as fate. Is there actually any responsibility to try if our best efforts cannot possibly change anything?"

"Could you do that any more than you could kill someone?" Joel's emotions whirled, guilt staining tantalising relief.

"I don't know. What I do know is it's something that's at least within our control."

"Enjoy our lives as best we can while we watch the world go to hell?"

"Yes, basically. Do you have a better plan? If so please tell me because I'm all ears. This is anathema to me."

Joel stared into space and eventually shook his head. "I don't, and I've been driving myself crazy trying all this last week. So that's it? We keep making contact with the jigsaw puzzle every day because that's the one thing that might make a difference, but otherwise we just try to ignore all of this and live what life we get? We try to be good people. We try to be kind."

Nat filled up their two empty glasses. "Joel?"

"Yes?"

"I forgive you for completing the jigsaw puzzle. I forgive you."

And suddenly tears were coursing down Joel's cheeks.

Saturday: they slept late, and again met in Joel's cottage so they could start the morning freer from reminders. Nat was carrying a pan.

"How's your head?"

"Not great. That second bottle was a mistake."

"I brought soup and bread."

They ate slowly, only occasionally breaking the silence with some bit of banal conversation. After lunch, with it being a grey sort of day, they moved into the lounge and attempted playing chess without any will to win.

It was almost a relief when insistent knocking started at the front door. Joel shrugged at Nat's questioning glance. "I've no idea. It's only you who visits, and you're already here."

He got up and went to open the door.

"Euan?"

"Nat in here then, is she? Oh that's very fucking cosy, yeah." Bitter sarcasm dripped from every word.

"I'll go ask if she wants to speak to you."

Ignoring Joel, Euan barged straight past and down the corridor into the lounge. Joel restrained himself from responding physically, but with the week's frustration bubbling away inside him it would only need Nat to give him the tiniest signal.

"I'm leaving Thurso," Euan announced.

Nat seemed at a loss for words, all her old awkwardness back in full squirm.

"I've got an off-Fringe gig at a pub in Edinburgh. It could really launch the band. Jamie's up for it. So we had a misunderstanding, but it's not too late Nat. I'm giving you this one last chance."

Now she was starting to shake her head.

"If nothing else then for the music," Euan added, his voice going up a tone.

If Nat had only spoken Joel would have kept quiet, but she seemed to lack any answer to the bullying whine in her ex-boyfriend's words. "For the music?!" he whispered, not kindly and not so sotto voce.

Euan turned on him. "Like it's anything you'd fucking

understand. I'm talking real music. Not whatever hip-hop gangster rap shite you're into."

Joel's eyebrows rose. "Do you know that's the first time anyone in Caithness has made assumptions based on the colour of my skin."

The Adam's apple bobbed angrily. "What?! Are you calling me a racist?! Me? I'm, like, the least racist person ever. O-fucking-kay?"

"If you say so. Either way I think I understand 'Tethered' well enough, and it's certainly not to my tastes."

Euan's mouth flapped open like a landed pike's. "D'you hear that Nat, eh? You're going to just sit there while this...fucking Sassenach new boyfriend of yours who knows nothing about music insults our artistic integrity, eh?"

And still she couldn't get herself together! Joel was almost ready to explode. How could this woman who'd skewered him so adeptly on the Thurso tennis court fail to find a response now?! How was she not raging that Euan dared show his face at her home?!

Aware that he was about to do something everyone would regret if he remained within fist-range, Joel made himself walk over to the piano instead. He sat down, raised the lid, and chose sonata number eighteen in D major.

The opening bars were typical Mozart, deliberately complex and unusual enough to capture any audience. Thereafter it turned full-on dazzling and bewitching, the pianist left nowhere to hide. Aware of the sweeping second hand on the wall clock, he played for less than a minute, but it was enough to wash his mind clear. When he finished he just sat there, his gaze out the window now calm.

"Fine then Nat. Fucking fine," spluttered Euan eventually. "Have a shite, boring, middle-class life then. With him. You know what? You're just like your mother! You don't know the meaning of loyalty."

That finally snapped her out of whatever stasis she was in, but she didn't hurl insults back at him, didn't even raise her voice. Instead she got up and walked out of the cottage, a hand on Euan's back to propel him in front of her. Joel could hear her voice from the front garden, calm and low, but not the words she chose. Euan's replies ranged wildly from squawking frustration through to childlike snivelling, but she met them all implacably. After some ten minutes of it Joel heard the gate go and then she re-entered alone.

"Are you okay Nat? I'm so sorry I interfered."

"It's fine Joel. I'm fine."

He waited while she thought.

"The only feeling I could find for him was pity, but it would have destroyed him to let him know. You can't be twenty-six and still be nothing more than you were at sixteen. The world won't allow it. I think something inside him understands that and it's turned him bitter and desperate, stifled the potential that used to be there. He's gone now, and that's for the best."

They lapsed into an almost dreamlike silence, Joel still sitting at the piano churned up by Mozart's genius and Nat's kindness. Her eyes were distant with whatever memories she was turning over. Then they snapped back into focus.

"How come you've never told me you can play? And like that! It was exquisite Joel."

He blinked and returned to the here-and-now. "Hardly. I fluffed two sequences, my pedal was clumsy, and try as I might I still can't get this poor old piano fully in tune."

"I didn't notice any of that. Why would you hide such a talent?"

And she was right, he had been, but not because of false modesty or any lack of desire to impress her. His mind slid back to when he'd learnt that piece, the Handel scholarship he'd applied for because Mr. Andreev insisted he needed a better tutor to continue his progress. He'd performed the audition well. It hadn't been quite enough but they'd encouraged him to try again next year. He never had though.

He sighed. "If you must know it's because I'm ashamed."

"Of ability like that? That's absurd."

He could have shifted this conversation on or closed it down, but those caring eyes of hers were on him and he knew she wanted to understand.

"I didn't take piano where I might have but I can't say I regret that. I guess I'm ashamed of how I treated the most generous friend I've ever had, Mr. Andreev. He gave and gave to me, and when it was my turn to repay I just turned my back and walked away."

She met his silence, her gaze constructing a safe space for him. Eventually Joel relented. "He was our neighbour across the garden wall. An elderly Russian man who lived alone in the same size house as the seven of us. I think it was all that precious space that was the attraction when I was eight or so and I was always hanging around there. He was kind and patient with a small boy, and one day he allowed me to try his treasured piano. I still remember it like it was yesterday. He permitted me to use only my right hand, showed me a simple sequence and asked if I could play it back. I did, and he gave me another, then another, each more difficult than the last.

"Outside the family, who don't count, I don't think I'd ever caused an adult to get excited before. It was addictive. I remember he came back to our house with me, marched in all determined. My mum looked worried, must have thought I'd broken something in his garden with a football. 'I wish to provide for Joel the piano lessons. Do you allow this?' He was so formal. My mum didn't reply and I knew just what she was thinking: money. We never had it to spare. 'He doesn't want paying,' I blurted out. 'Certainly not!' He seemed shocked at the idea. 'I am convinced Joel has the exceptional talent. It is my honour to assist that.' Well there was no way she could turn that down. To start with it was once a week, but soon twice, three times, and then almost every day. 'This will not do,' he declared that very first week when he was trying to explain something. 'For you to one day understand Rachmaninoff you must also have his language.' After that all the lessons and all our conversations were in Russian, which is why I speak it." Joel lapsed back into silence, remembering where that skill had led.

"And?" Nat's look was gentle encouragement.

"And I was a natural at the piano. I grasped melodies instantly and had all the feel, timing and co-ordination. By age thirteen I'd passed my grade eight and people were talking about career possibilities. The problem was that my heart wasn't in it anymore. I'd begun to like girls, started to take a lot of note of my appearance and how it influenced all my interactions with the world. Concert pianist seemed such a musty, cobwebbed profession. Elitist and prejudiced too. A half-caste kid from a working-class background behind the piano was a curiosity to be discreetly gossiped about, and I hated that."

"So you gave up? It was your choice to make Joel."

"I guess so. The problem was that Mr. Andreev refused to understand. And I recognised I owed him. In the end I shut him out completely, wouldn't even speak to him because I knew what he would always ask. I didn't mean it to be anything permanent. It was just a way of finding space again, the very stuff I never seem to get anytime or anywhere in my life. He died though. A heart attack at seventy-one that turned him out like a light. He had a son from a broken marriage but the estrangement was forgotten quickly enough when it came to claiming the inheritance. Within a week the clearers had been in and the piano was gone. Not long after that the house was sold to another family, and it was like none of it had even existed at all."

"But you were just, what, fourteen or so Joel?"

"Everyone is always some age. I'm not sure it's an excuse. I knew well enough what I'd done. I wasn't stupid."

She eyed him. "So can I ask what you think of me falling for Euan when I was fifteen?"

Joel paused, blinking, then gave a sharp laugh. "Okay, you win: you were just a kid. He probably wasn't like he is now though. You said he hasn't aged well."

"No, he hasn't. But then how do you assess my staying with him until six months ago?"

Joel bit down on his first couple of responses, finally smiling and shaking his head. "I don't know how someone as perceptive as you can be blind as a bat sometimes."

"Ouch! But that's fair enough I suppose. I felt a sense of responsibility I now realise was mistaken and I forced myself not to see. And anytime I failed in that I lacked your courage to follow my own path and make a break. I might never have if you weren't so good at remembering lyrics. So why should something you decided at age eight keep a grip over your life at fourteen and beyond? Why should something I felt eleven years ago that had long since withered away continue to apply, as Euan wanted just now? We change in life and sometimes that comes with consequences for others. If Mr. Andreev truly cared for you, rather than just what you could do, then in time you would have put things right. That you never got the chance was nothing more than rotten luck."

Joel studied his hands, remembered the mottled, wrinkled ones that had once guided them with such passion. "I guess so. I won't lose the regret though."

"Of course not, but regret is an essential building block of the grown-ups we become. And now you're here in Caithness, where there is all the space in the world." She walked over to him and bent down to link her fingers between his on the piano keyboard, alabaster pink and coffee brown resting on ebony black and ivory white. "And you and I will have to learn to live with regret, as we decided last night."

She paused, then: "I have one follow-up question to something you said."

He could feel her pulse rising crazily through their contact. "Do you still like girls?"

"Well, yes."

"This one?"

He could barely control his voice. "This one most of all. More and more each day."

She let out a strangled noise. "Achhh...I'm just going to admit all this. Oh god! So that first evening you showed up at my door I didn't trust you but I was besotted at first glance. You were the most beautiful man I'd ever seen and it completely threw me. The angles of your face. Those golden eyes against your glorious, healthy skin. Watching the way your body moved when you were running along the riverbank...it's just a vet habit, checking out the gait. I'm aware how superficial all this focus on looks sounds, but it's how I felt and I had no idea how to deal with it."

Joel blinked in flattered bemusement. "So when you invited me to live here...?"

"I convinced myself it was social responsibility, but also I would have done almost anything to get you close. Am I completely crazy?"

"Not really. It's only what most men are like most of the time. Why didn't you simply ask me out for a drink a year ago? I'd have said yes a thousand times over."

"Well I sort of tried to. I knew full well you'd joined that tennis league. It's why I signed up as Anastasia so you wouldn't recognise my name and pull out. And I did offer you a cup of tea in The Reay Arms, remember? But those two times I was still with Euan and I was scared rigid I was behaving no better than my mother...which is probably why those arguments happened. Sorry about that. Then since I became single and hatched my cunning plan of having you move in I've been worried you didn't feel similarly and wanting to avoid doing anything would make our living arrangement too difficult."

Joel blew out his overheld breath. "You really tie yourself in unnecessary knots, Nat. You could have just talked to me!"

"Have you not noticed that us talking never solves anything? So I have this new idea..."

She bent closer and now her face and her green-eyed gaze on him was the most astonishing thing he had ever seen and all that he wanted in the entire world. He tilted back his head so she could kiss him, the energy from it incredible. Her hands locked round his neck and pulled him towards her, kissing him again and again more and more hungrily. They stood, and clothes were suddenly a barrier to the closeness both needed. He shrugged his t-shirt then jeans away, her eager hands helping between shedding her own. Clumsy because they couldn't bear to turn away from close inspection of each other for even a split second, they bumped their way down the hall and up the narrow stairs to the bedroom.

21.

Sunday: trying out of habit, the instant their interlocked fingers touched the jigsaw it was different.

It wasn't a voice as such, although surely could be if it chose. More the distilled essence of communication that words were a cumbersome form of aiming at. The first impression that formed was a reluctant taking of responsibility, a caveat of severe limitations on what was possible from afar.

Next there was a clear and specific task: bring the host and the portal into close proximity. Within half a handspan. For at least six heartbeats.

Now a promise: do this and the parasite will be removed from your world.

But with a time limit. The planet's orbit around its sun. A year. After that would come a permanent severance, the destruction of every link with Earth. This would occur whether they succeeded or not. It was coloured by the regret of a project curtailed, a garden abandoned by its gardener. But preservation lay behind the decision. Fear of how uncontrollably strong the parasite might grow with all of humanity to feed on.

And then the presence was gone, and Joel knew he would never feel it again.

"Should we write this down?" he croaked.

"What's the bloody point?" Nat's face was raw and pained. "I feel worse than when I was reconciled to failure. It's impossible."

They still sat on opposite sides of the table from force of habit, so Joel rose and went round to take her in his arms. "We have a year and Campbell will be coming here."

"That's like saying it's better to die of one disease than two. We've been trying all week to think of any way we could get near him and got nowhere."

"I know, but we can still hope."

"Can we? And what about despair Joel? Last night was a physical and mental awakening I was completely unprepared for. I lay there afterwards, and the grim certainties of my previous existence - that no-one in my family should ever become a mother again; that I'm not like other people and can never find their happiness - now I was seeing all those prison walls from high above and they looked like nothing. I woke up this morning filled with enthusiasm for my future. It's the first time in my life I've ever felt like that. Now it's gone. Taken away. Don't you see how that's worse than never even knowing it existed?"

"A physical awakening, you say?" Joel forced a grin onto his face, made it widen.

"Come on, don't do that. I'm serious."

"So am I. You mentioned genetics; well three of my four grandparents were immigrants who came to Britain with only basic language, a suitcase or two of clothes for non-English weather, and barely a coin to their names. They lacked all qualifications and contacts and were horribly out of their depth, but they kept on trying anyway. Maybe they didn't become millionaires, but they found stability. They managed to give their children more choices than they'd ever had. My parents have done the same when I think about it. I'm from a family of reasonably successful strivers-against-the-odds, and that's what we need here. It is possible to just keep going anyway."

Nat paused, until eventually a rather forlorn smile crossed her face. "As opposed to brooding uselessly like Russian nobility fallen low?"

"We have a year. We'll keep trying. We'll also keep on living day-to-day. Speaking of which, I'm hungry after last night's exertions. So maybe the future is laden with dark clouds and we don't see a path, but how about I make breakfast all the same?"

She nodded, and he could see her strength recovering.

He got up. "Here. Be mundane while I fry something." He collected the Sunday paper from outside the front door and put it on the table for her.

And of course that was a mistake. It was always a mistake these days. Mere minutes later Nat let out a contemptuous hiss. "So that was his plan all along!"

"What was?"

"You know how we thought that deal for a revised UK Supreme Court with extended powers was too good to be true?"

Joel felt his narrow strand of stamina stretch closer to

breaking. In April's Westminster crisis, when Campbell had prorogued parliament during the country's precipitous exit from the EU, empowering the top tier of the judiciary to veto executive orders from Downing Street that were adjudged to breach the UK's unwritten constitution had been hailed as a victory by the other main parties. Of the eleven justices appointed four were Just Brit nominees, three more came from each of the main right and left wing parties, and one represented the combined nationalists. With life terms for appointees, all bar Just Brits had skewed their selections younger, surely neutering Campbell's anti-democratic agenda for the long term.

"Two of the justices were killed in a car 'accident' yesterday. Two of the left-leaning ones as it happens. And does this newspaper, which is supposed to be one of the last independent ones, ask questions? No. It just blathers on in a long editorial about Campbell's duty, as Prime Minister of the day, to nominate replacements immediately for the sake of national healing. They, get this, 'hope he will respect the previous composition of the court'." She tossed the paper aside disgustedly. "He'll have a servile majority by the time the court rules on privatising the BBC and on scrapping the competition and transparency rules covering media."

Joel could only stand there feeling numb. You didn't ask 'how can that be?!' anymore.

"While we were wondering if we could commit one murder, Campbell was arranging two. The killing has started Joel. The killing has started and the parasite's tightening its grip."

Joel walked over and embraced her. Much as they might wish otherwise, their shared belief was the fixing of it all rested upon their inadequate shoulders, and too many clocks were ticking.

22.

Reay, November 2017.

The days were growing shorter and shorter, the nights darker and arriving too early. To the extent they could ignore context their relationship had blossomed wonderfully. They slept together in her bedroom now, seeming to fit naturally into the same space, the innate tendencies of each helping the other almost all the time. Life might have been ideal were it not for the complete lack of progress with the task that hung over them.

Photos of Champ Campbell mid-harangue above waving Union Jacks and a favourable headline were ubiquitous. Rumour had it he had threatened to pull his entire range of TV content, newspapers and magazines from any search engine or shop offering 'enemy' titles. Those were now near-impossible to find, and thus there was nowhere to confirm such rumours.

The right to peaceful protest had gone. Only 'temporarily' of course, while the current terror alert level remained in place. Whipped-up paranoia that Brexit might be 'stolen' had reached new heights of frenzy, despite the fact Brexit had already happened. Hence new voting restrictions clamped down hard on non-existent fraud and the ethnic and age groups thought likely to commit it. Dissenting voices were unacceptable. Even the BBC had been neutered, the corporation now stuffed top-down with Campbell cronies who paid themselves big bonuses from its ever-shrinking budget.

But at least alcohol tax had been abolished and all the football was available free on 'CCTV', the dominant broadcaster belonging to the prime minister.

Nor was it advisable for one's health to admit dissatisfaction. 'The Red Shirts', they called themselves, an oath of personal fealty to Champ Campbell forming part of their enlistment ritual. Not that vigilante justice was officially condoned, but the way the press extolled the group's 'patriotic fervour' spoke clearly enough. In the police force neat little moustaches were much in vogue, solving lynchings less so.

Easily able to manipulate the chaotic and flattery-hungry administration of the USA as a cohort, Campbell's Britain led new world trends. Demagogues across the globe were feted as popular saviours, the right wing of politics courting their newfound influence. Fingers were crossed behind backs when the oleaginous endorsements were made, but a winning formula for power wasn't to be ignored when power was your raison d'être.

The opposing left, meanwhile, railed, hand-wrung, engaged in infighting, split, and lost. As for the political centre and the idea of consensus, such concepts were anachronisms. The single thing everyone could agree on – although they would never admit to having one iota in common – was the legitimacy of their anger.

For Joel and Nat the ceaseless propaganda exhorting yet more aggression towards 'Remurderers', 'Illegals' and an amorphous 'Liberal Elite Conspiracy' was a constant reminder. Its ceaseless battering could diminish even the sense of wonder felt standing on Sandside beach gazing hand-in-hand at the Northern Lights. Sometimes it was only what they'd found in each other that kept them going. But even that brought its own pain, the knowledge their good days together could not be so many.

At times after that second peculiar visitation through the puzzle they'd backtracked into doubt. Had it all been shared delusion? Could something so ephemeral and opaque justify action?

But the problem was real enough, so if there was the slightest chance to combat it they wanted to try. It was only bringing Campbell together with the completed puzzle. If they had in fact lost their sanity this action would cause no harm to anyone other than themselves.

They were, therefore, resolved.

Resolved and still at a complete loss for what to do about it.

On a cold Friday with the sun already gone, Joel finished work and picked up Nat in Thurso. They were at the Forss Water Bridge driving back towards Reay when her phone rang.

"Hi Jimmy... Take a breath and tell me what happened... Is she trying to move herself?... And she's whining in pain each time?... Listen, I'm on my way. Just stay next to her, and I'll be there in ten minutes. I know it's not easy, but show her how to stay calm, okay?"

"Do you want anything from the house or shall I go straight there?" Joel asked, speeding up.

"I have all I'm likely to need in my bag. Straight there."

For a while there was only the whoosh and rumble of the tarmac, flagstone walls zipping by on each side in the headlights. Joel knew how much she'd been dreading this call.

"Do you think it'll be this time?"

Nat sighed. "Probably. She has severe hip dysplasia, muscle wastage, and the last time I checked her I found tell-tale signs of cancer."

"You didn't mention that."

"There's no treatment option so there was no sense in worrying Jimmy. She's a seventeen-year-old dog and her body's worn out. I guess I don't want to face this either. I used to walk her on the beach when she was a pup and I was a girl, back when Jimmy still had his track. Gran wouldn't allow a pet in the house and I so wanted one. Jimmy said Kelpie liked me and she'd far more energy than he could use up. She was always such a carefree presence. She would listen to me talk about anything and not say a word back. Not try to correct everything I was thinking. Not judge me. I mean obviously, because she's a dog, but..."

Joel looked over at this woman he loved. He wished he could ease her pain, even though it was an impossibility because to care is to open your door to suffering and Nat cared so deeply. "Can I come along with you? Just to be there."

She looked back at him and began to cry softly. "Would you?"

Nat knocked once and walked straight in. Jimmy was sitting on the floor next to Kelpie, the dog's eyes pained and unfocused.

"Is it alright for Joel to be here Jimmy? He was giving me a lift. My car's in for its annual service, you know?" Nat could handle people too, distract them with reminders of the day-to-day.

"Eh? Oh your man? Of course Nat, of course."

Nat knelt, easing Jimmy to one side. "Hi Kelpie. Is it the back legs again? I'm just going to feel for what's wrong, get a towel between you and that cold floor too. I'll be very gentle."

Joel watched Jimmy watching Nat as she probed with knowledgeable fingers. You needed a careful intelligence to croft, and the deep lines on Jimmy's face evidenced that. He was short but still sturdy, the arm he was leaning on gnarled like an oak. He must have rarely, if ever, known luxury or even comfort, but that in no way diminished his capacity for love. It was so clear in the way he watched his dog yelp when Nat touched a sore part.

"Okay, okay. Easy. Sorry Kelpie, I just had to make sure there."

Continuing to stroke the dog, Nat turned to the old man.

"Has she been off her food?"

"Well a little these last days, aye. I know she's getting on and I know it's serious, but will she make it to Christmas Nat? She's always loved Christmas."

Nat shook her head. "Jimmy, I've never known a dog hold on like Kelpie has. I believe she's done it so as not to leave you alone, but I'm afraid it's time now. She's not going to recover and if you leave it she'll be immobile and in constant pain."

Jimmy wrung his hands, his lower lip trembling. "I can find the money for the operation. Even if it would just give her another month or two."

Nat placed a gentle hand on his shoulder. "If I could fix her I'd gladly do it for free. Listen Jimmy, the fibula's snapped on her right hind leg. Last time I saw her I thought there was cancer spreading but I didn't say anything because nothing could be done about it. For a bone to go like this, well it must be right through her. Even if you could somehow repair the leg her hips are bad and her muscles are barely there anymore. If she stops walking for any length of time she'll never recover the ability. We're at the end, and I'd rather see her go with an amount of dignity."

Now tears were flowing down the grey stubble of Jimmy's cheeks. "You're right Nat. I know you're right. What'll I do though? What'll I do without her?"

"You have a lot of friends round here Jimmy, and you'll lean on us until you work that out." She pulled him into a tender embrace, and for a long while the only sounds were the sniffs of Jimmy's quiet grief and the loud ticking of a carriage clock on the mantelpiece.

"Will it hurt her?"

"No. She'll just close her eyes and drift away. Then all the pain she's in now will be over."

"Nat...do you think there's anything after? Anything beyond this world?"

"Lately I've become sure of it. Whether we go anywhere after our lives here I can't say, Jimmy, but I'm certain there's more to the universe."

"And will it take long?"

"No. A minute. Less even."

"Then I'll talk to her now, and when you've what you need ready you help her on her way."

Nat gave a single nod, then stood and walked over to her vet's bag by the door. Her gaze met Joel's and he saw in her that delicate bargain of heart and mind: how to face loss without losing the ability to love again.

Jimmy was bent right down next to Kelpie's head, his eyes fixed on hers. "Seventeen eh girl? What an age you've managed. Is it true you've hung on just so I'd not be on my own, like Nat says? You can go. You can rest now. I'll be alright. Listen, if it's just me I won't need all this land anymore. Won't have to look after it all and get so tired. Maybe I'll move to Thurso, someplace small and easy to keep. Near all the shops. Wouldn't that be good, eh? Anyway I'd not go on the walks here without you girl. I'd never leave you behind for a walk. Never."

Kelpie seemed to be focused on him, even through the milk of cataracts, and now she gave a little whine. Jimmy leant closer and her tongue flicked out, licking a tear from his cheek. As the old man buried his face in the black and white fur, Nat was approaching, syringe in hand where Kelpie couldn't see it. Jimmy looked up, meeting her gaze.

"That's it girl, that's it. There. There! Nothing, was it? Nat's got a sure touch and she's just given you something to take the pain away. Ach Kelpie you've been such a grand dog. Such a grand dog. I swear there's never been another like you. What a companion you've been to me. If there is anything comes after all this I'll find you girl. You keep those keen eyes of yours out for me and I'll find you."

Nat, one hand on the dog's chest, reached for Jimmy's shoulder with the other. "She's gone Jimmy. Kelpie's gone."

The old crofter drew in a shuddering breath. "Thank you Nat," he managed.

"I loved Kelpie too," silent tears were streaming down her cheeks.

"I know you did. She used to hear when you were coming and get that excited."

The vacuum grief brings began to build in the room. The creaking of Jimmy's knees was loud in the silence as he stood. "What happens now Nat? With her?"

She wiped her eyes with her sleeve. "I can leave her here, Jimmy, if you want to bury her. Otherwise I can take her to the crematorium. Whichever you prefer."

"You take her, please. I couldn't put her in the ground. It wouldn't be right to keep her stuck in just the one place."

Nat turned to the body and drew in a ragged breath.

"Can I carry her for you?" Joel asked.

"You don't mind?"

"No, it's fine." Joel looked to Jimmy for his nod of permission, and then bent down to pick up Kelpie. She weighed next-to-nothing.

"Will you be alright tonight Jimmy?"

"I've my series on the TV...I'll be okay Nat. Don't you be getting worried about a sentimental old fool like me. You young folk go and enjoy your evening."

"You've my number if you need anything. Even just a chat. And will you come round for tea tomorrow afternoon? I know I'm fussing, but just so I'm sure you're alright."

"Thank you Nat, it'd be nice. I've said it before, but you really are an angel. You know that?"

She pulled him into another hug, then wiped her eyes again and went to hold the door open for Joel.

"Bye, Kelpie," murmured the crofter, reaching to stroke

her fur one last time. Joel couldn't bear to look at the old man's face as he walked out and Nat closed the door behind him. He lowered the dog's body into the car boot and soon they'd driven down the lane and out onto Reay's main road.

"Do you want to take her out to the surgery at Melvich?"

"No, I won't disturb Neil now. I'll call him tomorrow morning. She'll have to make do in the shed tonight. Not that she's here anymore. Not really."

They got home, went round to the low side-building, and together performed the macabre task of lowering Kelpie's body into the ancient chest freezer kept for this purpose. Putting his arm around Nat as she whispered a farewell, Joel managed to restrain himself until they were back in the house. Then it had to come out.

"I have a plan Nat. It's still a long-shot, but it might get me close to Campbell."

She spun to face him.

"The thing is I don't think you're going to like it."

23.

Nat had her hand over her mouth and Joel found himself talking like a salesman as he spelled out the details.

"The club is the one place I stand a chance of getting near Campbell but membership is invite-only. They're desperate for Jimmy's land, we know that. We, and they, also know he would never sell to them, right? You once told me the way in was being a sycophant who can offer them something they want, remember? Well the croft is something they want badly, and I can play the amoral money-grabber. I was halfway to being that once."

"We can't do that to Jimmy. Especially not after he's just lost Kelpie. I can't ask him. I won't."

They paused to hug each other, affirm this as discussion not conflict.

"But I got the idea from him Nat. When he was talking to Kelpie, telling her the land would be too much for him and he might move into a smaller place in Thurso. Derek's the architect on the Ormlie project so when they come on sale early next year I could arrange that Jimmy gets the best unit, the one with the view out over the Pentland Firth."

"But he didn't mean any of that. He was just trying to soothe Kelpie. He'd hate living in the town. He's Reay through and through."

"You may well be right, in which case we back off immediately. But is it so wrong just to ask him? He's getting on and that croft's cold, basic and not in great repair. I can see what a charming place it must have been once, but with that wall there blocking out the sea and the golfers going by, and now Kelpie's gone, does it still hold the same meaning for him?"

She was shaking her head now. "That all sounds eminently reasonable Joel, but I just can't live with it."

"We may not be able to live without it Nat. Don't forget what the stakes are here. We've thought and thought over this and come up with nothing. This one plan may be all we have."

"To betray Jimmy like that and probably still never get close enough to Campbell...I'm not sure I wouldn't rather just accept defeat with my integrity intact."

"But we wouldn't be betraying him." Joel was emphatic now, every word working on bending her will. "He would be in on it all. We'd tell him everything. It only needs to be a secret until we've done what we need to to Campbell or the year's up. Then he can tell everyone how he conspired with us to sell the knackered old house that he'd mostly kept for his dog to the rich golf club folk for a sky-high price. My guess is he'd enjoy that."

"He'd still lose his croft."

"Yes, but isn't that his choice to make?"

Even Jimmy's knock at the door was somehow in mourning.

"Hello Nat. Joel. Are you sure this is no bother? I'm not great company today."

"I'll be the judge of that, Jimmy. Come on in. How are you feeling?"

The old man sighed as she took his coat. "It's a terrible thing to admit but in a way I'm relieved. I knew Kelpie was hurting more and more, and I've finally done right by her. But I tell you, this morning when I saw her bed empty…my first thought was she'd managed to get up all by herself. I was just about to call and tell her 'well done girl' when I remembered, and then it near broke me. Dogs shouldn't live fewer years than people, Nat. If you ever talk to God you tell Him that."

"But what a life she had, Jimmy. What a great life you gave her."

"Aye, I suppose. She gave me the same or more back though."

"So come on into the kitchen, I'll pour you a cup of tea, and we'll raise a toast to Kelpie, never a collie finer."

Nat was failing to introduce the topic, and getting more and more flustered in the process.

"Jimmy?"

The old crofter turned to look at Joel.

"Do you trust me?"

Jimmy took a while to study him before answering. "That's a mighty strange thing to ask. Well if you must know, yes, but mostly because Nat trusts you. Maybe it's because I can't read a coloured face so well, but you've not half the openness about you that she has."

Joel's face relaxed into a smile. "Thanks Jimmy. For being honest."

"Well I hope I'm that. So are you going to tell me why you're asking such a question?"

"No. Nat is."

Jimmy turned back expectantly to the young vet, a frown wrinkling his brow.

She closed her eyes, breathed out, then opened them to look at him. "This is going to sound crazy Jimmy, but I believe it and so does Joel. It's only the two of us though."

She exhaled again, shrugging her shoulders loose. "I'll start at the beginning. No-one else here knows this, but the reason Joel came to Caithness was to get me to sell that old jigsaw puzzle we have in the family. The one Gran and I took to that Antiques Hunt programme. He has the missing piece, and he wanted to split the quarter of a million pounds the complete puzzle would fetch at auction."

Jimmy eyebrows shot up but he stayed quiet, just looking between the two of them.

"That jigsaw is creepy and I've always been afraid of it. With good reason, it turns out. When we assembled it..."

"When I completed it without giving Nat the chance to stop me," Joel interjected, making her shake her head in exasperation.

"When we assembled it a sort of tunnel opened and a shadow came through. A horrible parasite as dark and evil as can be. Then later, in the puzzle, there was this highly intelligent presence of some kind...I know how all this sounds, but it confirmed things. To survive and feed in this world the parasite needs to take over a person to do its work. We think it did and that person was Charles Campbell." She ground to a halt, exhausted.

The old crofter's face stayed serious and hard. "And what does it mean if this all happened as you say?"

"It means the destruction of society, because that's its food. The spread of hatred and conflict until it eventuality destroys humanity."

"And you truly believe this Nat?"

"I do. And I think the signs are all there already. It's almost two years since we completed the puzzle, and look at the way the world's suddenly turned since then."

Now Jimmy was nodding slowly. "Do you know I've always felt I understood this Earth of ours well enough, but the anger of recent times has been beyond me. And that Campbell's the one stoking it most, for sure...but are you going to tell me how I come into this?"

"If we can bring Campbell into contact with the jigsaw puzzle that presence can remove the parasite. But we've turned it over a hundred ways and we can't work out how to do our part. Also we've less than a year for it. We're at the point where we have to clutch at any straw even if it seems crazy and we don't want to, and, well..."

"We need your croft."

Jimmy turned to stare at Joel. "You need my croft?"

"I got the idea last night when you told Kelpie you might move to Thurso. The golf club wants your land, but they know you won't sell to them."

"They're right about that."

"So instead what could happen is Joel, the mercenary incomer who no-one was ever quite sure about, takes advantage of poor old Jimmy when he's shaken up by the death of his beloved dog. I pitch a great now-or-never deal on one of the new townhouses my boss is building up in Ormlie, and to make the finances work I offer a good price for the croft on the condition it's all done quickly and quietly. I even trick Nat into believing I plan to fix the place up and live there, which is why she helps persuade you to sell to me."

Jimmy's eyes were narrowed to slits. "But instead you sell my home straight on to them?"

"Yes. In fact they will have financed the whole deal, because before I even approach you I'll have been to get their agreement. That kind of premeditated betrayal and the fact I want a juicy big profit out of it makes them trust me because those are the only motives they understand. One more thing, I'll say that I'd also like one of their 'Gold Executive' memberships for a year."

"I'm hoping there's a good part you're getting to, Joel."

"I'll negotiate an excellent price and my cut will go in full to you, although that has to be kept secret for a while. But the point is that if I get access to that club I'm close to Campbell. It's the one way I can see of getting to him with that jigsaw puzzle so whatever we let in can be removed from this world. I'm not going to lie Jimmy, it's still a very long shot, but it's all we have."

Jimmy studied him a while longer and then turned to Nat. "Are you asking this of me Nat?"

Her face contorted uncomfortably. "I know it sounds ridiculous and I hate to, but I think I may have to."

"Okay then."

"Jimmy no! Take more time to think about it."

"Nat, I've known you your whole life and you've always been true. If you want this of me then you've my answer here and now. So what's it to be?"

Joel ached to go over and embrace Nat, try and share the load that had been placed on her, but there was no moving in this moment.

She shook her head sadly. "Yes, then. Yes Jimmy. We have to try and I can see no other way. I'm so, so sorry."

"Then it's settled, and you'll let me know what I've to do."

24.

Reay, January 2018.

"I detest this Joel. I absolutely detest it. Is this really how people think in the cities?"

"Not all of them, but when enough do everyone else is more or less obliged to either join in or lose out."

They were gaming scenarios, something Nat had never heard of before. For almost two months they had been researching the golf club and the Campbell companies' chains of command, and both of them were feeling pressure to act. A visit from Joel's parents and his sister had made a joyful festive interlude, but with the two cottages quiet and private again they needed a plan of attack. It was, by necessity, exploitative and devious. Joel loved Nat all the more for how she was struggling with that, and he was finding his own facility for it rusted since leaving London.

Nat got up and went to the window, where the low sun was harsh and red in the gap between leaden clouds and the southern horizon. "So it's today?"

"I think it has to be. I have just one bullet, as it were: Jimmy's croft. The whole hierarchy right to the top is going to want it, but the risk is I get stuck at a low rung and don't acquire the level of access to the club we need. We know Champ Campbell isn't at the castle, and I'd never get near him anyway. Chaz Campbell, on the other hand, docked his yacht in Fresgoe harbour yesterday. From what we've found he's desperate to try and please his father. He's even in some phase of hanging out with ethnic minorities and being loudly anti-racist, which could help me. So I talk my way in and as high up the ladder as I can, then if I need to I can demand Chaz be brought into the meeting and hope he'll agree to my terms. It's a gambit, but I don't see the odds improving if we sit on our hands any longer."

"This is repellent. I actually feel unclean. Unpleasant as he seems this is still a human being you're talking about here."

"I know Nat. I wish there was another way."

"But there's not is there, so I suppose you'd best get dressed for battle. When will you go?"

"After sunset. This is best suited to darkness."

"Isn't it just."

Joel had seen the turrets of Fresgoe Castle many times from a distance, but this was his first time driving up to its stone gate. A giant 'Champ' signature cast in fake gold flashed gaudily in his headlights as he approached.

The guard was out straight away, alert to the incongruence of a mass-market car here. He walked up to the window, shining his flashlight full into Joel's face as if to confirm he really was that colour.

"Can I help you with something?"

This was Malky Dunnet, a Thurso man who was ex-Dounreay security. Nat was confident he would ask limited questions before going higher up the chain of command. His Thurso knowledge should also see his superiors informed that Joel worked for Derek.

"I'm here regarding a matter of interest to the club. Is Rick Couzens free?"

"The Resort Manager? Do you have an appointment?"

"This isn't the kind of thing you make an appointment for. I can't give you details, but Rick will want to see me."

The flashlight went full in his face again but Joel kept his expression stolid. "He'll also get very unhappy if he's not told about this."

"Wait here."

Malky retreated to the tiny guard room built into the gatepost, and Joel could see him on the radio. After a short conversation he hitched his trousers up and came back out.

"Name?"

"Joel Elliott."

"Drive up to the castle. Round the back to the left, don't go to the front. Mister Menzies will meet you there."

As they'd predicted, next would come Donald Menzies, head of security. A grizzled Glaswegian who lived on site, little was known about him locally and the internet had been equally unrevealing. This one Joel would have to wing.

The barrier lifted and Joel drove under it and down the winding driveway through Fresgoe Castle's screen of gnarled, hardy forest. The castle façade was stone but its true colour was hard to tell in the glaring floodlighting. It was also defiled by the massive 'Champ' signature, burnished to absurdity. Just before the wide sweep up to the main door there was a narrow turning signposted 'Service Entrance'. Joel followed it round to an erratic collection of small buildings at the rear. On the top step of a door into the castle a burly man wearing a dark suit and with a nose like a pickled beetroot watched him park. Joel got out and walked towards him, sensing all the friendliness of a nightclub bouncer towards the unhot and penniless.

"Good afternoon, Mr. Elliott. You've no appointment but wish to speak to Mr. Couzens about a matter of interest to the club." The man's gaze scanned Joel's clothes openly. They were the ones from his trip to St. Petersburg, still by a margin the best he owned.

"Yes that's right. Is he available?"

"Well that depends, doesn't it Mr. Elliott. Would you care to expand on this matter of interest to the club?"

"It's delicate. I'm afraid it's something I can only reveal to the resort manager."

"I see." Without appearing to move Menzies was suddenly

closer to Joel, the combined odours of soap, whisky, eau-de-Cologne and cigarette smoke leaving no doubt this was a man who could overwhelm. "Mr. Couzens is a very busy man. I suggest again that you share a few details with me first."

Joel tried to both stand his ground and appear non-confrontational. "Do you happen to know what my job is?"

Menzies considered this. "You work for the Reay-area architect in Thurso. You're not fully qualified yet."

"So in my line of work you often get advance notice of certain properties available for sale. In this case we're talking about one the club is known to want to buy."

"And you're figuring on arranging that and making yourself a nice wee chunk on the side are you son?"

"Yes."

"Which property?"

"Sorry but I'll only reveal that to Mr. Couzens."

"Then I'll pass that message to him and if he's interested he'll have someone call you to make an appointment."

"Right now would be better. There's a narrow window of opportunity here you see."

Menzies wanted to hit him, Joel could see that. The sandpapered jaw ground left and right a time or two, but anything further was cut short by a crackle of tinny speech from the earphone nestled in his left ear. Only now did Joel notice the tiny camera pinned to the security man's lapel and realise that he'd already started his meeting with Rick Couzens.

Menzies didn't even blink. "Follow me."

Inside the door was a storage area where giant tins of processed foods were stacked. A sallow woman in chef's whites stamped past and gave them a glare for no obvious reason. They went down a dark corridor and into a wider hallway carpeted in a thick, tartan shagpile. A herd or more of deer heads gazed blankly into the far distance. Lower down, in a series of glass cases on slender antique tables, taxidermied smaller animals and birds were frozen in faux-natural tableaux. The hallway was even wallpapered with deerskin, and Joel was relieved to move onwards and out of it.

Guests might occasionally stray into this next portion of the castle, but it was for matters of business. The opulence was restrained now, and everything had a harder edge to it.

The office door stood open.

"Mr. Joel Elliott. An unexpected pleasure I'm sure. I'm Rick Couzens, the Resort Manager." Rick, a New Yorker implicated in but never convicted of several 'Champ Organization USA Inc.' intimidation scandals before being relocated to Scotland, was all Brooks Brothers elegance below his immaculate hair and shuttered eyes. "Thanks Donald. That'll be everything for now."

Both men waited for the security chief to make his unhurried exit and then Rick took Joel's elbow and guided him over to the desk.

"Are you drinking Joel?"

"Only if you're having one."

"Well that kinda depends on whether we're celebrating something or about to conclude this meeting, doesn't it?"

Joel smiled. "Can I assume you're familiar with Jimmy Bain's croft?"

Rick's eyebrow rose a fraction. "You can. D'you know I am in the mood for that dram now. Tell me Joel, are you a Speyside man or an Islay one?"

"If the quality's right, either. I'll go for a Laphroaig," he said, pointing at a bottle he knew to be expensive.

Rick moved to the side cabinet and poured two identical dark measures, returning to hand one to Joel. "Slàinte Mhath. This would be where you start talking."

Joel raised his glass and took a healthy sip of the peaty single malt. "I'm confident I can acquire the croft within the next month. Once I have I would like to sell it on to the club."

"Well isn't that good news. It won't make you so popular in Reay." Rick was measuring him now.

"I'm not pale enough to fit in up here anyway," Joel lied.

"Indeed. Not so fond of change in these parts are they? Anyhoo, talking change, what kind of number did you have in mind, Joel?"

"As you just mentioned, there are costs to me that go beyond the financial. Bearing that in mind, and with the unique and desirable nature of this property, I came up with a figure of half a million."

"Pounds?"

"Yes, pounds." Joel estimated the market value of the croft at around one hundred and twenty thousand if you ignored the golf club's interest in it. They'd agreed that one hundred and fifty thousand would be the recorded value of Jimmy's sale to Joel, a good price which would hopefully limit the damage to both their reputations until the full story could be made public.

"Now I do admire your entrepreneurial spirit, Joel, but I think we both know that place is almost falling down. It's probably not worth more than eighty grand." A wolfish light had appeared in Rick's eyes.

"I take your point about the house itself. The land's another matter though. In fact I believe it may even have a legally-protected historic right to a direct beach access."

"Which would cost you way more than your profit plus some personal risk to try and assert in court," put in Rick sharply. Apparently threat was never all that far below the surface at the Champ Scotland International Golf Resort at Fresgoe Castle.

Joel raised his palms. "Of course, of course. I was just musing out loud. Well I guess my half million could be flexible."

"Y'don't say. Listen Joel, you seem like a smart guy so let's get down to brass tacks. I assume you've researched who you're trying to deal with here. The thing about us is we never lose. We never get made to look like the schmuck. Now you and I both know that half a mil is chicken feed to us, but how would it look if we were to shell out that kind of dough to just any little mongrel nobody who comes up with a way to con an old halfwit out of his shitty house? Do you see my point?"

Joel raised his glass. "I do. And no offence taken by the way."

"I wouldn't give a damn if it was. So lose the dollar signs from your eyes, come down to earth, and then I've no problem with you feathering your nest here. Assuming this all checks out." Rick's eyes were now gauging continuously.

"It will. So I completely understand that Champ hates to lose, Rick, but in many ways that's the crux of the matter. What I'm offering is a way to triumph in a fight Champ's been...can we say not winning for these last seven years? It must annoy the hell out of him every time he shoots round the dogleg on that fifth hole. I could learn to live with four-seventy-five I guess."

Rick smiled coldly. "I bet you could. Now Joel if we say no what are your options here? Live in the place yourself? It can be a noisy, nasty, dangerous environment next to a golf course, and I can promise you that we'd be watching like hawks for any contravention of building or planning regulations if you tried fixing it up. The folks round here already know this and that's why you wouldn't find any other takers for the place. Now if that four at the front was to change into a two...?"

Joel sighed melodramatically. "I just feel I'd be underselling a once-in-a-lifetime opportunity Rick. There is another thought I'd like to throw into the mix: Champ's famous for driving a hard bargain but he's also known for looking after his friends, right? As you said, if this goes through I'm going to need some new ones round here. Maybe I'd find them at the club? How about I see my way to dropping to four-twenty-five and you throw in my first year of Gold Executive club membership for free? No-one'd look like they're losing out if you're just treating a friend well."

Rick had just started shaking his head in mock sadness, a precursor to the next round, when the door banged open.

"Alriiiight. Hey Rick. I just bumped into the old Donster out in the corridor and he said you were busy with some urgent matter of interest to the club. Need a little VP input on that? Nice to see some diversity happening here, by the way."

Charles Campbell junior, aka Chaz. His Sloane-voiced interference was the lucky break Joel had been hoping for, and he hadn't even had to ask!

"Mr. Campbell. It's an honour! Well I was just trying to interest Rick here in buying that old croft your fifth hole has to go round."

Chaz's face lit up with greed and need. "Fuck! Seriously?! Did that old wanker finally die or something? Oh yeah, totally, we WANT that. Senior would be like...fuck! So are we talking the numbers? Fill me in guys."

"I'm afraid you just missed all the fun, sir. Joel here and I already agreed on the terms of the deal." Rick's hand, thumb tucked in to leave the four fingers, was drumming discreetly on the desk in front of him.

Joel smiled a sycophant's smile. "Yes. I think I probably got a bit screwed, but that's just what happens when you negotiate against Champ isn't it? At least Rick was kind enough to throw in a one-year Executive Gold membership and three months of weekly lessons with the club pro." Joel glanced at Rick, who nodded once.

"Yeah? Cool! Nice! Sorry if you lost out Joel. Say, if you need to get screwed some more I brought a few girls over on the yacht. Fresh out of school in Czecho...what d'you call it, hardly speak any English, and like HOT, man. Nothing's too much trouble for the guy who gets that old fucker off our course. So how's about it bro? Call me Chaz by the way."

"That's very generous of you Chaz, but I'll have to take a rain check. Business before pleasure you know, and to bring the deal home there are a couple of things I have to go and get started on tonight. I'm scared to think what Rick here would do to me if I let this one go cold. Maybe I'll see you out on the links though?"

"Huh, Okay. Sure, could be. What handicap are you?"

"I don't have one."

Both Chaz and Rick looked nonplussed.

"Never played golf in my life. Just tennis. I mean lean sporty girls in miniskirts running themselves all into a sweat or old white guys trundling around in buggies? No-brainer isn't it?" Joel flashed a leering grin.

"Fucking-A to that!" Chaz laughed and clapped delightedly. "I like this guy Rick. Look after him okay? So, seems we've got everything sorted here then. Good job people. Listen Rick, leave it to me to tell Senior the good news, yeah? And now you'll excuse me if I go celebrate with a little white on white, know what I mean? Ciao."

As the door slammed behind Chaz, Joel looked back at Rick, who was assiduously erasing the traces of disgust from his features, and found he felt strangely sorry for both men.

"Can you advance me one hundred and fifty on my watertight purchase contract and a sale to you at the four hundred? I'll be using an Edinburgh solicitor for obvious reasons."

Rick nodded. "Sure. I think you'll take to golf well Joel; you don't seem unduly bothered by nerves."

"I'd like to believe I'll enjoy it here, Rick, and I mean to be a friend. That won't be a problem, will it?"

Rick glanced back towards the door. "Apparently not. Well played Joel, and let's keep in close touch on this one. Welcome to the club."

"How did it go?" Nat, her favourite giant chipped tea mug clutched between her hands for warmth, gazed at him like a tonic as he came inside.

"We agreed the deal. Chaz even got involved just like we hoped. I'm not sure he's as good a route in as I thought, but he did mess up the negotiation tactics in my favour."

"You got the membership?!"

"Yup. It's embarrassing to think how that kind of thing would have appealed to me two years ago. As would the four hundred thousand we agreed on for the croft."

"Four hundred thousand?! Seriously?"

"They wanted it badly. They have to win, always, or they're nothing."

"It's so ironic that Jimmy would have sold all those years ago if they'd just offered him two hundred at the start."

"He would have?!"

"Oh yes. He only refused to sell after they'd tried to lowball him. He's going to be so chuffed when he can tell people you got him double his price."

"He'll have to wait until we get what's in Charles Campbell back through the jigsaw first, remember?"

"I know. But it's good news Joel! We've – well you have, I didn't do a thing – we've finally achieved at least one step forward. Let's enjoy that. You smell of rich people though, so why not go have a shower...but don't worry about getting dressed afterwards. I reluctantly accept that you'll have to move back to Thurso as part of this whole charade, so I too have some plans for tonight."

25.

Thurso, March 2018.

"What's up with your knee?"

"Morning Jimmy," Joel said, checking no-one could be watching and then grimacing as he climbed over the garden fence between his and Jimmy's new houses. "Mrs. Shearwater in the Tesco car park with her Volvo's door. She claimed the wind caught it, but I've my doubts."

"Elsie?" Jimmy chuckled. "Well isn't that nice of her. Go in and get yourself a seat lad."

Joel limped into the living room, noting how devoid of character it still was. Jimmy's croft had been decorated by decades of his carefully hoarded and sorted clutter. In his new townhouse he was, as Nat had predicted, utterly lost, especially without Kelpie to keep him in orbit. True he'd only been in three weeks, but it wasn't going to change.

"Has anyone told you exactly how much that nasty young Londoner ripped you off for yet?"

"No. I'm still getting the shock and outrage that I've to live next door to you. It'll not be long though, not now your sale price is public in the register. I've headed a couple of people off letting me know already, including that poisonous shite Nat used to be together with."

"Euan? Is he back in Thurso?"

"Aye, seems so. Never so much as a word to me in his life before but now he spies me in the street and greets me like an old friend so he can fish for gossip."

Joel felt oddly perturbed by this news. "Jimmy you do remember every penny of that money's yours, even though for appearance's sake it has to stay in my bank account for now?"

There was genuine tenderness in Jimmy's face as he looked over from the kitchenette where he was slopping teabags about.

"Are you doing alright, lad? Holding up, you know?"

Joel shook his head. "Is it that obvious?"

"You've nice even teeth so it's a shame you've given up smiling."

"Everyone hates me Jimmy. Even Derek's gone ice cold. I doubt he'll renew my contract in the summer now. It was lucky I could sign the rental on the unit next door before he found out it was me who'd bought your croft. And all the clients know too. Can you believe I went to see how the build's going at Dot Andrews' and she didn't offer me a cup of anything?"

Jimmy's laugh was almost bitter-sounding. "Surely not?"

"Yes. Most of all I miss Nat, Jimmy. I mean we can video call, but..."

"But every time you think of her you realise you're deep in love with the greatest woman on this green Earth and every moment apart hurts like hell?"

"Exactly!"

"It'll not be forever. And how's your golf going? I suppose you've seen what they've done to my old place when you're whacking your wee ball between the holes?"

Joel thought of the speed with which they had erased all memory of Jimmy from that piece of land. Champ Campbell had flown up specially to watch the croft be demolished the very same day the club acquired the title.

"At least that wall's gone. You can see the sea from there again."

"Well that's nice."

"Other than that golf's actually quite good fun, but they're false, oily people there. I'm the toast of the place for what they think I did. And you Jimmy, are you doing alright? How are you finding life in Thurso?"

"Ach, ups and downs. But if you do what you need to out at Fresgoe then we can tell everyone and it's all fixed. As you said, I'll be the canny crofter that put the rich Sassenach in his place and you'll have been a good guy all along. I'm alright waiting out a few months for that."

"If I can do it. That's what scares me Jimmy. I haven't even told Nat this yet, but when Champ..."

"You're not calling him that now?!"

"Sorry. I have to keep in practice though. I can't risk blowing cover. The whole place is this kind of paranoid, jealous court all sucking up to the big baboon to have favours bestowed upon them. Don't play along for even a second and they'll turn on you like vipers. I've already seen it happen to one person."

"Sensible of you then. So when Cha...I cannae do it! When Campbell... what were you going to say?"

Joel gave a resigned smile. "It sticks in the throat, doesn't it? There are portraits of him everywhere, and his stupid gold-plated signature all over the place, so there's never any escape. It's like he has to prove something constantly right in your face. Anyway, he was up last week so I took the jigsaw in hidden amongst my clubs. I had this thought that maybe I didn't need some big plan, I could just grab a chance and do the deed. I've cut a sheet of plastic to mount the puzzle on, and my idea was to assemble it and then just run at him, see if I could press it against him long enough. I got everything in past the scanners fine and then I tracked him as best I could through the club and out around all eighteen holes..." He paused, remembering it; the slow burn of terrible realisation.

"And? Did you try it?"

"No. Because there's just no way. He has a huge entourage around him the whole time. They're constantly prepared for an attack of any kind, those Special Forces guys and all their tech. Try to make any kind of move towards him and they'll taser you or worse without a second thought. Also Champ's a fully-fledged germophobe so he uses his own private dining room and toilet, and no-one, not even his wife until she gets home and is disinfected of the public or whatever, is allowed within five yards of him. Damn it Jimmy, life was going so well up here and I've thrown it all away for something that I just don't see any possible way to attempt now."

Jimmy's face was sympathetic but also contained the toughness of a crofter who'd endured hard winters. "And junior, young Chaz? Is that angle going anywhere?"

"No. He picks people up on a daily basis and drops them on a whim, and I think he rarely sees his father. I could have tried harder there I suppose, but he's so messed up that I kind of feel sorry for him. Also staying close to him would have meant...some unsavoury things I'm not prepared to do."

"I see. And what does Nat say about all of this?"

"She says keep on going and hope that something turns up. That this pretence is temporary, one way or the other, and that whatever happens she loves me for trying."

"Well there's that then. I wish I could help you lad, I really do."

"You've already done too much Jimmy. It was me that let that thing through to possess Champ so it's me that has to try and fix this, even if I've no idea how to do it."

Jimmy patted him on the back, consolation the only thing on today's menu. "So you saw Campbell up close... Can you tell? Is there any sign of what you think's in him?"

Joel pondered this for the umpteenth time. "I don't know. Even once I force personal opinion aside I see a wrongness there. It's this seething hate and fury, dangerous but almost broken, a desperate quality that wants revenge against the whole wide world. I thought maybe that was the parasite showing, but when I looked at some old video of him from four of five years ago, from long before any of this, I got the same impression. So I just don't know. Maybe it was drawn to him because he was already its kind of evil. And he is, and I reckon always was."

Now Joel could feel the perplexity that was part anger and

part fear rising in him again. "And then I think of his eyes and contrast them with Nat's, the way hers show you that caring soul she has, and I feel that surely anyone with a heart must be able to see the difference. Do you know what I mean?"

"Aye, I do."

"Then why do so many people keep falling over themselves to help Charles Campbell tighten his grip on the world? Why do they say nothing and do nothing when he trashes our shared heritage and sets us at each other's throats?"

Jimmy shook his head, his face saggy and resigned in a way it had never been in Reay. "You've got me there, lad. I've no answer to that kind of question."

Joel's tiny new lounge still smelt of paint, and as he sat in the single armchair he felt the strongest urge to take Jimmy off to The Reay Arms right this minute and regale the locals with the full story. He'd be a hero. Accepted in the far north. He'd never be able to pay for a drink in Reay again. Just like Nat, who'd he'd get back along with the rest of his life in Caithness.

He angrily forced his mind away from temptation.

It retaliated by recalling Euan's presence.

It made no sense to feel paranoid about him being back in town and doubtless trying to drive any wedge he could between Nat and Joel. But it was still another worry to weigh the spirit down. Her ex was a clever liar who would play the wronged cuckold and exacerbate what and where he could, and the longer Joel was trapped in this enforced isolation the more Euan's kind of poison might fester and stick. The town already believed him an immoral conman. What else were they saying about him Thurso? Could Euan even leverage that, his and Nat's long history, and her innate kindness to worm his way back into her life?

Of course not, damn it!

He was just dwelling on everything too much and getting irrational. It was the thought of her that he lingered on to renew his resolve. What they might have together in a long future. How could he even consider bailing out when there was so much at stake? Tell anyone of his and Jimmy's arrangement and Caithness word of mouth would mean he'd be out on his ear from the club within days.

As for Euan, whilst it might be useful to know what his adversary was saying there was no way to find out, so forget it. No, he just had to see all this out. If nothing else, come November the one year would be up. They could tell everyone then and it wouldn't matter.

But that would mean they'd lost the much bigger battle.

Swearing, he levered himself out of the chair. He pulled on shoes, jacket and gloves and set out for the riverbank. Not the hard run he would have preferred, because of his injured knee, but even freezing-cold fresh air was preferable to sitting here with the modern, for-profit architecture closing in.

By the time he'd reached the cemetery bridge, that same one Nat had intercepted him at to whisk him off to Reay, he was feeling calmer. The hollows in the brown reed tufts would soon be clear of the last of the ice, and even though the trees still looked bare you could see buds coming.

Gazing down the river he spotted a figure approaching, and for a split-second déjà vu made him wonder if it was Nat. Ridiculous! She knew they couldn't be seen together at the moment, and anyway this figure was taller and larger.

In fact a lot larger.

Shane Oag! Joel felt the blood ice up in his veins. An aggravated assault conviction had returned Thurso's resident hitman to prison just weeks after getting out the previous year, but he was clearly a free man again. And he was here, and from the way he was looking across he was tracking Joel.

But that 'accident' Calum had tried to arrange was almost a year ago and Joel hadn't so much as caught sight of Freya since. Surely he wouldn't have hired Shane again now?

Then it hit Joel that any number of people in this tight community might want to see that nasty, swindling incomer who'd ripped off old Jimmy paid back. Harming the different was the prevailing zeitgeist these days, and he'd made himself the clearest of targets with his profit on the croft. How had he got so complacent that he'd missed this risk?!

It was going to hurt badly. He knew it. On any other day he would have turned and run, confident in his fitness and head start to give him an edge. No chance of that with his knee though. Shane would catch him easily. He could only try to limit the damage.

Could he fight back? Maybe, but he had no talent for violence and would be a distant second favourite. Should he fight back? That was the more pertinent question. If he did, how mad might resistance make Shane? How far would he take things? Suddenly Joel was acutely aware of the vulnerability of his limbs and joints.

He made himself walk towards Shane rather than turn and encourage pursuit. It was better to get clear of the bridge just in case Shane decided to throw him off it into the icy brown water that slid by fast below. He also wanted the least adrenaline possible in the big thug for the assault that was now inevitable.

There were only some twenty yards between them and there wasn't another soul in sight. Was that by design too? Had the whole damned lot of them clubbed together for Shane's services and absented themselves from the scene? Joel considered phoning the police, but everyone in town complained how that would connect you to a clueless operator down in Glasgow these days. No help would arrive in time there. Nat? She could do nothing, so why cause her that angst?

"Youse are Joel, yeah?" The guy was huge and Joel had to hide his hands in his pockets because they were shaking.

"Yes." There was nothing else to say. Joel could only wait for whatever form the attack would take.

And then, amazingly, Shane Oag melted into deference. "I was hoping youse could mebbe do us a favour, like?"

Was this some sort of cruel cat-and-mouse game? Make the victim think they'd got away with it so the eventual size twelve boot to the groin felt all the sweeter? No; subtlety surely didn't figure in Shane's armoury.

"What did you have in mind? Shane, is it?"

"Aye, 'tis. Look, I've tae get a job. I cannae go back to the jail again. No one'll hire me in Thurso but I heard youse are right close wi' the folk at the golf club out at Reay an' I know they're looking for people for security. Could youse put in a word for us? I'd owe youse."

Birds were singing in Joel's head and it was a struggle to keep himself from laughing out loud at this reprieve.

"I can try Shane, but I'm less 'in' there than people think."

Shane gave a forlorn grunt. "Uh. 'Kay. Well, 'preciate it like, then." He turned and started on his way.

Between the surges of euphoria the chance of also answering a nagging question popped its way into Joel's head. "Oh, Shane. One thing you might know..."

He looked round, brow slightly unlowered in question.

"I heard Euan Pettifer's back. Is he saying anything particular about me?"

"That moaning gobshite? A thing or two mebbe, but he's a twat an' no-one listens to him. Anyway he's been trying tae worm his way into Freya Patterson's knickers and he'll like as not be gettin' a kickin' for it soon."

"So he's not mentioned Nat?"

"Nat Sinclair the vet? Nah, or only to call her a whore."

Joel's face must have given him away, because Shane suddenly brightened at his reaction. "Do youse want me to do him for youse?"

"No! Seriously Shane, if you don't want to go back to prison then you can't keep 'doing' people."

The big man shook his head mournfully. "Aye you're right, you're right. I know you're right. It's like the Restart woman at the jail said: if I want tae be a winner I've tae stop hangin' around wi' losers."

"That's sensible advice I guess. Listen Shane, I promise I will ask at the club for you, and I'll let you know what they say. I can't give you any guarantees they'll be interested though."

Shane nodded in a quite touching way, there was a brief uncomfortable silence, and then he was lumbering off again.

Joel, meanwhile, was starting to tremble from head to toe. It was no longer due to his escape from imminent bodily harm. Rather it was because of Shane's desperation to be a 'winner' and the image it had brought to mind: Champ Campbell, trophy in hand, waving to his adoring lackeys at the Champ Invitational Charity Golf Cup.

Pulling out his phone with unreliable hands, he dialled Nat. "Hi. It's me. Can you talk?"

"Yes. How are you?"

"I know how we can do it now Nat. I've worked it out."

"Oh Joel! Tell me!"

"You know Champ's golf tournament each year? You know how he's guaranteed to win it?"

"Uh-huh."

"And then they do the whole traditions of the noble and ancient Reay club thing and use that old podium for the winner receiving the cup?"

"The flotsam fish crate and fake humility thing? Yes, it's pathetic. Where are you going with this?"

"I'm going to fix the puzzle underneath it. It's the guaranteed proximity we need. That crate's even had his 'Champ' signature set into it so if they pass a metal detector over it the platinum wire won't show up as anything unexpected."

"Joel that's genius! That's brilliant! Oh, I've been so down. I've even been wondering if all of this is worth it and whether we should just grab what time we can and enjoy it together."

"Me too. Especially because everyone loathes me in Thurso. I've only got Jimmy for a friend. Oh, and Shane Oag, who just unwittingly gave me that idea."

"Shane Oag?"

"He's going straight and wants a job in security out at the golf club, where I'm apparently known to be influential. While he was locked up I guess they were brainwashing him through some rehab program to become a winner. I thought it sounded cheesy and lame, and you can see how that and mention of the golf club might lead to an image of Champ receiving his annual trophy."

She laughed. "Joel I'm missing you so much. But we can do this, can't we? Stay the course."

"And rig the trap. I believe so Nat. For the first time in all of this I believe we can."

"I love you, Joel Elliott?"

"And I love you Nat Sinclair. I love you so much that every moment without you is torture. But maybe there's a way now. Maybe these awful days of being apart are numbered."

26.

Thurso & Reay, April-June 2018.

Soon after coming up with his plan Joel began faking an architectural interest in Fresgoe Castle. What he'd noticed, beyond its mid-Victorian 'misted-Highlands-of-yore' chocolate-box vernacular, was that a lot of it was badly built.

Spotting the tell-tale signs of a roof leak, he dropped by the maintenance manager's office to mention the incorrect way some lead flashings were fitted. It turned out he'd solved a persistent irritation and it earned him the moniker 'our resident architect' and a decent amount of goodwill.

He then affected further professional curiosity about the hodgepodge of different era add-on buildings tucked around the back. Just for good measure he identified and solved one more annoying building issue for them, and now his presence more or less anywhere around the castle could be explained away. He encountered one staff member whilst casting his eye about, and there seemed no problem with it.

It took him a whole month to find the podium. It was a wooden fish crate retrieved from the beach in 1927, back in the days when there'd still been a sense of humour in this place. Some long-dead wag had daubed the number one and a crown of laurels on it, and it had served as the winner's rostrum for the annual championship ever since. This object was now treated as a venerable relic steeped in glorious club tradition. Not with how it was stored though. Joel finally located it in a dank stone shed, rusting paint tins piled up alongside it.

As luck would have it the shed had an unlocked side window. Joel took photos of the five cameras at the back of the castle, looking up the specifications online to get lens angles and then triangulating the fields of vision in CAD as best he could. If he entered from the rear and stayed pressed against the shed wall there was a route to access the window unobserved.

For his first foray inside he stayed late at the driving range, the approach of twilight giving him the place to himself. Then he was quick, cutting through the dense stand of trees, getting to the window and clambering in. He used a tiny pencil-beam flashlight to pick his way to the podium, which he turned upside down and took detailed measurements of. Also, having to risk that the camera flash from his phone might be noticed outside, a single photo.

With new light at the end of the tunnel, he and Nat risked only a couple more illicit liaisons, the last of which was a nine-month-iversary hike up Ben Hope. Even then they only met near the summit after they'd checked it was clear. They were taking no chances and reconciled to this time apart by the magnitude of what was at stake.

Three weeks from the end of his contract with Derek, Joel broached the subject with the boss he liked so much and barely saw anything of now.

"Derek?"

The architect returned reluctantly to the open office door he'd just walked past.

"Yes? Can you make it quick." His eyes studiously avoided genuine contact, rather like Nat's once had.

"We need to talk about what happens at the end of the month."

"I'm not sure that we do."

"I love working for you, and I've done all the applications and been approved to do my RIBA Master's from here. I want to stay on."

"Then you've a bloody strange way of showing it." At last the months of pent-up fury were visible

"I know that's how it looks. Can I ask for your opinion of the work I've done since February when the sale of Jimmy's croft went through?"

"Oh it's been exemplary. Don't imagine I doubt either your ability or the lengths you're prepared to go to to get the job done. Thing is I see other factors as more important when it comes to an architect's practice in a place like Caithness. Trustworthiness, for example."

Joel just kept looking straight at his boss, and Derek must have seen something there because indecision clouded his anger. "Derek you took a big chance on me once and I came through for you. I'm asking you to do the same again now. I can't explain why, I'm afraid. I'm asking you for one more month. I don't need a contract and I'm happy to do it unpaid. I just want to keep what we have in place a little longer. My hope is that something will happen in that time that will change what you think of me. If so I'd like to continue here indefinitely."

Derek's face was a mixture of affronted, sceptical and unsure. "And if this something doesn't happen?"

"Then at the end of that month, or whenever you want, I'll leave without fuss. You tell me the best way to play things to help your business and reputation and I'll go along with all of it."

For a long while Derek just kept looking at him. "Alright then Joel. Shall I tell you why? Because for all these months I've been wrestling with a question that I still can't answer: having abused your relationship with a wonderful woman like Nat to con a decent old man like Jimmy; having done all of that and banked your quarter of a million in blood money, I've never been able to understand why you would stay on a day longer in Caithness. I would be thrilled to get a good answer to that question, Joel. Thrilled. Although a little saddened by the fact you'd felt you couldn't trust me."

Joel almost spilled the beans there and then, but his and Nat's resolution held him back. This was too important to take even that slight risk.

"If I could tell you then I would, Derek. You've been almost like a second father to me during my time here, and these last months have been as painful for me as I know they've been for you. I'm sorry for the situation."

"Well you have your month. One way or another it'll be good to resolve this."

Seven weeks had passed with no sign his reconnaissance trip to the shed had been detected.

From the photo he'd printed a thin sheet of adhesive-backed plastic that was a visual match for the underside of the crate's planks. Cut precisely to the interior dimensions, it would cover the jigsaw puzzle, hopefully well enough to pass at least a basic inspection.

His 'resident architect' access would end as soon as the Special Forces security team and all their highly-trained suspicions arrived for the tournament. Dounreay airstrip gossip via Nat said they were due tomorrow, three days ahead of Champ and his entourage, so today was as late as Joel could leave it to fix the puzzle in place. Once there it would just have to risk discovery for the best part of a week.

At the end of June, with the summer solstice barely behind them, there would be no darkness this far north until after eleven. He'd therefore chosen five o'clock for his mission, banking on the call of the nineteenth hole and dinner preparations to give him the best chance of going unnoticed.

As the hour arrived there were still three other people at the driving range. Watching their rhythm – endless little balls from a bucket being walloped far away – he picked a moment of synchronisation and ducked amongst the trees. There he paused, breath held to a trickle, looking back through the tangle of trunks towards the range. If any of the three had spotted him there was no sign they cared. Bending to his golf bag, he slid a cardboard tube from it and then was moving forwards, prioritising silence over speed.

He came to the edge of the copse just metres from the shed. Here he had a narrow angle of view beyond the buildings to the castle's drive, and a movement there caught his eye.

Suddenly his heart was pounding in his ears; a convoy of dark green Land Rovers was pulling up, and getting out of the first he recognised the grim face of Tom Faulkner, ex-SAS head of Prime Ministerial security. They were here a day earlier than expected.

Cursing under his breath and scuttling like a crab down to the back of the shed, he risked going round to the side without a thorough check first. Luckily it was all clear, and he ran to the window, eased it open, and levered himself inside.

Going over to the podium, he willed his body calm as he set up on an old trestle table next to it. Inside his cardboard tube the puzzle pieces were stacked in order. Hurriedly slotting them together, he pulled out three wide strips of double-sided adhesive foam which he fixed in marked places over the upper surface. He'd cut them so they would hold the jigsaw perfectly together and in place but not show white through the thin gaps of the fish crate's planks. Flipping the podium over he moved the jigsaw into place, pressing with the palm of his hand to ensure it was well-stuck and all the pieces exactly aligned.

"...keeps everyone on the hop you see. The commander likes to stay a step ahead of the bad actors." A clipped Sandhurst voice. Footsteps moving across the courtyard outside.

Joel pulled out the adhesive photo of the planks that was rolled inside the tube and spread it flat.

"Well, you've your ways and I'll not waste my breath arguing with them." Donald Menzies. Joel was convinced the Fresgoe Castle head of security still disliked and distrusted him.

Bending to the photo, he picked and picked at the corner of the sheet with his thumb but couldn't get the backing paper to separate. He felt desperation beginning to choke him.

"So what's this building?"

"Just a storage shed. You want to take a look?"

Finally the sheet peeled free. Joel forced himself to take it slowly, make no mistakes and no noise.

"Got to check them all. Can you believe we have twenty-nine ongoing credible assassination threats against the PM?"

"Aye I can. I'd have expected a lot more."

As both men laughed outside Joel, teeth gritted, put the sheet in place and smoothed it flat so it stuck securely. His measurements had been perfect and the puzzle was completely obscured, but he had no more time to admire his handiwork. Flipping the podium back over, he returned it softly to its place.

The door handle lowered, had no effect, and then there was rattling in the lock. Joel stood like a rabbit in the headlights, scrabbling through his brain for any kind of excuse but knowing this was a lost cause.

"Ach. Not that one then." There was the jangling of a keychain.

Glancing desperately around, Joel spotted an old boiler enclosure in the back corner and made a terrified, tiptoed scuttle for it. There was just enough space to sandwich himself in between the tank and the brick wall around it, but they would see him if they came over here.

The door crashed open as a boot helped it.

"Wasn't even locked after all that."

"Well what would be the need? It's just junk in here."

Joel had a plan of sorts now: if they saw him he would claim he came here to do drugs, had in fact just snorted the last of his cocaine when he heard them arrive. It was one of the few advantages of a coloured skin: that the average white person in a position of authority would believe without question almost anything bad about you. It might be enough. The true story was too incredible, which meant no-one would ever suspect it. He'd be ejected from the club, but that was fine because he'd done what he needed to here. Would they run extra checks on the podium just because he'd been caught in the shed? That was the crucial question. Surely they would see no reason to, not as long as they didn't find the suspicious cardboard tube with the backing paper in it. Softly as a mouse, he pushed it far into the dark, damp void behind the boiler tank.

"What's that?"

"That?"

"Yes. Isn't it what he stands on to get his cup each year? Why's it in here with all this junk?"

Joel moved his head a fraction so he could see.

"Because it's a fucking fish crate." Menzies stood hands on hips behind the suited man who was bending to look closer at the podium.

"Indeed. Still, get it straight into proper storage once I've checked it."

He lifted it to peer underneath, then pulled out some kind of handheld detector. It made small bip-bip noises as he ran it over the ancient wooden podium. Then the bips raced faster and louder.

"All okay?" Menzies asked.

"Just the iron nails. And that damned signature he puts on everything. They play merry hell with my instruments. You know they're brass not gold?"

"I couldn't give a shit. I only stand to look at the things because I've my daughter's mortgage to pay."

The security man laughed. "Well quite!" He picked up the podium, and Joel squeezed into his hiding space just in time before a high intensity torch beam flashed round the room. "That does for here. Christ this thing's heavy. Let's go dump it somewhere secure."

As quickly as they'd appeared the two men were gone. Joel wanted to laugh with manic relief until he melted, but there was a new nervousness building inside him. He'd done it! He'd actually done it! But now there was something tangible to lose. Now the stakes were higher.

Squirming out of his space and brushing himself clear of cobwebs and dust, he checked that he'd left no trace, then returned to the window. He could hear the voices of Menzies and the other man outside, then another door opening. He counted to ten to give them time to enter and then inched the window open. All seemed clear so he jack-knifed through it. He landed softly, shut the window, and was soon back in the trees, his head boiling fit to explode with the release of tension.

Forcing himself forwards, he made his way back to the driving range, saw it was clear, retrieved his bag and walked out into the open.

Now he was exultant. How good it was going to be to calm himself by driving an entire bucket of balls as far down the range as possible, he thought.

"Well, well, well. Mister Elliott. The very man we've been looking for."

Rick Couzens, and walking next to him Tom Faulkner. They must have been just out of view when he checked, but would have seen him emerge from the trees.

Rick came closer, his hard eyes unreadable. "Something interesting in the woods, Joel?"

Think fast! "Er..." Come on! "Well it's a little embarrassing, but I had a call of nature."

"Our members' bathroom doesn't have enough gold-plating for you?"

"Oh I really couldn't wish for a toilet with more. It's just there were a whole lot of security guys in there checking it, so resorting to nature seemed like the easiest option. Sorry."

"Sounds like I should be apologising for the inconvenience

then. Anyway, this here is Commander Tom Faulkner, head of the PM's security team. He has a few things that he isn't clear about on some of the building blueprints and I said I was sure our resident architect wouldn't mind lending a hand. Can you spare a few minutes?"

"No problem at all."

Tom leant forward. "Appreciate it. Do pardon all of the fuss, but yours truly has to make sure this whole show with the cup goes off smoothly."

Rick rolled his eyes.

Tom winked at him. "Best not to go there old chap. Rather unhealthy if you get to thinking about it all too much. Shall we, gentlemen?"

Joel nodded and fell in alongside Rick behind Tom's long stride.

"Thank you Joel." The resort manager's eyes showed truth for once.

"It's no problem at all Rick. I said I'd be a friend to the club and I meant it."

"Noted. And will you be coming to watch The Cup? All the thrill of wondering who's gonna win this year?"

Joel laughed. "Do you know what Rick? I wouldn't miss it for the world."

27.

Reay, July 2018.

It felt so good to drive up to Nat's cottages again. Would he have been observed turning off the main road in Reay? Without a doubt, but that didn't matter anymore; at last they could come clean to the community.

Or fairly clean at least. If things went well the parasite would be removed from Champ Campbell, but that wasn't an explanation for public consumption. Instead it would just be their story of Joel – with Nat's blessing – helping Jimmy beat the golf club, the intervening months explained away with vague mentions of legal completion periods and a non-disclosure agreement.

And if things didn't go well? Joel wasn't sure they would even know, but either way they were reconciled to this being their one and only attempt. Crucial bills were due before Parliament, the eradication of the last democratic threats to a Campbell autocracy. He would surely not return to Reay before their year ran out at the start of September. It was now or never.

Nat emerged from the door as Joel turned the car round.

"I hate this dress."

"Good morning to you too!"

"Sorry Joel. I'm already on edge today for the obvious reasons. I could have done without the whole getting dolled-up palaver too. I've never wanted to be a doll."

He leant over to kiss her as she got in. Then unclipped his seatbelt to be able to do it better.

"Don't mess me up! But oh this feels so good after all these months."

"Do you know that's what you were wearing the first time I ever saw you, on Antiques Hunt. I'd never have guessed in a million years that I'd end up with you."

She made a face of mock affront. "And why not?"

He became serious, thoughtful. "Because who you are didn't show in that context. And because even if it had I wasn't mature enough to appreciate it."

Her springwater-clear gaze considered him. "Then here's to growing."

"Indeed."

"Shall we go watch the show then?"

"Let's."

At Fresgoe Castle gate Special Forces had taken over and four men, a sniffer dog and various scanners made a very thorough search of them and their car before they were allowed to drive onwards.

"There's security absolutely everywhere," Nat observed. "We never would have stood a chance any other way than the one you found, would we?" she added as they drove through the trees.

"Not one iota of one, no."

"Are you sure they won't have discovered the jigsaw under the podium?"

"No, but there's nothing we can do now so let's try not to think about it. At least we don't need to worry about who'll be standing on the thing."

There was a posturing melee at the main entrance composed of hard-faced foreign tycoons, flushed members of the English ambitious classes and a scattering of the county's most odious social climbers.

"Ah," sighed Nat with mock reverence. "What glorious sporting spectacle this day promises."

Joel had to force a straight face as people glanced long enough to dismiss them. An attendant directed him round to the rear, where a sign declared "Overflow Parking" and all the less salubrious vehicles were hidden away.

"Will you behave yourself please! I know how you feel about this kind of charade, but you've only to suffer it today and then you can get back to chopping off cats' testicles in your jeans and t-shirt on Monday."

Laughing, she put a hand on his thigh. "How have you stood it, ingratiating yourself here these last months? I don't think I would have lasted a day."

"Actually I have a confession to make."

"Oh?"

"I like golf."

"You like golf?"

"Yes. I mean playing it, not all the frippery and one-upmanship that goes with it. I've managed a couple of early morning and late evening rounds with the entire course to myself here and it's magical. It's the one thing I'll miss when we tell everyone and I lose my membership."

She considered him. "There's no shame in that in Scotland. It's why we invented the game. It's just a pity the uniforms, rituals and money crowd moved in and stole it."

"Indeed. And we'd better go join them I guess."

She bent in and kissed him. "I love you Joel, and I'm so glad to have you back. From now on we're together whatever."

There was a small, unhappy-looking film crew doing their best to make the crowds look bigger and more enthusiastic. As soon as the director spotted Joel and Nat he had them placed in the front row, muttering about optics to a production assistant in passing.

It meant they had a good view of the cup entrants as they emerged, were presented to the crowd, and teed off.

There were the habitual three groups. First the 'invited field', thirty-four individuals who had paid the one-hundred thousand pound 'charitable donation' because the show of fealty made economic sense to them. These were the people who wanted a boon in Champ Campbell's gift and could offer something in return. Some looked like fair golfers to Joel, but all would ensure they lost heavily, future profits and the greasy pole trumping any such triviality as pride.

Next there were what could generously be termed the genuine competitors of the 'open field'. These were the people who fancied a shot at taking down Champ Campbell on his own course and were prepared to fork out half-a-million apiece for it. There were nine this year. Locker room gossip had it many hundreds had tried to enter – the PM making a tempting target for big egos who could lose this amount like pocket change – but all candidates had been thoroughly vetted to ensure they posed zero risk. They would be trying to win, but even on his worst day Champ could easily beat any of the permitted entrants on his own course.

These, mixed in with the less-favoured bootlickers, formed the opening succession of pairs who teed off to go about their business unwatched.

Now came the paid-to-play ex-pros, of whom there were four. Joel knew one, Jack Bainger, who had won some major tournaments ten or so years back. That must have been before the rolls of fat and clear signs of alcoholism, but his name still brought applause from the crowd. He and his peers would not make the mistake of playing to win either. These were sportsmen brought low, and they'd learned which side of the bread today's meagre butter rations were to be found on. Discreet speculation at the club bar said one or two of them might give it their best for the first few holes, but then they would ensure their scores rose back up above Champ's. Complementing him on his stamina and staying power was a well-known way to assure a lucrative repeat booking next year.

Lastly Champ Campbell emerged, toupee shining jet black in the sun below a Union-Jack-coloured 'JUST BRITS FOR BREXIT' sports cap. Dwarfed by four lizard-eyed security men who kept everyone at germ-defeating distance, he was pumping his wrinkly fist in the air to loud cheering from the crowd.

Champ and Jack Bainger were the final pairing. After his excellent lessons from the club pro, Joel could spot how Jack took all the edge off his drive. When Champ stepped up to the tee his swing was the mechanical, reliable product of decades of the best instruction and golf tech money could buy. It was uninspired but straight, and bounced about ten yards further down the fairway than Jack's shot.

"Woah! Out of sight. I'm not feeling good about my chances today! This guy, eh?" Jack mugged to the crowd and a grinning Champ.

Joel squeezed Nat's hand. "Having fun?"

"Please tell me there's alcohol."

"There should be. It cost me two hundred and fifty pounds for the tickets today."

"I'll bet you the drinks aren't free," Nat said through a rictus smile as they moved on to the second hole, where the whole ghastly performance was re-enacted.

The fifth hole was a hard one to bear because all traces of Jimmy's croft were gone. In its place was a chain of three bunkers and a patch of dune rough, a tempting shortcut from the crooked fairway to get ahead of the hole's par five. Jack took it on and made the shot. Champ tried it, but fell a long way short. There was a search for his ball, gold coloured with his personal 'C' moniker on it, and it finally turned up a good twenty-five yards further on than Joel reckoned it had travelled. There were no complaints from the club-salaried officials though.

After the ninth hole there was a cut, the field being halved to the top twenty-four. Jack had been out front after the eighth but was now two shots back after a badly acted pantomime with a water hazard and two dropped balls. It left Champ tied for the lead with the only one of the 'open field' competitors left, a William Nolan.

And this, Joel noticed, seemed to be causing considerable consternation. Rick was frowning, murmuring angrily into his phone as he glared at the slight, elderly man dressed all in black and his giant, implacable, red-haired caddie. Champ had also delivered a couple of murderously-hissed asides to a panicked flunky.

Joel was shaking his head. "How is this guy Nolan playing so well?" he asked Nat. "He's an atrocious golfer. He doesn't let other players past either; I got stuck behind him going round here once. It's like he wants to force them to watch how bad he is. All elbows-out arsehole stuff."

"Sounds like he'd fit right in."

"I guess; suck up kick down is the way...although now that I think about it he was decent with his caddie. Maybe it's because the man looks like a Viking warrior."

Nat was frowning. "It's strange. Nolan's reputation locally is better than that."

"You know him?"

"He's a rich American. Owns Meadie Castle, one of the hunting, shooting and fishing estates inland from Tongue. I've never met him but I do know his caddie, John Robertson. He's the ghillie at the estate and very good about reporting any endangered animal they find injured or dead."

"Do you reckon John would tell you if there's something going on? There's no way Nolan should have scored like he has so far. He's been a shot or more up on the 'open field' standard every hole. It's too consistent to be just luck."

Nat's worried expression was mirroring his own now. "Maybe. Let me go and ask him."

There was a refreshment stand set up to cater for the pause before the back nine, and Joel bought two extortionately-priced glasses of white wine while Nat worked her way over to the ghillie. Watching the gentle way the two fell into conversation he had to bite down on an irrational flash of jealousy: he knew this quiet, considered Highland way of being now, and that he would never quite master it himself.

She came back over, accepted a glass from him, and made a face as she took a sip. "What is this?"

"I don't know but it's not what's on the label. Do you see how all the full bottles have the corks pushed back in instead of being unopened? You learn to watch for that in London. Did you find out anything?"

"Unfortunately we're not the only ones who've been playing a double game. John decided there was no harm in telling me now: Nolan absolutely loathes Campbell and seems to think publicly upstaging him is the best outlet for that. He joined here and even goes to his Cape Cod club to play badly in order to fool Campbell's checkers, but over at his Scottish estate he's made some practice links and has had a private instructor living in-house to give him secret intensive golf lessons. He's been doing this for an entire year all just for today. If he can win he will."

Joel tried to keep calm but he felt his composure fraying. "Bloody Americans always taking it upon themselves! If Champ doesn't get on that podium...I mean..."

"I know. I don't see what we can do about it though. It's Campbell's course so he must know it back to front. Also Nolan's older and shorter than he is and can't hit the ball so far. Surely all that counts for something?"

"It should, but... Nat, how can Earth's future rest on a grudge match between two doddering old men?! It's too surreal, too ridiculous."

"Isn't it all these days?"

"Smiles please," growled the director as he stomped past them.

There was a palpable air of tension running through the crowd now. Picking up on it, the assorted sycophants and ex-pros making up the first eleven pairs were scattering in mishits liberally. All of them wanted to keep their names well clear of the leaderboard and the mounting fury of the Prime Minister.

By the fourteenth hole Campbell and Nolan, paired together for the back nine, were four shots clear of the field and the challenger was leading by one. Nolan teed off first and his drive, as expensively grooved as Champ's, was on the weak side but found a true line. Reay was a tight course and it suited his careful game.

Aiming to recover the deficit on this par-four hole Champ planted his feet wide and, belly rolling in counterpoint, took a series of big practice swings.

"He's going to mess this up," groaned Joel, and sure enough seconds later the shot was shanked off to the right and into a swathe of coarse grass.

The officials scurried off down the fairway and into the rough. Soon one called out that he'd found the golden ball, but Joel could only watch in increasing horror as John the ghillie bent to whisper in Nolan's ear, his long arm pointing to exactly where the mishit drive had actually fallen.

"Think your guys marked that one wrong, Chump," Nolan called out loudly.

"Did he say Champ or Chump?" Nat whispered to Joel.

"I think that was the general idea. Damn it Nat, this makes him clear favourite to win this now. We have to do something. What can we do?"

"I don't know."

A row was brewing as Nolan and the official argued over which ball was the real one, the one John was now standing over or the one thirty yards on and in a much better lie.

Nolan was looking smug. "Hey TV guy. Since no-one else was watching, apparently, can you wind back on these cameras and show us where that shot landed?"

"Sorry, that's not convenient."

Nolan snorted. "This how you want to do it then, Chump? You don't even have the guts to play the game fair, like a man?"

The two were squaring up now.

"Whatever," snarled Campbell. "No-one knows which is the real ball, because everyone wants my gold balls and so there's lots around. But you know what? I'll play your fake lie and I'll win anyway."

Joel studied Champ Campbell's rage. Was it just the way this man's life had grown him? There was simply no way to tell. Was that separate presence watching all this and guiding the PM like a golem? If it was so clever and cunning, such a master-manipulator of whole populations, could it not do better than the absurd spectacle playing out here? Maybe not. Maybe it saw just the broad sweep. Set the route but could not navigate the bumps and turns in the road. Maybe it was reliant on its flawed host for that.

Champ took his shot, trying too hard, and it was another bad one. Nolan, meanwhile, hit another of his tame drives straight and true towards the green. With horrible predictability the hole was played out to leave Nolan up by two. Even worse, Champ carried his loss of composure forwards. Where his much longer drive should have reduced the deficit, he only managed to tie the fifteenth. With only three holes remaining, the result was looking ominously certain.

"Let's try and talk to Nolan, Joel. Come on."

"What good will that do, Nat?" Joel was shaking his head, despondency draining him.

"What else can we do? He's going to win as things stand, isn't he?"

Joel nodded, but he barely had the willpower to put one foot in front of the other as the crowd, now prudently thinning, made its way to the tee for the sixteenth.

Nolan and John were an island of two, the ghillie's stern face unnecessary to maintain their ostracism.

Nat walked up to him and the big redhead turned to bar their way. "John, I'm sorry to ask this but we need to talk to Mr. Nolan."

The ghillie pursed his lips, not fond of the idea.

"Who are these people, John?" Nolan, approaching behind him, was all atwitch.

"This is Nat Sinclair from the vet's practice at Melvich, sir. She was out with us at Meadie twice last year, for a wildcat and one of..."

Suddenly Nolan was all smiles. "A Sinclair, eh? So was my great-great grandmother. Then you'll know that today's the three-hundred-and-thirty-eighth anniversary of the Battle of Altimarlach, when loyal Sinclair men were butchered by the treacherous – wait for it – Campbells! I'm gonna kick the ass of that son-of-a-bitch for clan Sinclair and for every man and woman who believes in decency, truth and democracy."

Nat just shook her head. "You don't beat this with more fighting," her quiet murmur.

"Mr. Nolan," Joel jumped into the pause. "I know this will sound crazy, but there's a reason Campbell has been able to do so much damage to all you just said: decency, truth and democracy. It's because something's possessing him. A parasite not of this world. There's a plan to remove it, but for it to work we need your help, sir. Campbell has to win today."

Nolan laughed nastily. "Nice try kiddo. You one of these butt-lickers of his trying to rattle me off my game with this nonsense? Ain't gonna work. John, remove them would you please."

The big man gestured for them to step away. Desperate, Joel measured the distances, bunching his muscles to lunge at Nolan and try to injure him so he couldn't play on. Instantly the ghillie was between them. Joel looked him up and down and knew the giant man would prevail in a fight. He felt his last energy seep from him like a string-cut marionette. To have got so close only to see it end like this...

Shaking his head in defeat, he walked away with Nat, glancing across at her with all hope extinguished from his heart.

And there, by way of answer, was that utter compassion he'd fallen in love with her for. The gaze he'd seen when she caught him after he'd completed the puzzle and blacked out. Suddenly he knew they had a single chance left.

"Nat you have to ask him."

She was frowning now. "Come on Joel. Maybe he'll make a big mistake in the final holes."

"He won't. You have to let him see your soul, Nat. All of it. Like you just looked at me now. Like you did when we made the puzzle and I regained consciousness. That honesty. That caring. The love. That's what Nolan claims to care about, so show him. Show him every bit without concealment or deflection, and ask him to lose."

"Please stop this Joel."

"No Nat. You have a special kind of power. It's why you can calm animals the way you do. You're the vet. They know you're going to inject them and cut them open. There's no possible way you can explain to them why it will help. They should fear you, but instead you show them what's inside you and they see it, trust you and grow calm. I've watched you do it. Ask him using that. All of it."

Nat was shaking her head as if being ranted at by a madman.

A low voice came from behind them. "For what it's worth I'd say he's right about you." John must have been listening. "If this is genuine and as important as you both say then go and ask Nolan now. Just you though Nat. He's a decent man. Maybe he'll see and accept your truth."

Nat's face was four seasons in quick succession, a Caithness summer's day. She turned and went back the way they'd come, leaving the two men standing watching her. Nolan looked up, surprised at her approach. She said just a few words that Joel couldn't make out, then bowed her head and walked back over.

"You asked him?"

"Yes."

"What did he say?"

"He didn't reply."

"And the final player to tee off," the announcer's voice was terrified. "Leading by two, William Nolan."

John nodded to them and returned to his employer's side.

The challenger's opening drive on the sixteenth fell well short of Campbell's, but on a short par four that didn't matter much. Nolan reached the green in three with a longer distance to putt, but his technique was solid and the two men tied the hole to leave the lead unchanged.

Joel reached for Nat's hand, felt hers wind around his.

The seventeenth was the same story. For a moment Nolan seemed to pause on the fairway and reconsider, but then that groomed technique took over and again the hole was tied and his two-shot advantage intact.

At the eighteenth and final hole, a par four, Campbell put every ounce of power from his bulky frame into his drive. This time he connected properly and he was a full forty yards ahead of his competitor's cautious strike. As Nolan stood up after his tee shot he looked around. Joel observed the faces glaring back at him, livid repulsion at this gate-crasher in their ritual. Nolan's gaze, however, was searching for Nat. Their eyes met, and then his dropped.

If that set growing a tiny shoot of doubt in Joel, the American's next shot razed it, a perfect drive taking him to the end of the fairway. Champ's second shot came past to almost make the green, but the deficit had been reduced to no more than twenty yards and Nolan's putting was stronger than his rival's.

Both men took a pitching wedge next, Nolan's shot leaving him only six yards from the pin. Champ's was further out, but he holed on his first try for a par four. As he retrieved his ball and stood there was no satisfaction at a good shot and a decent score for his round, just slathering fury contorting his face. He stood in front of Rick, watching at the front of the nervous crowd, and stabbed two fingers at him like a gypsy casting a curse.

Nolan looked serene as he came to stand over his ball. He took two practice swings and then straightened up, worked his shoulders loose before bending forwards again and taking the shot. The ball had a reasonable line but was going too fast. It went six inches to the right of the hole and then carried on, the slope taking it a yard past the pin.

Joel clenched Nat's hand, a sliver of optimism returning. Campbell was watching eagerly too. Nolan had just one chance left to win the match, but surely he wouldn't miss a putt of three feet?

This time he took an absolute age preparing the shot. Finally he hit it, and Joel groaned as he saw that its line was true. But it was slowing, losing speed. As it trickled towards the hole its legs were running out. 'Stop!' breathed Joel silently, and two agonising inches before the hole it did.

Nolan raised his hands up to the sky in exasperation. He could now only tie the match. He looked at the crowd again and once more he sought Nat's gaze. Joel turned to study the woman he loved, and saw her whole soul there in her eyes.

The challenger walked up to his ball, then looked at Champ, asking for the obvious gimme. The Prime Minister pouted skywards, pretending he didn't see his opponent. Nolan smiled, shrugged, then flicked his club one-handed to send the ball the tiny distance into the hole. Incredibly, it missed.

"Yes! Yes! Yes!" Champ was cavorting across the green. He danced up to Nolan and shook his fist in front of his opponent's face. "Yes! Yes! Who's the champ, uh? Who's the champ, uh? Who's the champ, uh? Who's the champ, uh?"

This jolted Rick into action and he hissed at the stunned announcer. Triumphant music blared out across the eighteenth green, the grotesque, sycophantic carnival suddenly restored to full merriment.

Nolan, a leper at this party, walked off behind John, his face offering no clue as to whether he'd lost deliberately. He glanced over at them and they both nodded back gratefully, but Nolan only saw Nat.

Scuttling groundsmen emerged carrying the Reay Golf Course podium into position. Joel gripped Nat's hand, all his attention fixed on the ancient fish crate. Nat leant against him. It was all either of them had left. So much of their past together, so much of their future, came down to what happened next. It was too incomprehensible, and they had no capacity left for anything beyond the simple contact of their human love.

"Ladies and Gentlemen." The grinning announcer was trickling hair dye from his recent sweat. "For an incredible sixth year in succession, may I present to you the winner of the Champ Invitational Charity Golf Cup. Titan of business; Prime Minister of Great Britain; deliverer of the Brexit promise; always the winner; Sir Charles Campbell...which might be why, round here, we all know him better as Champ!"

The entire congregation had reformed and there was a manic air to the cheering. They pressed forwards, jostling for the front row face space to better suckle at Campbell's savage glory. Waving and fist pumping, he stepped greedily up onto the podium with its number one and laurel wreath in faded white paint.

Nothing. Had the puzzle been discovered? Had they only imagined a promise made? Had it been broken? Had it all been delusion from the start?

Then the fabric of the world seemed to stretch both outwards and inwards from the podium. Campbell's hands flew to his chest, convulsions shaking him as if shot. He clutched at his head, fingers tearing the toupee off to expose shrivelled, glue-covered pink skin below. A high-pitched shriek ripped from his mouth, cutting above the growing gasps from the crowd, then he was sinking down to his knees, shaking and groaning, a yellow stain of urine spreading across the front of his white golfing trousers.

'Three, four, five…' Joel was counting out the heartbeats in his head. On six Champ collapsed as if his strings had been cut. Joel made it to eight before Shane Oag and another security man had forced their way to the podium. They each pulled one of Champ's arms across their shoulders and lugged him the short distance to the clubhouse that extended out from the castle.

Rick had recovered and was yelling at everyone to move away from the building and round to the side. Weakness could never be admitted, especially when it was on display; that was the iron rule.

Freewheeling and milling people passed by. Their voices came as if from underwater, but all the clearer for that. Not concern for their fallen leader, but anger. Rage at having shelled out good money only to find they might now be cheated out of their just favours. Fear too. That of rats assessing whether this constituted an opportune moment to jump ship.

Joel and Nat remained like an island amongst all of it until finally, incredibly, they stood alone. Joel could still find no words. He wrapped Nat into his embrace, and it was as if all good emotions co-existed in him at once.

"I felt a change," she whispered. "The evil is gone."

Finally they drew apart. Spotting a chance to do the last thing needed, Joel ran over to the podium. He was anticipating a bite from the air as he upended it, but nothing came. He began to tug the jigsaw free from its underside. Nat knelt by him, and working together they pulled away the strips of adhesive and dismantled the puzzle, stuffing everything into her handbag.

"Here." She held out the centrepiece to him. "It should never be all in the same place again."

He pocketed it wordlessly. The nightmare was over. The life he hadn't dared consider now stretched out ahead.

"Come on my love." Nat's hand was in his again. "Let's go home."

Twenty minutes later they stood in Nat's dusty lounge.

"Together?"

"Yes."

They linked fingers and moved their joined hands to where the air had been scarred.

There was no shock. Only the sensation of benign, unremarkable air bathing their skin.

"We did it! It's gone! It was all real!"

"Or none of it ever was."

Epilogue.

"Okay, fifteen minutes," Joel whispered, and ended the call. He tiptoed to the hall to get his shoes, hoping not to wake any of his family. Easing open the front door, he went out into the bright morning sun.

Reay looked glorious today. It wasn't the kind of beauty you noticed at first. Rather it was something that grew as you learned to see it. He walked down the main street and took the turning to Fresgoe Harbour.

The fences around the club were still there, but the new owners had lowered them to something that didn't shout disrespect. They'd even implemented a community access plan allowing locals like Joel an eighteen-hole round each month. This quiet lane had ceased to be a jail keeping the greater portion of the world prisoner.

Campbell's collapse at his tournament had been hushed up completely. He'd been up and about again just days later, but all he did no longer worked as it once had. Some necessary energy had gone out of his vitriol, and the fightback mounted from every side. In the face of rising protest his Just Brits party staged a coup d'état to oust him. Blind with hubris, their new leader called a general election. Now the public could speak freely, and the governing party lost all bar forty seats.

The ex-PM, beset by mushrooming debts and lawsuits as his companies unravelled, continued to cry fake, foul or whatever to any who would hear him. Few did now.

Because whatever had made his malevolence potent no longer steered him? Or was it simply the nature of a burst balloon?

And despite the desperate pleas of ill health and diminished capacity from his remaining lawyers, prison was beckoning.

Following the explosive allegation that Campbell had ordered Geoffrey Petard's murder, detectives were re-examining the deaths of the two Supreme Court justices and even, going way back, Charles' own brother. By all accounts former employees were turning on Champ and spilling their guts. It...

Joel exhaled, sweeping such thoughts from his mind. Not today, of all days! He turned onto the beach and walked along the line of dunes, looking not at the azure sea but in between the hills of sand. When he spotted her he broke into a run.

"Quick, in here so we're not seen! This fuss is ridiculous. I don't know why I agreed to any of it."

"Because the entire population of Reay ganged up on you Nat, and they're your adopted family." He leant in to kiss her.

"But I don't want to sleep in someone else's house and not see you until later today. It's stupid."

He laughed. "At least you've avoided the hair, nails and makeup session they had planned. They're still not happy about that you know."

"It's unfair that I'm expected to submit to all that nonsense. All you have to do is put on a suit. Why can't I be a man?" But she was smiling now too.

"I'm glad you're not. It's because they love you Nat. Sometimes they just express it with dubious taste."

She rolled her eyes. "I come bearing news actually. A wedding present from Jimmy and Dot. Something very surprising."

"Surely not more surprising than them tying the knot before us?"

"That wasn't a surprise at all. Everyone knew how they felt about each other. They'd have done it years ago but that cat of hers wouldn't tolerate Kelpie, so that was that. Anyway, they sat me down first thing this morning and informed me they're giving back the two hundred and fifty thousand extra you got for Jimmy's croft."

"They can't!"

She shrugged. "I tried saying that, but they've already decided and there's probably no use trying to fight it. They pointed out they're well set up and neither of them has children. And Joel it would mean we can clear your loans, even buy me into practice with Neil and you a partnership with Derek. I confess I've also been thinking a lot about your idea to knock the two cottages together into a proper family home. I went and sat in Dot and Jimmy's conservatory to watch the sunrise and it's a perfect space. I'd enjoy seeing what you can do to our place with a decent budget." Her eyes were shining, but without a trace of greed. Just enthusiasm for the future.

"Wow, then!"

"Yes, that pretty much sums it up. Does it also erase the last of your regrets about the jigsaw puzzle?"

Joel was about to protest that he had none, but she knew him better than that so he smiled ruefully instead. "It did hurt, setting fire to a quarter of a million pounds. Especially if it was harmless with the ending of whatever link there was."

"But we've never understood that. Nor what we did nor how it was undone. Thus you agreed it was the right thing to make sure. I'm glad of that, because it reaffirms that I'm marrying a good and careful man. What defines us if not the whys of our choices?"

To that he could only nod further agreement, and feel the warm glow inside that they'd also chosen each other, which would be celebrated today in the village's church in front of the Elliott clan and the massed ranks of the populace of Reay. Whatever future lay beyond that was gloriously uncertain again, theirs to help forge.

After a hungry kiss au revoir, she went off back between the dunes and he walked out into the salt breeze of the beach. He thought he could remember the exact spot, soon three years ago, where they'd come at low tide to dig a fire hole in the sand.

It had been dark that late evening, the silence only disturbed by the take-off of the Campbell jumbo jet leaving Reay for what would turn out to be the last time. As they'd fed the puzzle pieces to the flames of the baron's diaries, their two faces had taken on a peculiar hue: shades of red from the embers of the lignum vitae wood as it burnt and the perpetual glow of summertime night sky in the far north. It had been the light of hope returned.

The sea had soon come for their night's work, scooping up the grey cinders to disperse across Earth's wide oceans.

The hope, though, remained.

In that first year together Nat and Joel had known how it felt to live without it, and there could be no greater lesson. Not in the sweetness of hope's taste. Nor in the absolute need for it that courses through the very fabric of our human souls.

The end.

Acknowledgements.

My dad, Mike Imrie, was this book's first reader, the printer-out of its many versions, and the writer of heartwarming words in 6am emails when he'd sat up all night with yet another new manuscript. I miss you.

Denise Imrie provided the kind of glowing feedback mums are renowned for, but accompanied by a playwright's insight and perceptiveness. It's been a genuine pleasure discovering such a shared interest at this point in our lives.

Anna Dahlberg, my wife, supplied me, and our two boys, with every kind of nourishment and the resilience of the loved throughout the writing of this novel. She even made the book cover and video trailer. We're in this together, and I couldn't imagine anyone better. Älskar dig.

A small group of friends, acquaintances and fellow writers gave of their time and thoughts to hold up a mirror to early versions of The Lost Piece. Test readers truly are gold. I won't go into names here, nor list the various realisations and improvements your feedback prompted, but thank you so much for your generosity and perspicacity.

Although all characters and the version of Reay in this book are fictitious, I hope I've done Caithness justice. It's the unique place I grew up in and inevitably some part of me.

Last but not least, thank YOU for reading this book.

I hope you enjoyed it. If you did then online reviews, ratings and recommendations help me no end. In this modern world's endless sea of novels, only by standing out do I have any chance to justify writing more.

About the author

David Imrie was born in Oxford, England, in 1973. During his childhood his family moved first to Dorset and then to Thurso in Caithness, where he lived between ages 10 and 18.

He read psychology at Oxford University, an arbitrary choice of subject made hastily at 17 and perhaps something of a pattern. After a few years in psychiatry research and Manchester, David stumbled into IT in search of a way out. He ended up in software integration and error management, and for 3 months in 2005 knew of a simple way to kill every Nokia Series 40 colour phone in the world.

David's (very 2000s) plan behind returning to university to study architectural technology was to set up in Galicia, northern Spain, restoring old farmhouses for foreign buyers. Then Brexit nobbled that whole idea.

In 2017, getting kind of desperate, David asked a publisher acquaintance if he needed any proof reading doing. "If you want, but it's awfully dull stuff," came the reply. "Why not give editing a bash?" So he did, and it was a fit. Soon, of course, he started itching to do a bit of writing himself... The Lost Piece is his first novel.

David lives with his wife Anna and their two sons near the Galician town of Pontedeume. On lucky days he spots dolphins from his study window.

Coming soon...

The new novel from David Imrie, 'Ghosts', will be released on
October 1ˢᵗ 2024 and is available for pre-order.
Find out more at davidimrie.com

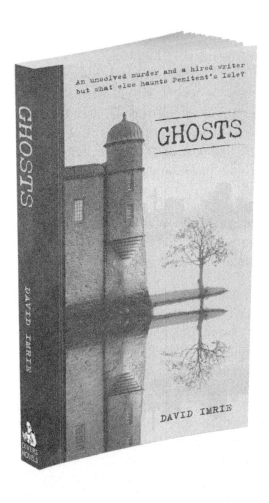

Printed in Great Britain
by Amazon